BETWEEN
HEAVEN AND HELL

L A Michaels

LML BOOKS

For my late mother, Lisa Marie. This book wouldn't exist if you had not introduced me to Erica Kane, Vicki Lord, and Luke Spencer. I will love you always and forever. Very Much. More than Anything.

CONTENTS

Pastiche:

An artistic work in a style that imitates that of another work, artist, or period.

Soap Opera:

An ongoing drama serial on television or radio, featuring the lives of many characters and their emotional relationships.

FORWARD

Like sands through the hourglass, there is a destiny that makes us brothers in tragedy and triumph because you only have *One Life to Live* ...

Whether it be from a mother, grandparent, aunt, uncle, or possibly father many people inherit at least one soap opera in their lives. I, like many people, inherited them from my mother...

One of my earliest memories is sitting on the floor in my house in Troy. My mother would have *General Hospital* on. I couldn't tell you a single plotline that was going on because it was all over my head. I knew it was *General Hospital* from the theme music, known as *Faces of the Heart*. She watched all of *ABC's* daytime lineup from the time she was a little girl to the time she passed away. Nurse Jessie Brewer was often mentioned in conversations involving the soaps.

As a young child, these shows did nothing for me. They would be on while I played with toys or what have you. It was as I grew older and could recognize who *Carly Corinthos* or *Jessica Buchannan* were that I started to take an interest in these characters. It's straightforward to get hooked on soap operas. They are on five days a week and you watch people fall in love, get married, have children, and send those same children off to college in the matter of a year in some cases. It's indeed one of the most fascinating genres for that reason next to comic books for me.

Over the years I'd be sick or I would get home from school earlier each year and have nothing to do. I'd tune in to other networks shows myself. My mother was an *ABC* soap purist. I'd discover *Guiding Light, As the World Turns, The Young and the Restless, The Bold and the Beautiful,* and *Days of Our Lives* by myself. It truly is fascinating to watch these characters play out their lives on screen, and the histories of soaps themselves are fascinating. We wouldn't have a majority of prime-time dramas if it were not for daytime soaps.

When I was in eighth grade around the time that *Guiding Light* was canceled, I looked up online "how do you write a soap opera." I found an article that essentially said write what you know and what is around you. Well, that is a different novel to be released at a later date… I sat on the idea for a while thought of what to write until one day around 2010, I came up with a reverse *Beverly Hills, 90210* story of a New York family that loses its wealth and is forced to move to the mid-west. However, instead of going to just some middle-class town they are put in what is perceived as upper-class but completely different than what they are accustom to. I'd sit on the idea for some years and come back to it every so often. The supporting characters just didn't mesh well.

A few years later I realized they didn't mesh well because as much as I liked the family I created, they didn't work as the primary leads. A name randomly popped into my head… Vivica Fitzgerald. An Erica Kane type who seeks fame, she doesn't think she is doing anything wrong, but everyone else would disagree. I had to quickly change the last name from Fitzgerald to Fitzpatrick due to a real-life friendship, but I found myself creating a world for this Vivica woman. I was really into *The Bold and the Beautiful* at that point and couldn't for the life of me figure out why people hated *Brooke Logan* aka *The Slut from the Valley* so much and yet her biggest rival, *Doctor Taylor Hayes* could literally do anything (or anyone) that Brooke would and get away with it… I knew that Vivica needed a rival in this form, but I wanted her rival to be related to her and be her sister. I didn't want them fighting over *Ridge Forrester* though. I thought that *Phillip Spaulding* of *Guiding Light* was more interesting and loved his relationship with *Beth*. Especially, during their teenage years. This got me thinking about Vivica and her love interest as teenagers… I'd create a series that would feature different timelines.

I didn't know how to execute that though. Would I focus on one-time line at a time? Would I have extended flashbacks? Fast forward to 2014, and I'm reading a novel by the late great Jackie Collins. *Chances,* I wanted to learn how to write dirty, and I thought who better than the queen of smut herself? I didn't, but it finally clicked though reading through the pages. This needs to be multi-generational and tell multiple parts of a story. Also, throw in that Kingsley family that I really enjoyed from that *Grosse Pointe* series I kept writing. Oh, and that's where it will take place.

This novel is pastiche. It's a loving tribute to a genre that is often overlooked or not given the credit it deserves. While it takes much inspiration from many soap operas, it is an original work. If, however, you as a soap fan need to be sold on it from a soap perspective, imagine if the Spaulding family lived at Llanfair and rivaled the Quartermaine family whose humble beginnings mirrored that of the Ryan family. Tracy Quartermaine was strongly against Brooke Logan who as a teenager had Erica Kane tendencies that she now recognizes in the new girl in town, the Luke and Laura or Bo and Hope or Holden and Lily are now the Joe and Ruth of the town and Taylor Hayes' abduction is often referenced but never explained (at least not yet...). If you are not a soap fan, my pitch to you is this... Rich people with problems that make it easy to escape your own.

From the Flames of a Fire to The Blue Skies Above,

We Are All Just Somewhere

Between Heaven and Hell…

VIVICA – 2018

Detroit is far from the only city in Michigan. It seems that people only ever mention Detroit when talking about Michigan. There happens to be many towns and cities worth talking about. In the same county, there is Grosse Pointe. A lux town filled with history. Every city has their prominent citizens. Doctors, lawyers, businessmen, and women. You also have your fair share of socialites depending on the town. Grosse Pointe is definitely one of those towns… Vivica Weston – Fitzpatrick - Knight – Fitzpatrick -Fitzpatrick looked out the bay window in her home's library. The redhead was doing a final rundown on her dress for that night. The Grosse Point General hospital annual gala. Vivica was known for dazzling people with her outfits and legendary parties. She wouldn't usually touch such a low-key event like the hospital gala, but her husband Nial Fitzpatrick was chief of staff at the hospital. It also happened that Vivica's event planning company was a conglomerate of *The Fitzpatrick Group*.

The Fitzpatrick Group was the family company that stretched back three generations. While it started as a very modest company that sold steel to the local car companies, now it was a fortune five hundred company within the first decade of being in business. This was all due to good investments on the late family patriarch and Nial's grandfather, Seamus. Nial's sister Margot was the current CEO and had the most shares within the company next to her father. Margot would be at the gala that night. Margot hated Vivica with a passion. Vivica hated Margot even more.

Vivica had been in charge of the event for the past five years. The first year she did it willingly because she used it as a chance to announce to the world that Nial and her had decided to remarry. Margot realized how much her sister-in-law dreaded the yearly event, so she continued to give her the bid even if she didn't want it. After all, Vivica technically worked for Margot.

1

The dress that Vivica would wear was gold but not shimmering. Sleeveless and went to the floor. Nothing with a floral print. Vivica hated any type of print on a dress. She found it tacky and reminded her far too much of the eighties. An era that she wished she could leave behind her. She smiled as the dress was being fitted to her perfect figure. She had average but perky breast that were completely natural and legs that didn't end. Her overall look was always completed with her green eyes which you could swear were emerald. Vivica was supposed to be listening to her assistant Lucy Kingsley. The twenty-eight-year-old blonde could talk all day long. The redhead never really bothered to listen.

"Earth to Vivica. Come on pay attention. We need to finish this seating chart. We only have a few more hours. Where do you want Cliff and Tiffany? It would be appropriate to have them up front." This was the third time that Lucy had brought up the subject of where Tiffany would be sitting. Vivica kept trying to dodge the subject.

It didn't matter where Tiffany sat, Vivica thought. "Sit them in the back. I don't want to hear another word of it." Lucy tried to speak, but Vivica kept speaking. "Now don't remind me of how *Knight Motors* gave its largest donation yet to the hospital last year. I also don't want to hear how Tiffany is a head surgeon at the hospital. My bitch of a sister is not going to get the spotlight. My husband is chief of staff. My company put on the event. Tiffany doesn't need the exposure." Tiffany was Vivica's older sister. They hadn't grown up together. Their parents had divorced when they were young. Vivica was forced to go with their mother while Tiffany got to stay in California with their father. They had never been close. Vivica doubted that they ever would be.

Lucy sighed. She knew better than to question Vivica's word when it came to Tiffany. She had worked for Vivica for five years since moving from Manhattan. Lucy knew that another year or so working with Vivica would be all she needed to get her career on the right track. There were other positions at The Fitzpatrick Group that could easily put Lucy in the corporate spotlight herself. She worked well with Vivica though. They were just two people with two completely different agendas. Two agendas that strangely aligned at the end of the day. Lucy kept Vivica from falling to pieces and Vivica gave Lucy contacts in the business world. "So, then for your table, you have yourself and Nial, as well as Brad. Then Nial instructed me to leave one seat open."

"What do you mean, he instructed to leave one seat open?" Vivica looked at Lucy. "I know it couldn't be for Margot. She always sits at a table with the mayor." Vivica wondered why Nial would want another seat. Brad, their son, was sixteen and away at an in-state boarding school. She only saw him on holidays and then this event. He seemed to grow five years every time she saw him... "I guess I will just have to talk to him about that when I see him for lunch today."

"He actually called to say he is canceling lunch..." Holly mumbled as she put pins in the dress. Holly was Vivica's maid and best friend. "He had to go to the airport or something."

Vivica looked down at her maid. "Well isn't that wonderful of him. He cannot even call me himself. Whoever this mystery guest is better not make any disruptions for the evening." Admittedly Vivica and Nial had been a bit more distant than usual lately. This was a tad concerning but she knew how Nial was. Their love wasn't exactly conventional. They were perfect together on paper, similar personalities but neither of them was the other's soul mate. No Vivica's soul mate was Cliff Knight...

Knight Motor Company was part of the big four regarding the American auto industry. It was just as old as the other three companies. It tried hard to keep the company family run. Clifton Knight had been groomed to run this company since birth. Cliff was the only reason the company had survived through the 2008 crash and since then had brought the company back on top. The other three companies were hardly his rivals or worth his time in his honest opinion.

Cliff wasn't your average looking CEO. The man had curly brown hair and perfect cheekbones. His eyes matched the blue in Lake Saint Clair to a T. At six foot three inches he towered over many of his peers and rivals. Cliff managed to work out at least four times a week and was in perfect shape. Sure, he had put on one or two wrinkles, but by all means, he had the exact body he had at eighteen years old.

The most important thing about Cliff though was that he had a heart of gold. It always shocked people when they met him. His father and grandfather were far from saints. His grandmother often lamented as a child that Cliff had all the best qualities of his great-grandfather Heathcliff, who himself was far from a saint.

If his great business ethics, amazing looks, and personality were not enough. He had a near perfect family. His wife Tiffany was a head surgeon at Grosse Pointe General Hospital. His daughter Hope was on her way to being a doctor herself, and son Harry was on point to graduate high school top of his class. His other daughter Hannah, who was the identical twin sister of Hope, on the other hand, had been a little lost for the past few years. He loved all his children the same though.

It was lunch time for him which meant that he was still working. Work didn't stop just for food in his mind. He was a great multi-tasker. Someone knocked on his door as he was in the middle of typing up an email. "Come in."

Tiffany walked in. She was wearing a black turtleneck sweater with dark gray dress pants. She wore stilettos though Cliff still towered over her. She walked over to his desk and kissed him. Cliff kissed back. They happened to be madly in love at the moment. "How has your day gone?" She asked him. It was her lunch hour as well. She had a surgery that afternoon before the gala was to take place.

"Our stock fell by two percent," Cliff stated.

"I'm sure it won't take long to recover."

"Yes, but none of the other companies had a fall. Being at the top doesn't mean anything. Knight might have had top sales two years in a row for the big four. I want it to go for three." Cliff explained Tiffany was always so fascinated how Cliff could be the perfect husband but such a fierce businessman. It only made their love for one another stronger.

Cliff looked at Tiffany. He could tell she wasn't happy about something. "What's wrong?"

She didn't want to sound like a broken record. "I know I'm head surgeon, but do we really have to go to the gala tonight? You know Vivica is just going to throw us in the back corner like she does every year."

This was true. Cliff knew that Vivica was bound to mistreat Tiffany the entire evening. He learned five years ago when he renewed his vows to Tiffany that the best way to keep Vivica and Tiffany happy was to keep them apart. Each year at the gala, however, the two sisters were forced to interact with one another.

It had never been a secret that Cliff had been with Vivica first. He had been engaged to Vivica right out of high school. At one point they were married, but it turned out to be an invalid marriage. He did love Vivica, but he married Tiffany first and had his family with Tiffany. Vivica was fun, and he never regretted a moment of the time they spent with one another. Tiffany, however, he never really had to think about if he made the right choice with her. She was a wonderful wife and an even better mother to their children.

"I promise you, darling; tonight will be just fine. Plus, we can't not go. You could win doctor of the year." Cliff pointed out. Tiffany smiled and kissed him on the forehead. Yes, Tiffany was the perfect wife and mother. He did not doubt that. Vivica was his past...

VIVICA – 1986

"Mother! Mother!" Vivica screamed at the top of her lungs. She made a screeching noise before running down the stairs of their modest home. It was on the edge of Grosse Pointe and Detroit. Many would argue that it was Detroit, but Vivica always won the argument against that. It wasn't as if they didn't have money; it just happened they moved here once her mother Gale married DJ Brash, who had lived here since his birth and wasn't going to give up the home. "Mother! Did you not hear me from upstairs?" Vivica asked with curlers in her hair but otherwise dressed for school.

Gale Brash, previously Weston, born Harwood was always a simple woman. She never enjoyed living in Beverly Hills with Vivica's father when they were married. She didn't fit the mold of the other women there. It was a regret of hers that she never could get that mindset out of her daughter's head. "Vivica, honey I'm sure that the entire neighborhood has heard you by now. What's wrong?"

How could her mother not see what was wrong? bIt was so obvious. "The hem on my skirt. Did you lower it?" She barked. It looked hideous.

"I had no choice. Father Harold's secretary called last night. She informed me that they are strapping down on the dress code this year. We've already talked about this Vivica. I'm not going to be at your school every other day because you cannot behave yourself. I have a job. DJ has a job." It seemed that the older Vivica got the more trouble she got in. Gale thought that sending her to Catholic school would keep her under control. It didn't …

This was unacceptable as far as Vivica was concerned. She hated wearing the same outfit every single day as it was. "My skirt length shouldn't be any-one's concern."

"Well, it can be a distraction for some of the boys." Gale pointed out.

"Well, that's the point mother…" Vivica rolled her eyes.

DJ walked in. He was an Olive-skinned man with dirty blonde hair and deep brown eyes. As well as a perfectly chiseled body. He worked at the *Fitzpatrick Group* as a construction worker for one of the many companies that they owned. His half-sister Nadia was married to Brandon Fitzpatrick. They had been working on a new dealership for *Knight Auto* that would go up in town. It had gotten off the ground last year, and he was put in charge. Some claimed nepotism. He didn't care. DJ had to work hard for what he had. He didn't have the Fitzpatrick name attached to him as his sister did. "What on earth is going on in here? Vivica are you alright?" He genuinely tried to have a good relationship with Vivica. He loved her like his own daughter, even if Vivica herself didn't care for him very much.

Vivica looked at Gale. She made a moaning noise and looked in the mirror as she took off the curlers. "It's just this town… I cannot stand it anymore." They moved here when Vivica was ten. She was sixteen going on seventeen at this point. She still missed living in Beverly Hills.

"Vivica I don't understand why you dislike Grosse Pointe so much. It's not that far from the city, and there is so much going on during the week here." DJ pointed out.

"Beverly Hills is not all that it is cracked up to be," Gale mumbled.

As she took out the last of the curlers, she handed them to her mother. She turned to DJ. "Grosse Pointe is a far cry from being Beverly Hills. Heck, Manhattan would be an upgrade." Her mother and step-father just didn't understand. Vivica was destined for greater things. "If I were in Beverly Hills right now, I could be posing for photos that could end up in a major magazine. Get discovered."

Gale wished that Vivica would give up on her obsession to go back to Beverly Hills. She wasn't going to so long as she lived under her rules. "You were offered the chance to be in the Trusdon fashion show just last month." Gale reminded her.

The Trusdon fashion show… Vivica scoffed loudly. "Oh, how quant. A bunch of locals and myself modeling clothes for other locals. What's even the point?" Sure, she would get to keep most of the clothes, but where would she even wear them? She was stuck wearing her hideous uniform at school, and on the weekends the farthest she ever ventured was Troy.

Before the semi-argument between the three of them could continue someone knocked on the door. Vivica looked at her mother and step-father. "You can both leave now." She knew exactly who it was.

"Remember, you need to bring the bag of clothes to Sister Mary Newman tonight for the rummage sale this weekend." Gale reminded her as she walked into the kitchen. Vivica gave her a look of acknowledgment.

She opened the door. "Hey, Weston." Cliff Knight said. His striking eyes were blinding to Vivica. He looked particularly good in his school uniform. He might have been the only one in school who could actually pull it off. Vivica loved the way his ass looked in dress slacks. It was the one advantage to having to be stuck in these ugly things all day. "Are you ready for another exciting day of learning?" Cliff joked to her.

She couldn't help but smile. "No... But we might as well get going." She grabbed her backpack and closed the door behind them. She didn't even bother calling to her parents in the kitchen to say goodbye. "Cliff, where is your car?" She wondered.

"I thought we could walk today. It's only four blocks from your house." He said as they made their way up to the sidewalk.

This was true. Her house was close to the school. "You live like a mile away though." Vivica pointed out.

Cliff was hoping she wouldn't point that out. He was well aware of that. "Well, we had another fight last night. So, I'm walking for the next week or so." Cliff and his father Rodrick had always been two very different people. Rodrick cared about one thing, and that was making money. Cliff cared about other people and wished he would realize that his employees deserved better working conditions.

"He didn't hit you again? Did he?" Vivica asked. She stopped as the two walked up the street.

"Not this time. Don't worry. He hasn't hit me in a while. Not since I started hitting the gym." Cliff explained. Vivica frowned and Cliff noticed. "Hey, don't worry. I know how to take care of myself. My mom and grandma won't let anything bad happen to me. So, what if I get hit every once in a blue moon?"

Vivica wished that there was something she could do. It wasn't as if she could call the police on Rodrick Knight of all people. He was the CEO of *Knight Motors*. They would probably come to arrest her instead. "Well, you can always come to my house tonight if you want to study."

Cliff smiled. He was glad that Vivica wasn't going to make a bigger deal of this than she needed. He knew she probably wanted to. "I can probably come over for a little bit, but Brianna and I are supposed to hang out for a little bit as well around five."

Brianna Belle was both Cliff and Vivica's best friend. Lately, however, it seemed that Brianna wanted there to be more going on between her and Cliff. Vivica could easily see it. It all started when Vivica finally admitted to Brianna that she had feelings for Cliff. "Well, why don't you invite Brianna over as well? We can all just hang out together." Vivica suggested. If Brianna thought, she was going to get private time with Cliff she had another thing coming. Brianna might have been her best friend, but Cliff was the man of her dreams and when push came to shove she would be the one to win over his heart.

"Yeah, that could be fun," Cliff said with a smile on his face. Vivica could easily tell that Cliff was oblivious to the crush that both girls had on him…

LUCY – 2018

Lucy sat at her desk in Vivica's home office. She was finishing up a quick email. She looked at the time. She needed to start heading to the airport. "Vivica, I'll be back tonight." The blonde assistant grabbed her bag and headed towards the door.

"Where do you think you are going?" Vivica asked her as she was picking out different earrings for the evening at the vanity in front of her. "We still have so much to go over before tonight."

"Everything is set. You have to arrive at six – thirty. The doors open at seven – thirty. I have to go pick up my brother and sister from the airport." Lucy explained. This was the hundredth time she had reminded Vivica of this. Vivica never remembered anything.

Taking a deep breath, Vivica nodded. "Alright, but I expect you there tonight. You know I couldn't do this without you. This will be the first program that has your name right next to mine as an organizer." Vivica took another deep breath. "Look, I just need you there tonight." Vivica didn't know why, but for some reason, as of late she had become very nervous. Nial had been more distant than usual lately. He was coming home later, and it seemed on purpose so he could slip into bed while she was asleep. She very much doubted anything was wrong, but she needed to know she had someone on her side that night. Tiffany and Margot were not going to be the highlight of the night. Nial also never stood up to his older sister, so even if they were in a super loving mood, he would just lower his head while Margot and Vivica went at it.

It was nice to hear Vivica admit she needed Lucy for once. She almost never heard Vivica talk like this. "You know I will be there. I just need to pick up my brother and sister from the airport. That said, remember I have taken off Monday next week, but I will have my phone on. I have to enroll Langley in school."

"Alright," Vivica said with a reluctant smile.

***

Lucy stood in the airport waiting to see her brother and sister. She felt guilty for some reasons. The number one reason being that she hadn't been there for the past five years. They spoke on the phone now and then, but that was it. Once Lucy and Austin moved in together, she ended up spending holidays with him, and she could never justify getting off work for random family events. She always sent gifts though on birthdays and Christmas. She wished she had known what their father was up to. Well, no she knew what he was up to, and that was why she left.

Their father, Alexander Kingsley made the majority of his money as a stockbroker. The issue was that he was completely corrupt with mob connections. Lucy had been aware of the rumors since she was in sixth grade. She learned very quickly it was best if she stayed out of her father's business. Lucy became responsible for taking care of her brother and sister though when their mother disappeared. Lucy still wasn't even sure if their parents were legally divorced. It had been so long since she had seen her mother. So, long in fact that her mother was all but dead to her.

It took longer for Lucy to realize that her father was just as useless in her life. When she turned twenty-three, she had been out of college for over a year. Lucy was working in the executive level of an international hotel chain. She came home while her brother and sister were at school one day, to find her father in his dirty dealings. Lucy wasn't going to confront him about it, but she knew that the FBI or IRS or someone was on their tale. This was five years ago. It took five years, but the past finally caught up with her father. He was arrested a week earlier.

Lucy came to the realization five years earlier that had she stayed around she would probably be in prison with him. It turned out that the reason she had gotten her job was through a shady business deal that her father had a connection with. While the hotel got off scot-free, her father was probably looking at five to ten, with additional charges that could earn him up to thirty plus.

When she found out what exactly was going on, she goggled the best way to remove herself from the situation without completely erasing herself from existence. She decided the best thing for her was to quit her job and find work in the Midwest. Michigan was far from a stable job market, but she had once run into Margot Fitzpatrick at one of the hotels she had worked for. They hit it off one afternoon and gave her a business card. Luckily, Margot had remembered her. Unluckily, Margot didn't have any jobs that matched her qualifications at that moment. Lucy had flown out though just to talk with her. She accidentally bumped into Vivica who had previously had such careers like housewife and model. She had worked for a defunct cosmetic company owned by the *Fitzpatrick Group,* but that had been years earlier. Vivica needed someone with drive. So, Lucy immediately moved to Michigan. She had to live in a small one bedroom in Warren for the first two years before she moved in with Austin. Lucy only took the money she had in her personal account from work. She hadn't touched the account set up by her father. Which as of right now was blocked by the FBI.

People started exiting the plane. She noticed a lot of people who clearly had been tourists or on business trips. Then they walked out. It only took a moment for them to spot her. Xander had a smile on his face the moment that they made eye contact. He was twenty-one years old with short blond hair and sky-blue eyes. He had clearly been working out because he was much bigger than when she had left home. Then there was Langley. She had naturally curly blonde hair, a fake tan that had clearly faded, with brown eyes. Langley was the ultimate junior socialite. "Hi, guys," Lucy said. She didn't really know how she should react. It wasn't as if this was a positive reunion.

Xander walked right up to her and gave her a quick hug. "Hey, Lucy. I've missed you. Thank you so much for taking us in." He said.

Langley looked at her sister from head to toe. "What have you done to yourself? Lay off the avocado…" She scuffed. To Langley, this was all a large inconvenience. Her weekend plans had been ruined.

"Well, we better get going. I have a work thing I need to get back to." Lucy explained to her younger siblings. She was just going to ignore the fat comment. She weighed the same as she did before she left…

"Oh joy, I get to sit in some strangers' house all evening while you are at work." Langley rolled her eyes.

"Austin is my fiancé, Langley. He is hardly a stranger." She said as they headed for the exit.

NIAL – 2018

After making his midday rounds, Nial Fitzpatrick returned to his office. Nial was a complicated person to describe. He was a miracle worker regarding his medical practice. There was a reason he was chief of staff at Grosse Pointe General Hospital. His family was genuinely shocked when he declined an active role in the family company to be a doctor. He did so though because he wanted his sister Margot to get the chance she more than deserved at running the company. While Nial might have sounded like a saint in that regard he also was known as a womanizer with an addiction for a certain redhaired vixen. Vivica or Viv as he would call her, was his greatest conquest but also his greatest regret. It was the fact that their relationship had never been two-sided. She gave him his children though.

Nial had known from the beginning that Vivica only married him because her sister stole Cliff Knight from her. Vivica had never had any interest in him. It wasn't to say that he thought Vivica didn't love him now. Nial had been known to cheat on Vivica regularly. Sometimes, he was able to keep it a secret sometimes he wasn't. It was hard to find women who would just keep their mouth shut. Nial didn't understand why women couldn't just accept that sometimes regular sex with someone was just that. Regular sex. He still came home to Vivica at the end of the night. Though, Nial also wished that Vivica would grasp that sometimes herself. He took care of her. He is the reason she had her name in the spotlight at all. It wasn't because of Cliff Knight.

Nial realized his phone was ringing. He looked down. It was Vivica. He just let it ring. She had called three times today. Nial had better things to do than listen to his wife. This was the first time all day that he had to himself and really wasn't in the mood. When the phone finally stopped ringing, he noticed a series of texts from her as well. Nial didn't even bother reading them.

He just sat down at his desk and looked at his agenda for next week. Then someone knocked on his door. "Come in." He said.

"Doctor Fitzpatrick." Austin Martin nodded. Austin had just turned thirty and was one of the better doctors at GPG. He was well on his way to a very successful career. "I just wanted to tell you that your um… Well, your visitor has been secured."

"Good. Yes, very good." Nial stated. He looked up from his desk. "I trust that she has been put in a nice hotel room?"

Austin cleared his throat. "Yes, she should be fine there. The guard you hired took over as soon as I dropped her off." Austin had been hired by Nial to do some extra work. Austin grew up the middle class. He would be paying off student loans into his fifties When Nial offered him the work; he was pitched with the prospect of having his loans paid off by thirty-eight. While the concept of having that sort of money did worry him he knew he couldn't pass up such an offer. "She is pretty excited about tonight. I'm not really sure why. It's just a silly gala."

He couldn't help but smile at knowing she was excited. "Well, remember this girl isn't used to getting out much. This evening should prove to be most entertaining."

Before anything else could be said, someone else walked in. Hope Knight. Nial's niece by marriage. "Uncle Nial, I need to talk about getting my rounds changed. I cannot deal with one of the older gentlemen I've been assigned to. He has pinched my rear end twice now." She didn't even notice Austin until she turned to her right. "Oh, hi Doctor Martin." She said. She then turned back to Nial before he could even acknowledge her. "It just won't do anymore. I can put up with just about anything but not that. I realize this is only my first year in the student doctor program, but still."

"Hope, darling don't worry. I will assign that patient to someone else. Now if you don't mind, I was having a conversation with Doctor Martin." He explained.

Hope wasn't used to being skirted around, but fine. She seemed to get what she wanted. "Well, alright. I guess I will see you later then."

"Yes, tonight at the gala," Nial explained.

"Not this year. I'm scheduled to work. I couldn't get anyone to switch shifts with me." Hope told him.

That just simply wouldn't do Nial thought. He wanted his entire family there tonight. "Well Hope, I do hope that you have an outfit picked out anyway. I will get you off tonight's shift."

This was unexpected Hope thought. She really didn't mind working tonight. It wasn't as if she wanted to watch as her mother and aunt fought once again. "Oh, that's fine, uncle Nial. I don't want you to give me any special treatment."

"Don't consider it special treatment. You should be there with the rest of your family." He told his niece. "Now hurry along now."

Hope left, and Austin once again cleared his throat. "So, anyway I just wanted to catch you up. I should probably get back to rounds myself."

Nial nodded his head. "Yes, that is probably for the best. I'll have your next payment in your account by Monday. You've done good kid." Nial expressed.

HANNAH – 2018

Hannah Knight exited the elevator of *Knight Motor's* world headquarters. She was on the executive level. It had been a year since she had walked these halls. Hannah had moved to Royal Oak and had been living with a group of friends' Well ex-friends as of today. She couldn't believe they kicked her out. Sure, she had been late on the rent, but it wasn't her fault she been laid off at the bookshop she had been working at. Hannah had long black hair with gray almost silver looking eyes. She had a natural tan about her. At twenty-four she had accomplished nothing she thought she was going to accomplish. It killed her to be back here, but she had no choice. She ignored her father's secretary and walked in any way. "Dad, we need to talk."

Cliff had been on the phone. "I'm going to have to call you back," Cliff explained to the person he was on the phone with. He stood up. He had not seen his daughter in forever. "Hannah, what on earth are you doing here?"

"I need to borrow some money. I got kicked out of my house and haven't had a job in several weeks." Hannah just blurted out. She hated having to admit that, but she really didn't feel like skirting around the facts with her father today.

The last time Cliff saw Hannah, she had pierced her eyebrow and lip. It would appear that both those piercings were now gone. "Well, you are more than welcome to move back home. Your room is just as you left it."

"There is no way I can move back home." Hannah had finally escaped the nightmare of the North Pointe last year. North Pointe was the name of the family estate. Which was reason enough not to want to go back. Hannah tried to make it in the world on her own. She didn't want to be known as the rich girl handed everything. It didn't help that her parents thought of her being just like that. Which wasn't the case what so ever.

When she was growing up, she learned quickly that her sister Hope was the favorite child above her and her brother Harry. She never understood why. Hope was fake. She kissed everyone's ass. She did everything the proper way. Sure, Hannah had a history of bad choices, but it wasn't always her fault most of the time.

"Well, are you expecting money? I clearly remember a conversation in which you said you never wanted another cent from your mother or myself." Cliff reminded her.

"I was younger and stupid." She admitted. "Look, don't think of it as an handout. I will gladly pay you back once I get a new job." Hannah explained. The fact is that she actually would pay him back and he knew it. Hannah never left a debt unpaid. That wasn't her way. "You know what. I'll figure something else out."

Cliff wished that Hannah wasn't so stubborn. He wanted to help his daughter, but he wasn't going to just let her waltz back into his life after a year of being left in the dark not knowing if she was actually alright or not. "Hannah, where do you plan on staying tonight?"

Hannah hadn't thought about that. "Well, I've never slept in a car before, but there is a first for everything I guess." Hannah said off the tip of her tongue. She wasn't even looking to get pity from her father, but if it came down to it, he could feel bad. Hannah didn't care. It wasn't as if she was living off her parents like Hope still was. Sure, Hope was in medical school, but that was Hope's choice to get into medicine. Hannah had a business degree from U of M.

"Oh, for crying out loud Hannah, you are moving back in. I will get you a job here." He told her. "I'm not offering you this. I'm telling you that is what you are doing."

"I'll accept your demands on one condition. You get me a job at one of the Knight owned dealerships. I want to start at the bottom and work my way up. I'll move back home, but the moment I have enough money, or a better offer comes along I move out." Hannah was only agreeing to this because she really didn't want to sleep in her car. Like, that was ever actually a choice. She didn't even know where she would be able to park.

"I can agree to that. That said until you move out you will have to act like a member of this family. So, tonight you will be attending the hospital gala. I assume you have no proper dresses. So, you can either take my credit card and buy yourself a new outfit or borrow one from Hope." He held out his credit card. She growled almost and took it. Hannah walked out. Cliff knew that she wouldn't borrow something from Hope…

CLIFF – 1986

"I guess, we will have to cancel our plans to go to Belle Isle tomorrow. I mean we really can't go without your car." Vivica pointed out.

"You could always borrow one of your parent's cars," Cliff stated.

Her mother would never let her borrow her car. Even if Cliff or Brianna was driving, she wouldn't trust them with Vivica in the car. Vivica was notorious for being an absolute terrible driver. DJ would be working, so that also eliminated his car. Though, she did suspect that he would offer it up if it meant earning points towards Vivica. "We might as well see if any decent movies are coming out. My parents are not going to be an option. We know Brianna's parents won't let her drive with me in the car." No one trusted Vivica in their car.

Cliff nodded. "Yeah, I'm sure there is a decent movie playing." They walked up to the school. A familiar Knight limo pulled up beside them. "Vivica, go inside." He said. Vivica looked in his direction. "Vivica, go inside now." He instructed his friend.

Vivica knew better than to get in between Cliff and his father. There wasn't much she could do anyway. She headed towards the doors walking up the steps. She looked back for one second as Rodrick got out of the back of the limo…

"Clifton Knight. How dare you leave North Pointe before I was done speaking to you this morning." He spoke yelled. Rodrick only had one tone of voice. It wasn't normal talking, but it also wasn't screaming. "Well, boy what do you have to say?"

He didn't say anything. Cliff looked to the ground. He really wished his father hadn't come to school. "Why couldn't you have waited until I got home to talk about this?"

Rodrick knew better than to wait for him to come home. "I'm not stupid. You would hide out at one of your little friend's houses."

Cliff didn't want to do this right now. He just wanted to go to class and get through the day. He could have dealt with this when he got home. At that point, Rodrick would be plastered and more than likely with whatever call girl he was currently seeing. "Can we please just do this later?" Cliff begged his father.

"Boy, we are going to do this now and later. I'm your father, and you will listen to me. I don't understand why you cannot be the son I wanted. You are not worthy of the Knight name." Rodrick screamed loud enough that people probably could hear from inside the building. Nobody was going to come. They all knew who he was and what he could do for or to them." He got in the face of his son and then slapped him across the face hard enough it left a red mark. "I'll see you later." Rodrick got back into the car and drove off.

Vivica, who had been watching from inside, quickly ran out dropping her books halfway down the path from the front entrance. "Cliff are you alright?" Cliff said nothing. He just stood there. "Cliff, say something. I don't know how to help." Vivica shouted at him. Cliff fell to his knees and continued to say nothing. Vivica squatted down next to him and hugged him. She didn't know what else she could do.

The Fitzpatrick mansion was a four-story (basement included) home. The fourth floor had not been used in years. It was initially a maid's quarters; however, the Fitzpatrick family had never possessed a full staff. Anyone who was anyone knew the kitchen was the heart of the home though. This is where Vivica spent most of her time frantically trying to not have a panic attack amid getting this gala together… "Holly, why is there no food in this fridge?" Vivica asked as she looked through the fully stocked refrigerator.

"You need to calm down for five minutes Vivica. I don't know why this event always works you up so much." Holly told her friend and employer. "I realize that Tiffany is going to…"

"That right there is the issue!" Vivica shouted as she turned around and faced Holly. "This is the one event a year that I know that Tiffany will be at. It can never just be simple with her. She always ends up ruining things for me." Vivica had always been compared with Tiffany. It wasn't fair she thought. They were so different even if they were sisters. Tiffany dreamt of being a doctor. Vivica dreamt of fame and fortune. Which, apparently wasn't noble enough for some people. Vivica wished people would look past Tiffany's supposed sense of maturity and actually look at her as a person.

When Holly was growing up, she had limited interaction with the Knight and Fitzpatrick families. She knew of them of course. Vivica was a legend in Grosse Pointe. She was a legend in general really. None of this really ever mattered to Holly though. Holly only went to work for the Fitzpatrick family after her husband was temporarily laid off. She thought that she was going to hate every moment of it. She was partially right. Nial was a complete and total asshole. Then, there was Margot. She had a true talent for pissing people off. It confused Holly to no end as to why Vivica would want to live with this man or be around his sister. Vivica was better than them.

"Holly, why aren't you listening to me?" Vivica screamed as Holly appeared to be nodding off into darkness. "I just hope that Nial shows up and that Margot doesn't team up with Tiffany. I swear people need to open their eyes to the person that Tiffany really is!"

Tiffany was another story altogether, Holly thought. She wasn't really a bad person. Though, it was clear she belittled Vivica any chance she got. Her achievements always had to outshine Vivica's, even when they could have been equal. Still, it wasn't hard to tell that if Vivica had something Tiffany wanted it more. She knew that the bulk of Vivica's hatred for her sister came from the fact that she stole Cliff from her. Which, she honestly found ridicules. It had happened ages ago. Why did it still matter that much? If it did, then why did Vivica stay in town? Though, Holly did wonder. Did Tiffany love Cliff? Or did Tiffany love the fact that Vivica wanted him?

Years ago, Holly had read about Tiffany being kidnapped for several years only to return to town. Vivica had been illegally married to Cliff and had been raising Tiffany's children as if they were her own. Tiffany apparently came back into town as if nothing had happened and just expected Vivica to leave. It made sense to some extent. However, Tiffany had been so cold in the articles about the situation. Holly was in eighth grade when this happened. Her friend and her used to come home from school and read up on all the latest drama that had transpired from this. Vivica for whatever reason though seemed to stay silent aside from saying she was happy that her sister had come home. Holly never actually asked Vivica about any of this when she did come to work for her. It always was on her mind about what happened though.

"So, do you think I should go to the spa?" Vivica looked at Holly. "Holly? Earth to Holly!" Vivica sighed. "Yup, this is how today is going. My personal assistant went MIA to attend to family, and my maid is ignoring me. Why is it so hard to have loyal friends that you pay?"

Holly rolled her eyes. "Will you relax?" She told Vivica. "Tonight will be fine. It goes over well every single year. It isn't like you don't see your sister or Margot other days of the year. Heck, Margot was here yesterday, and you didn't get into as big a screaming match as usual. That must be a good sign."

That was true Vivica thought. Then, she remembered that Margot had just gotten Botox and was trying not to talk. It didn't stop her from trying to taunt Margot a little bit. She would admit that when it came to Margot, it was a two-sided battle. That bitch just downright hated her for very little reason. Vivica never even knew what it was precisely that Margot hated about her. She assumed it was because Margot didn't think she was good enough for the Fitzpatrick family. Though, Margot had no issue with telling that to her face. There had to be more she thought.

It always bothered Vivica that people thought she was so bad for the Fitzpatrick family, or the Knight family for that matter. In a way, she had been connected to the Fitzpatrick's for years though. Her mother had been married to DJ Brash. The younger half-brother of Nadia Bloom-Fitzpatrick. Who happened to be the mother of Margot and Nial. She had retired to Florida several years ago. The two of them had a love-hate relationship themselves, but it seemed to be more love than hate. Especially, after DJ died.

"Holly let's go into the office for a bit," Vivica said. She needed someone to drive her.

LUCY – 2018

They were finally home. Thank goodness, Lucy thought to herself. Langley wouldn't shut up the entire drive home. She realized that her sister had just lost everything basically, but for goodness sake, she needed to take a reality check for one second. Just one second. She complained about anything and everything under the fucking sun. Lucy couldn't handle it for a second more. "Alright, welcome home!" Lucy said. Xander smiled at her. Langley gave her a sour look as if she had just been told she was going to be sleeping in a meth house. "Your rooms are upstairs, at the end of the hall. You can decide who gets which one. The social worker said that your things would be here within the next week or so. They still are going over what they are withholding until the trial.

"Thanks again Lucy for letting us move in. I'm going to spend the weekend getting a lay of the land and plan to start looking for a job on Monday." Xander explained. He would have loved to have applied for graduate school too, but he knew that there just wasn't enough money. Technically, Lucy had told him that Austin and she had talked it over and they had the money to help him out a little bit. He didn't want the help though. Xander planned to become his own person in light of all that had happened. Which included paying his own way.

Langley took another look around the room. It wasn't small, but it wasn't large either, and the furniture looked so early 2000's. It just was one more thing she would have to deal with. It seemed that since her father had been arrested no one really thought about how this actually was affecting her. No one thought about how this would affect her at all. Which was really starting to piss her off. "So, when are we enrolling me in school?

"Monday morning," Lucy said.

"Please, tell me this uniform is not going to clash with any part of my body. I got off so lucky that my old high school's uniform didn't clash. I just bet you I don't get off lucky this time around." Langley stated. She knew very well that she was going to have to reinsert herself as queen bee of this high school. She had one up on everyone already. She was from Manhattan. That was basically all she had to say. It would take some dodging around her parental issues, but she knew that she could make it work probably.

Lucy and Xander looked at one another. Lucy was making a look that said, Xander better be the one to tell her. "Um, Langley… You won't be wearing a uniform at your new school." Xander admitted.

No uniform? Langley thought. Well, that just made things even better. She didn't have her full wardrobe as of yet, but she did have enough of it to show off to these people. "Well, that works perfectly. This just better not be one of those progressive schools though. I need some tradition." Langley laughed. Like she gave a damn.

Once again, the two older siblings looked at each other. Lucy sighed. "Langley, you are going to public school…"

"Come again?" Langley asked her sister. "Did you just accidentally say public school? Oh, Lucy how funny." She looked at her sibling, and Lucy said nothing. She was laughing awkwardly though. "Right, it's a total joke I assume?" Langley stopped laughing. "Oh, for fuck sake!" She stormed upstairs and slammed a door. "I'm taking the room on the left!" She screamed to Xander.

Xander sighed. "She hasn't been taking this very well." He explained.

That had to be the understatement of the year Lucy thought. She knew that Langley had always been a little needier than herself or her brother but Christ she was taking things to a whole new level. It had been a few years, but still. "I think she need to just cool down a little bit. I have to get ready for a gala that my boss and I organized tonight. It shouldn't last past eleven if that. You can use one of those websites to order take out if you want. My card information should be on them. I'll leave my login." She frowned. She hated that she would be leaving her siblings in a little bit, but she had no choice. Life moved on around them. Lucy suspected that Xander knew this.

"Yeah, that should be fine. I'll order Langley sushi. That always calms her down a little bit. She can check her social media, and I'm sure she will be fine." Xander explained.

It seemed apparent to Lucy that Xander was looking for the good in this situation. She wasn't sure that she would have been able to do the same if she was being honest. However, she was a completely different person. "Well feel free to watch TV down here or go up to your room." She said as she walked upstairs. She was going to be in the bathroom for at least an hour getting ready.

TIFFANY – 2018

One thing that Tiffany Knight always knew was that she was a good surgeon. In fact, if she were honest with herself, she was a fantastic surgeon. The day before she successfully operated on a patient that if she were being honest probably had no hope of survival. Yet, somehow, he pulled through. Tiffany couldn't help but take the credit. She walked down the hall of Grosse Pointe General with a smile on her face. Sure, she wasn't looking forward to tonight at all. That said, it would only be a few hours and then she would come home and not see her idiot little sister for probably a few weeks. That is how these things tended to go. Tiffany looked at her phone for a moment as she walked. Cliff had texted her that he loved her. That's when she accidentally bumped into someone. She looked up. It was Margot Fitzpatrick. "Oh, I'm so sorry Margot."

Margot smiled at Tiffany. "Oh, it's no problem what so ever. I was just meeting a few board members for lunch here today. We order out. Obviously, we might have the best hospital food in the state, but it's still hospital food." Margot explained. Margot was a tall woman with broad shoulders and dark auburn hair. She came off as being a lot stronger than she probably was. Which Margot liked. "I'm sure you are looking forward to tonight."

Tiffany tried to crack a smile. "Well, it is for a very good cause," Tiffany admitted.

"Yes, that is a very good way to look at it. Don't worry. It should be an evening of surprises in a good way as far as I'm concerned. I've been speaking with Nial about it lately. Trust me; you won't want to miss a moment of it." Margot explained. She had a mischievous smile on her face.

The main issue that Tiffany had with this evening was that her sister was sure to piss her off at an event that was supposed to be about her and her fellow doctors. Sure, Nial was there, and technically Vivica was there to support him. Technically. She wasn't foolish. Tiffany knew very well that Vivica was still madly in love with Cliff. Which drove her up a wall to no end. Why couldn't Vivica move on? Nial was a good man who seemed to love her. Sure, they had been divorced several times over, but Vivica could be blamed for a lot of that as far as Tiffany was concerned. She wasn't a very good wife in Tiffany's opinion. Tiffany felt that Cliff was always her first priority along with their children. Which was another thing that Tiffany didn't understand. Vivica never really tried very hard to be in her children's life.

"Well Tiffany, I do have to get going. I'm sure there will be much to talk about tonight though. I cannot wait to see you there. Seriously, you are in for a big treat." Margot blew her kisses goodbye and then walked away somewhat giddy.

Normally, she would question what Margot was up to, but Tiffany still had to focus on work. She continued walking down the hall when she noticed Hope was studying on a bench. "Hello, honey." Tiffany said to her daughter.

Hope looked up from her book. "Mom, hey!" She said. Hope stood up and smiled. "I didn't see you leave the house this morning." She explained.

"Early morning surgery and what have you." Tiffany explained. "So, how is your day going?" She wondered.

"Fine, I guess." Hope admitted. "Nothing out of the ordinary." Hope liked to play this game where people asked how she was doing and she would be vague about it. That way the conversation was sure to be about her. "I'm just not very fond of my rounds. Uncle Nial said he would take care of it but I don't think he took me very seriously."

Tiffany put her hand on Hope's shoulder. "Well dear, if you don't like your rounds I will make sure that Nial changes them up for you. Don't you worry about a thing." She explained. Tiffany thought that Hope was such a good child. She had always been growing up as apposed to her sister and even brother. Hope never was a problem child. It was always Hannah who was getting herself into trouble. It never ceased to amaze her some of the things that Hannah could manage to do to herself. "Don't worry about a thing. I will get it all fixed up for you."

Hope smiled. "Thanks, mom. I really hate to be a bother, but it's just hard dealing with certain elements of my current rounds if I'm being honest." Hope explained.

"It's no trouble at all dear." Tiffany smiled at her daughter. "I have to go meet with a patient. I will see you later." She explained. Tiffany walked off.

VIVICA –1986

It was lunchtime, and Vivica sat down next to Cliff. He hadn't said any-thing all morning. It sorts of worried her that he said nothing. This wasn't uncommon with Cliff though. He never liked to speak about things involving his father. It was apparent that people around them were talking. Vivica hated that Rodrick would hit his own son in public. Though, it was far from the first time. "Are you doing alright?" Vivica tried to ask her best friend.

Cliff didn't want to answer. If he answered, then Vivica would probably not get off the subject. "I'll be fine. Let's just pretend that nothing happened. Ok?" He gave her a look that screamed drop it.

If he really wanted her to drop it, Vivica would. For, the moment anyway. She started to take a bite of her sandwich when Brianna sat down. Brianna with her brown hair and brown eyes. She looked so pure and innocent with her almost baby-like looks. Vivica wanted to hate her so much but she couldn't. She was her best friend "Hey, guys!" Brianna said. She had a smile on her face. Vivica was sure that Brianna had heard the gossip about Cliff. She also knew that unlike Vivica, Brianna knew how to just leave it alone. "So, Cliff are we still hanging out after school?" She asked.

"Vivica invited us to study at her house actually." Cliff said. He has a slight smile on his face.

"Oh really?" Brianna said. A normal girl would be pissed off, and secretly Brianna probably was a little bit. However, instead of showing it she just sounded a little bit sad. "Well, I guess that should be fun as well. We do have a big study load and all." Brianna explained.

Sometimes, Vivica pictured messing up Brianna's perfect hair. Vivica took the high ground though. If she were any other girl, she would probably have slapped her silly by now. They were such opposites, and if Vivica was honest, they were only friends because of Cliff. Still, it was weird. Vivica did love her like a sister. A better sister than her real one. She rarely if ever thought of Tiffany. It was strange that she was even thinking of her now to be completely honest. She loved her sister but considering it had been years since they had really spoken it was almost like they weren't even sisters. Vivica sighed. "I'm sure that we can order a pizza or something. It will be a fun evening I'm sure."

"Yeah sounds like a plan." Cliff looked at his watch. "I have to meet a few of my basketball friends for the rest of the period." He picked up his tray and walked off.

"I feel so bad for him." Brianna said.

Vivica nodded in agreement. "I saw the entire thing. Rodrick drove up and told him off for no good reason." She still didn't even know what had happened. "I wish he would let us help him out sometimes."

"Well, to be honest Vivica I think we do as much as we possibly can. Brianna admitted. She had known Cliff most of her life, and he was just the sweetest boy ever. The only issue was his father. Brianna tried not to judge people, but Rodrick Knight might be the one person on the planet that she could honestly say she hated with a passion. "It was nice of you to offer Cliff, and I come over tonight. It makes a lot of sense, to be honest. He needs both of us right now." Brianna smiled.

If she could just slap that girl silly... Vivica thought to herself. Why was she so chipper towards Vivica? Yes, they were friends, but it wasn't like Vivica was a very good friend if she was really being honest with herself. "Well, like you said. He needs us obviously."

VIVICA – 2018

"I don't understand why you were being so slow, Holly…" Vivica said. The two just walked into executive level of the *Fitzpatrick Group.* Vivica's office happened to be on this level. It was in a thirty-floor building just outside of Detroit that was completely owned by the Fitzpatrick family. "I just need to get a few papers and maybe answer a few emails. Then I can go back home and get ready for the event in peace."

"Do you think we should stop by the banquet hall before going home?" Holly suggested.

"No, I'll be there three hours early regardless. My entire staff is there right now minus Lucy. Though she should be getting there before we do." Vivica was glad to have Holly in her life. She was the best blend of maid, driver, and best friend. If it weren't for Holly, Vivica probably would have gone insane.

The two friends continued to walk down the hall as they made their way into Vivica's office. When they walked in Margot was standing there with a measuring tape. Margot instantly looked at Vivica. "What the hell are you doing here?"

Vivica scoffed. "Well, it's my office. I should be the one asking you that." Vivica pointed out.

Margot walked over to Vivica with a giddy smile. "Sweetheart, I own the whole damn building. Which means I can go any damn where I please." Margot informed her less than favorite sister-in-law.

"Why do you have a tape measurer?" Vivica asked.

"I'm thinking about expanding my office into yours." Margot explained. She had wanted to expand her office ever since she took over as CEO of the *Fitzpatrick Group.* This office had been occupied by one moron or another over the years which was always the issue. It wouldn't be for much longer though. She couldn't tell Vivica that. "You don't even like working from the office. You prefer doing so from my childhood home."

Vivica scoffed. "Yes, Margot you are right. I do prefer working from home. That way I don't have to deal with you." She crossed her arms. Margot looked at her and just laughed as she walked out of the room. Vivica had never gotten along with that woman even before she had married Nial. "Alright, we just need to do a tiny bit of work before the gala, and then we will get back home." Vivica walked over to her desk and sat down logging on to her computer. On the screen was a picture of herself and Nial with their son Brad. It had to be a few years old. Brad practically looked grown at this point.

It was the hardest thing in the world for her to send Brad to boarding school, but his father insisted upon it. She wanted him to go to Saint Agnes. The local Catholic school which she had attended, and she was pretty sure that the rest of Nial's family had attended at one point or the another yet, Nial was sent off to boarding school from a much younger age than Brad had been, and he fought with her about it for years. Ultimately, he won. Vivica had grown so distant from her son and absolutely hated it. She knew that Brad blamed her for being sent away. The only time they saw one another was on holidays and birthdays, and even then, it was getting harder as he grew older to actually get him to come home.

She needed to stop thinking about Brad. He would be at the gala event tonight. While she knew that he would shrug it off and probably go sit with his cousin Harry, it would still be nice to see him if only for a minute. "Holly, can you check to see what time Brad is arriving?" She wondered.

Holly went on to her tablet and checked. "He didn't really give you a specific time or at least no one updated it. I'm sure that he will be there Vivica." Holly put the tablet down. She knew that Vivica had been looking forward to seeing her son. She remembered how badly New Year's had been for Vivica. Holly was actually home with her own family, but Vivica had given her all the details. Brad announced he was leaving a week early to go skiing in Denver with a group of friends. Vivica had attempted to get him to stay, but Nial had already said ok to it. Vivica was an emotional wreck for the rest of the week. Had Holly known she was essentially spending New Year's Eve alone, she would have invited Vivica over. Not that she would have accepted. Vivica was under the impression that Holly lived on eight-mile. She didn't...

"This event needs to be perfect." Vivica stated. "That is why I have decided you and Lucy have to keep me as far away from Tiffany and Margot as possible tonight." Vivica knew she was asking her maid and friend to basically do a suicide mission for her. She didn't care. Vivica needed to fix her relationship with her son and figure out why her husband had been so distant over the past few months.

HANNAH – 2018

North Pointe was a hauntingly beautiful mansion. Hannah could at least admit to that being true. She walked in through the front door. Hannah used to remember her grandfather telling her as a young girl that Knight's always entered from the front. The back was for the help. This apparently meant nothing to her as an adult. She actually found it rather offensive. She looked to the right and noticed the same portrait that had hung in the foyer since before she was born. It was a family portrait that had to have been done back in the early 60's of the Knight family. Her great-great-grandfather Heathcliff, her great-grandparents Benton and Delia, her father's uncle for whom he was named after Clifton and then her grandfather himself Rodrick who was about twelve years old in the portrait. None of them looked to be very happy in the portrait. She never understood why they continued to hang such a depressing portrait in the front of the home. Especially, since her father and grandfather hated one another so much.

Hannah continued on her journey up the grand staircase. As far as she knew no one was going to be home. Her father she knew was still at work. Her mother was probably looking to pick up extra shifts for the night, and hope was probably a fake bitch somewhere. She had no clue what time Harry got off of school. She heard noises though as she passed his room and knocked. "Harry are you in there?" Whatever noises she heard completely stopped and then she heard footsteps, and the door opened. "Hannah? What are you doing here?" He asked his older sister. Harry looked like a real Knight man. He had striking brown-black hair with blue eyes, and incredible bone structure in his face and on the taller side but only 5'10. Harry was the sibling that Hannah could deal with. Probably, because he was no Hope and that was perhaps the only reason.

"Well, I'm back home for the time being." Hannah said unenthusiastically. Just saying it made her feel like she was drinking poison.

Harry smiled. He hadn't seen Hannah in like a month or so. She didn't even come home for the holidays. "That's awesome Hannah! For me at least. Hope has been such a bitch lately. I don't get how the two of you are twins." He realized that she was probably thinking the same thing right now.

"I'm going to be spending the next couple of hours rearranging my room. It needs not to look like I'm still in high school. I also have to research our family's dealerships… So, if you hear a lot of loud noises and swearing don't be shocked." Hannah explained.

"I could always help you out." Harry offered. He needed a distraction so badly.

Hannah smiled. "No. I need to do this on my own. I don't want to hear that I should ask for help. I'm independent." Hannah said. She just had to keep telling herself that this would be temporary.

Her brother shrugged. "Well alright. I'll be here if you need me. The gala doesn't start until later on tonight. I'm sure that it will be super fun." He said. He knew it would just be his mother and aunt fighting all night. Harry assumed the entire town knew this. Probably, the entire state really. "Well, I guess I will see you in a little bit."

"Do you want me to drive you?" Hannah asked.

"Well normally, dad has one of the cars take us." Harry reminded her.

"If you would prefer to drive with mom, dad, and Hope be my guest. I'm driving myself though." Hannah told her brother.

He thought about it for a moment. "Yeah. I think I will take you up on your offer." Harry said.

She nodded at her brother and turned to her room which was across the hall. Hannah would have assumed that it must be filled with boxes and be used as storage. Much to her surprise, it was actually clear of storage. Hannah did realize that the house was large enough that there was no need to use her old room for storage, her family would have to be crazy hoarders. She walked over to a poster on the wall of a singer she had liked when she was in high school. That was the first thing to trash. Hannah looked at her old desk. It had been her father's teenage desk at one point. Her parents had offered to buy her a new desk so many times growing up, but Hannah always likes the idea of it being her father's. Mainly, because of what it had etched in the corner, *CK + VW 4ever*. Hannah would never admit this to anyone, but as much as she really did love her mother and she did. They might not have gotten along, but she knew at the end of the day they loved one another. That said, Hannah always thought that her father would have been so much happier with her aunt, Vivica.

Hannah had always been closer to her aunt than she had been with her mother. It was probably this was because Vivica had raised her for several years when her mother had been kidnapped and thought dead. Vivica had always treated her like a daughter. When her mother came back all of a sudden, it was such a weird experience. It had been like putting an old toy in storage that you loved very much but couldn't play with anymore. Then getting a new one that you loved just as much, not any more or less, and then being told you can play with both but the old one more than the new one. Hannah and her siblings had a very different upbringing, to say the least.

This was probably why her and Hope never really got along. Hope needed their mother. Hannah never did. Harry was oblivious to what was going on at the time. She suspected he would have kept quiet regardless. Harry always tried to remain indifferent. Hannah never could, and that is what would get her in so much trouble.

It seemed that every time Lucy got ready for a work event in her bathroom, she missed the days of having her own bathroom in Manhattan. She had the most amazing bathroom ever back then. In, the present she shared one with Austin. Which might have been bearable if he wasn't so sloppy. Lucy loved the man, but he was not capable of picking up a towel to save his life, and the master bathroom was so tiny. She realized that when Langley found out she would be sharing a bathroom with Xander, she would more than likely throw a fit. Lucy wanted to feel bad for Langley, but it was becoming increasingly harder and harder by the minute. As she thought about Langley, someone knocked on the door. "Lucy, can I please come in?" Langley said from the other side. Lucy was working on her hair. She wasn't so sure that she needed any extra stress right now, but she didn't need Langley going anymore nutty than she already had been. "Sure." She said.

Langley walked into the bathroom and noticed how small the space was. She took a deep breath. "I just wanted you to know… Well… I mean… Look, I'm sorry for how I was acting earlier." Langley stated. Xander had just ripped her a new one for being so bitchy. She couldn't help it. Langley was a self-proclaimed queen bitch. "This is just going to be an adjustment period for me."

"Well, you didn't have to say you were sorry." Lucy lied through her teeth still focusing on her hair. "I do realize it is an adjustment. It was for me too. I had to learn how to drive when I first moved here. You can only imagine how well that went down for the first year… Or so." The two sisters giggled at this. "It will be an adjustment." Lucy said. She hoped that Langley was actually willing to adjust to this. She doubted that Langley was and realized that Xander probably knocked some sense into her head. "Will, you be alright while I'm at work tonight? I'll have some free time tomorrow and Sunday, so we can get to know the town a little bit more. Then on Monday, we will enroll you in school."

While she was trying her hardest, Langley couldn't help but shudder at the concept of public school. She had read up a little on the school she would be attending. West Grosse Pointe High School. On paper, it sounded mediocre at best with the programs she was in at her old school. Langley would try her hardest though. "So, what is this event you are going to?" Langley wondered.

"It's this super boring but very important gala for the local hospital. My boss, Vivica Fitzpatrick's husband, is the chief-of-staff, and she was hired to plan the entire event. Since her husband has to be there she has to double her time as a guest. So, I have to basically run all the behind the scenes things for the night." Lucy explained.

"Did you just say, Vivica Fitzpatrick?" Langley practically shouted. "Vivica Fitzpatrick as in the famous cover model? The famous runway model? Obviously, she is retired, but her career is legendary." Langley was star struck. She had never realized that Lucy worked with Vivica Fitzpatrick. She knew that Lucy worked for an event planning company, but that was about it. She never bothered asking her any more information. "Lucy, you have to let me come!"

Lucy quickly turned to her younger sister. "Langley, I'm not really sure that is a good idea. Like, I said. This is far from the event of the year. A gala here is not the same thing as a gala in New York City. I mean, yeah it will be nice and all, but it is a gala celebrating doctors and nurses. This also remains in this room, but Vivica Fitzpatrick is bat shit crazy!" Lucy told her sister. She liked working with Vivica and was grateful that Vivica gave her a job when she did, but for fuck sake, Vivica was the craziest nut she had ever met. Vivica would call her at all hours of the day and usually bitch about random things such as her sister Tiffany or sister-in-law Margot. Once, she called up sobbing because it was her anniversary to Cliff Knight from when they were teenagers…

Nothing that Lucy just said got through to Langley. "Please, I have to go. I won't talk to her. I just want to say that I have been in the same room as her. I want to see if she still has her figure from the last runway show she did in New York."

"She does…" Lucy knew this because a majority of Vivica's day consisted of Vivica on a treadmill and under eating. Lucy was forced to go with her to doctor's appointments, and the doctors were constantly chastising her for being underweight. Lucy tried slipping her food, but Vivica burned so many calories a day and was on so many laxatives. Lucy was seriously worried about the woman. "Langley, please just stay home, and order take out. Rent pay-per-view. Heck go online shopping and put me in debt. Just don't come to the gala. It isn't going to be worth your time."

"Well, if you insist I guess I will stay at home or at least stay away from the gala." Langley lied through her teeth.

Lucy turned to her sister putting down the curling iron. "Langley look at me." Langley looked her straight in the eye. "You need to promise me right now that you will not show up at the gala."

Langley rolled her eyes. "Lucy, you have my word." Langley said in a very fake voice. Lucy looked at her sister. "You have my word that I won't cause a scene…" Langley smiled.

"Langley… Oh, who am I kidding? Vivica will have caused a scene far before you manage to get in. You have to have an invitation. This is the mid-west. The security guards have no life at these events, so they get all territorial." Lucy for the first time in five years sounded like her old heiress self. This was why she didn't miss that world.

TIFFANY – 2018

Such a daunting day, Tiffany thought to herself as she walked into her kitchen after a long day at work. She had an hair stylist coming over in a half hour to do her hair. She hoped that Hope would be home by then so she could also have her hair done. Tiffany honestly could have cared less about what she looked like that evening. She just wanted to get it over with as quickly as possible. Vivica was sure to make the event a nightmare.

Tiffany was about to walk up the stairs when someone started to walk down. She couldn't believe her eyes. "Hannah?" Tiffany practically croaked. "What are you doing here?"

"Dad didn't tell you? I moved back in." Hannah said as she made her way to the fridge. Hannah wasn't in the mood to get sentimental with her mother. Not that she expected Tiffany to become so anytime soon.

"You moved back in? When? Today? Why didn't you call me to let me know?" Tiffany asked entirely blindsided by this.

What did it matter to her? Hannah thought. This house had over forty rooms in it. It wasn't as if Hannah moving in was going to be an inconvenience. A family of immigrants could live in the entirety of the east wing, and Tiffany would probably go six months before interacting with them. So, why was it that having her back almost sounded like she was putting her out? "Well, gee mom it is great to see you as well. Don't, worry I didn't get any money from dad. He is making me work for it. I know you will be happy to hear that!" Hannah rolled her eyes.

Why did Hannah always have to treat her like this? Tiffany thought. She was a good mother to all her children. Hannah had always been a problem child. It didn't help that Hannah acted so much like... Well, Vivica. "I'm happy to see you, dear. Really, I am." Tiffany said. If she were being honest. She didn't know how she honestly felt.

It really didn't matter to Hannah if her mother, father, sister, or even brother for that matter wanted her home right now. Until further notice she was going to have to live here. "Well, we can stop this awkward charade that is small talk. I'm just getting an apple or something. I don't want to overeat when we have hospital food to look forward to tonight." Hannah explained.

"What do you mean by that?" Tiffany put two and two together. "Oh, are you going to the gala tonight?"

Hannah rolled her eyes. "Yes, dad is making me go. Sorry, if that ruins your evening."

"Hannah, really it doesn't. I just honestly didn't expect to see you. I really have missed you. We all have."

She imagined that Harry missed her to a small extent. She could imagine her father and even maybe her mother missing her because she was their child. That said... "Oh really? Well, that explains all the calls I got from my loving sister Hope over the past few months." Hannah made her way up the stairs taking a bite of a juicy red apple as she did.

Tiffany sighed. Things would never improve with Hannah, she thought. She went over to the fridge herself. She didn't plan on eating anything, but she just needed to focus on something . She needed to keep her mind off of the coming evening. As she was looking through the fridge and then cabinets, the back door opened. Tiffany turned to find her husband, Cliff. Tiffany walked over and gave him a kiss. "Why, didn't you tell me about Hannah coming back home?

It took Cliff a moment to remember he had said Hannah could move back home. He had been spending the afternoon in his past. Which was never a good thing. "Oh, well it is honestly for the best. It's time that girl grow up a little and realize that her family is the most important thing." Cliff stated. He for whatever reason had his father on his mind. He had no idea why. "Shouldn't you be getting ready for tonight?"

"Oh, right well I guess so. If you run into one of our staff just tell them to send the hair dresser to our room to set up. I'm going to be in the shower."

Tiffany explained. Cliff gave her a mischievous look. "You are welcome to join me if you would like." Tiffany stated. Cliff snickered. Cliff grabbed her hand, and the two ran upstairs.

CLIFF – 1986

"Alright, the Chinese food is here." Brianna said as she closed Vivica's front door. "It smells so good." She said in an overly chipper voice.

Cliff was lost in his studies. At least, that is what it looked like to the two girls in the room. He was busy thinking about his family life. Cliff wasn't so sure he could handle this lifestyle much longer. He hated being rich, and he had no one to talk with about it. Brianna would just nod and give him puppy dog eyes and probably hug him. Vivica wouldn't understand him what so ever. She would go on about her life in Beverly Hills and how she wished she still lived in a large home. Cliff seriously considered running away sometimes.

"Earth to Clifton Knight!" Vivica shrieked.

He looked up. "Oh, sorry… I was just studying." He said.

"Well, aren't you hungry?" Vivica wondered. She was smiling.

"Oh, Vivica he is probably just concerned about the test on Monday." Brianna said with a smile.

He nodded. "Yeah. I don't understand why a teacher would schedule a test for Monday. That just eliminates the entire weekend."

Vivica could tell there was more going on. She selfishly didn't want to confront him about it with Brianna there though. She wished that Brianna would remember some family event and leave them alone. That wasn't likely to happen though. Vivica suspected that Brianna was too goody-goody even for her own family. "Well, we can always study together the entire weekend if we have to." Vivica explained.

Brianna frowned. Which was rare for her she had to admit. "I wish I could. I have to go visit my grandparents tomorrow and Sunday though. You two should totally study together though! We are all going to ace this test. I just know it!"

This was one of those rare occasions where Vivica could hug her dear friend Brianna. The idea of being able to spend an entire day with the man she secretly loved? What a concept… "Oh, definitely! We could go to the library tomorrow if you wanted and Sunday I guess. Though, I think my mother wants to go to church this week." Gale had been going on and on about it for weeks.

"I wouldn't mind going to church." Cliff said. He honestly thought it sounded like a good idea. He needed some time to reflect on things, and Sunday Mass would be the perfect place to do so. "Would your parents mind if I come along with you guys?" Cliff asked.

Vivica found this question strange on two levels. For one thing, no teenager unless they were Brianna jumped at the joy of going to church. It also made no sense as to why he would want to spend time with her parents. She didn't even want to spend time with her mother and DJ. Especially, DJ who had been trying to speak to her like he was hip on the current lingo as of late. It was really starting to concern Vivica that something was wrong with him. "Well, I guess if you want to come they won't have an issue with it. At, least I don't see them having an issue. Heck, my mother is so desperate to get me to spend time with her and DJ that she will probably welcome it."

"Thanks, Vivica!" He hugged her.

The warmth of Cliff's body made her shake a little. He smelt of Halston Z-14. Vivica couldn't get enough of that scent. "You're very welcome Cliff." She said blushing. Vivica definitely knew something was up though when she came back to reality. Cliff just hugged her after the offer of going to church together. It wasn't as if she had offered him a billion dollars. Which she was quite sure he had or close to it anyway.

Vivica knew that she was going to have to confront Cliff about what happened earlier and what was on his mind now. She would just have to wait until the next morning to do so. Which would be agonizing for her, but also it concerned her that Cliff would be in a worse place because of it. She wasn't so sure that it was smart to wait if she were being honest. They had been studying for two hours so far. Brianna needed to take the hint that three is a crowed… "Oh, no!" Vivica said. "I totally forgot to drop off the bag of clothes for Sister Mary Newman. Fuck…"

"Oh, well I could drop it off on my way home." Brianna looked at her watch. "I actually should probably get going. My parents want us leaving bright and early for my grandparent's house." Brianna explained "Plus, I love Sister Mary Newman. I wouldn't mind doing it at all."

Clearly, God was paying attention to the fact that Vivica actually planned to go to Mass on Sunday. This was her reward she thought. "Well, if you wouldn't mind." Vivica said looking sympathetically towards her very dear friend Brianna.

Brianna smiled. "It's no problem. Cliff, do you want me to give you a ride home?"

Well, now it made sense Vivica thought. Brianna just wanted some alone time with Cliff. The back-stabbing bitch...

"Actually, I kind of wanted to stay away from home a little longer." Cliff admitted.

"Oh well, that's fine. I guess I will see you both on Monday then!" She got up and grabbed the bag of trash by the door. "Bye Cliff! Bye Vivica!"

The two friends smiled at Brianna as she left. "She is such a nice friend." Cliff said.

"Yes, the nicest..." Vivica said. She wanted to brush her teeth from all the sweetness she had just endured. "Cliff are you alright?"

Cliff sighed. "Yeah, Vivica I'm fine. I promise you I am."

She didn't believe him. "I've known you since forever, right?" Vivica knew he knew the answer. She had been mentioning the fact that she was originally from Beverly Hills since the day she showed up. "Cliff, if things are as bad as they look at home, we always have the spare room upstairs. I realize this house is not as glamorous as your home but still. I feel like DJ would jump at the chance of making me happy."

"Weston, I don't want to rock the boat. Plus, my father would never allow it. He could never bare to have his son living with..." Cliff didn't finish the sentence.

"With what? Me?" Vivica asked somewhat offended. She knew that Rodrick wasn't fond of her, but he wasn't fond of any woman. He was a huge misogynist.

"No. Not you. A Fitzpatrick..." Cliff explained.

It took a moment for Vivica to realize what he was talking about. She was far from being a Fitzpatrick. Those people were known to the town as new money even though they had been wealthy for at least twenty years. Out west it was a bit of a different situation; everyone was new money in some way. "DJ is hardly a Fitzpatrick. I mean yeah, his half-sister is Nadia Fitzpatrick, but it isn't as if we socialize with them outside of holidays ... I don't think Nadia likes my mother very much. When we do end up interacting it is always so awkward. Nadia's daughter Margot is estranged from her husband and the son Nial or whatever is a little perv..." Vivica was asked very last minute to babysit him once when he was home from boarding school. He tried to unhook her bra. She slapped him. Gale yelled at her when she found out. Brandon, Nial's father though? He seemed to think that Nial deserved it. She didn't try to piece together what the family dynamic was at that house.

Cliff laughed. "Once upon a time, Nadia Bloom went to school with Brandon Fitzpatrick. She also went to school with Rodrick Knight." He looked at Vivica hoping she was seeing where this was going. "My father wasn't exactly very fond of Brandon, but he did have a thing for Nadia. At least this is what grandmother has told me. Apparently, Nadia and my father were pretty close at one point, but Brandon was the better guy."

"Love triangles are confusing and silly..." Vivica said with a straight face. "Your father has your mother though. Why, would he still be wrapped up over Nadia Fitzpatrick then?"

"I don't think my parents are going to be together for much longer. They have been fighting a lot lately. I mean, I doubt it has to do with Nadia or the Fitzpatrick's, but I mean who knows..." Cliff really didn't want to get into the fact that his father had been cheating on his mother again. He had accidentally caught him around town with other women several times. "That said, the argument I was having this morning had to do with the fact that my dad wants to fire your step-dad from building the new dealership. He didn't realize that DJ was involved. I told him that wasn't fair, and he shouldn't be punished for some stupid failed relationship."

As indifferent as she was towards DJ, she didn't want him getting fired from such a large job. He had been so proud of it. "That's just not right. DJ worked hard to secure the account for his construction company." Vivica frowned.

This was why Cliff didn't want to tell Vivica. He didn't want her stressing out. As much as Vivica played up being this rich girl from Beverly Hills. He knew that she only got so much money sent to her from her birth father. He knew that her mother worked as a secretary for some Fitzpatrick owned company. DJ was the breadwinner. "I'm sorry Vivica. The thing is though is that you can't tell DJ or your mom. I'm trying my hardest to get my dad to reconsider things. If DJ goes to him, then it will just be the end of things there." Cliff explained. Vivica leaned in rested her body on Cliff's chest. Just as they were having a moment, the front door opened.

"Howdy, kids!" DJ said with a smile on his face.

Vivica planted her face into the coffee table. "Way to ruin the mood DJ..." She rolled her eyes.

VIVICA – 2018

Vivica was dressed to the nines with not a single hair out of place. She quickly checked herself out on her tablet's camera. "No… You cannot be wearing white socks. You have a half hour to change your socks boy…" Vivica told a teenage waiter. She turned to Holly. "Where in the literal fuck is Lucy?"

Holly checked her watch. As of right now, Lucy was only three minutes late. "Vivica you need to relax. Lucy will be here." As if, Holly were secretly a witch seeing into the future she proved right. Lucy walked in through one of the doors of the ballroom at the hotel. She ran over.

"Sorry, I'm late traffic was a bitch plus I was dealing with my sister," Lucy admitted. She probably should have kept the second part to herself.

"Are your siblings doing alright?" Holly wondered.

Why on earth were the two of them talking about children? Vivica wondered. Right now the most important person in the room was her. They both knew that and needed to focus on her. "We have so much more to prepare for. We can have small talk tomorrow after *Minute Detroit* posts their article about the event online."

Lucy nodded in agreement. She quickly entered work mode. "What do we have left to complete? As far as my agenda is concerned everything should be on schedule."

Looking at her own notes Vivica sighed. "The awards for the evening haven't arrived yet."

"The supplier called. He is five minutes from being here." Lucy said. She had almost forgotten. "We don't have Mrs. Templeton sitting by the Costa's against? We don't need old money mixing with crime money again." She reminded the two.

"Don't worry. I checked each table when Vivica and I got here. Mrs. Templeton is in the front row to the right. The Costa's are three rows back but center. It should be respectable for each." Holly still remembered last year when Anthony Costa got into Mrs. Templeton's face. It wasn't pretty. She honestly thought they would have read about Mrs. Templeton's less than shocking death on the news the next day. The woman was old as dirt and everyone in town hated her. She hosted the best book club in town though.

Vivica looked down at her notes once again. "Parking shouldn't be an issue this year either. I had to pay a little extra to the hotel, but the entire section closest to the ballroom has been reserved. All attendees have been made aware of this. So, they have no room to complain if they try parking somewhere else."

This might actually work. Vivica thought. The three of them were more than prepared for whatever the evening would hold for them. "Alright, the two of you gather around." Holly and Lucy stood in front of her with their eyes on her. "We all know that by the end of the evening I will have gotten into some form of an altercation with either Tiffany and or Margot. Possibly, Mrs. Templeton. The bitch stole my parking spot last week. That said, I think we gave it our all. Thank you. Both of you."

Holly gave Vivica a hug, and Lucy patted her on the shoulder. It was rare for Vivica to be human for a moment. It always genuine and nice when she was though. It had been stressful on all of them. Holly knew Lucy was going through a lot at home herself. That said, Holly had arranged her schedule around her husbands who was a police officer to watch their children when Vivica went on a tirade. Holly was just glad that tomorrow would be calm. Sure, Vivica would be in a bad mood due to Tiffany and Margot, but she would quickly move on. Every other event for the year would come and go.

HANNAH – 2018

It was dusk in Grosse Pointe. It was indeed a beautiful night in the town. Hannah drove her car down the street. It was banged up a little on the side, and it happened to be Japanese. She knew that her father hadn't seen it yet. When he did, he would insist on her selling it and being gifted the newest from Knight Motors. She had no desire or interest. Hannah noticed from the side of her eye that Harry was looking at his phone in a fearsome way. "Girl, troubles?" She asked.

Harry put his phone down. "Not really... Well, sort of. I guess." Harry said. He brushed his hand through his hair. Harry always did this when he was nervous. "I don't know. I think I'm having life troubles in a way."

"Do you need to talk about it? I realize I haven't been around as of late, but I am your sister, and I do care about you." Hannah felt guilty. She had hated leaving when she did because of Harry. Even though, their mother really wasn't a bad mother in the slightest Hannah had always been more maternal than she needed to be with Harry. Hope had never been. Hope seemed to suck up all the attention from their parents. "Why, don't you catch me up a little on your life. Tell, me about this girl or girls for that matter.' She giggled.

"Eh, well it isn't as if the girl is really that big of an issue." He looked at his phone. If it were girl issues, it would be so much easier. "School has just been sort of stressful." Harry went to Saint Agnes the same school his sisters had graduated from and his father, grandfather, and great-grandfather had all gone too. He had always liked being Catholic. He believed in God, and yet as of late, there had been things that were troubling him. Harry wondered if he could be Catholic and be himself.

"High school tends to be stressful. School, in general, tends to be stressful. I spent the better part of my time in school trying to get out. I think Hope cried for a week when high school was over because she was going to miss it so much..." Hannah rolled her eyes. "How are your friends?"

Harry had to think about it for a moment. Did he really have friends? Sure, he had people he spoke to in class when he was supposed to be studying. He had a group he would eat lunch with and have casual talk with. He even had someone he would walk to with between classes. Did he really have friends though? It didn't seem like people came to his house. He was the one who had to initiate text messages to people. He received a text message once from someone saying *hey* and he responded back the same but with a question mark. At the time he didn't think it sounded rude. Harry was just genuinely shocked that someone had taken the time to text him. "They seem to be fine." That was all he really could respond with. The people he did hang around seemed to be fine. They never confided anything to him, and when he tried to confide in other people, they eventually would block him out of their lives. It was always a slow but cold distancing.

There was something definitely off Hannah thought. She didn't want to push though. Their parents pushed her, and it ended with her distancing herself more than she ever wanted. "Well, if you ever want me to drive you and your friends anywhere or even buy you liquor just ask. Heck, we can get you a fake ID." Hannah was trying her hardest to be a cool big sister. The fact that she even called herself that in her head made her want to bang her head against the wall. Cool big sister? Oh, totally...

He thought about it for a moment. Could Harry tell his sister what was really going on? "Hannah, I have to tell you something." He started to say.

"All ears!" Hannah said as they came to a stop light.

"Well, I'm kind of g-glad that you are home. You know it was so weird having you away." He put on a really weak smile. Harry couldn't do it. It just wasn't the right time. It was never the right time with anyone. Except for that one time with Todd Roberts. He should never have trusted Todd. Harry just wanted to feel normal for once. Harry had just wanted to do what all the people around him were doing. Todd had been willing to do it with him. Little did he know that Todd had been filming what they were doing from an angle that only showed Harry on screen... Now Todd was threatening to not only reveal to the world that Harry was gay but basically destroy his entire life with a homemade sex tape.

Hannah nodded her head. "Well, I mean I'm not glad to be home. I am glad to be able to spend more time with you though." She pulled into the hotel parking lot. They both groaned. "Do you want to skip it?"

Harry shrugged. "I mean, I totally would, but I'm pretty sure that mom or uncle Nial is winning person of the year this year. So, we really can't miss it."

"Damn it." Hannah rolled her eyes.

Tiffany – 2018

Sitting in the back of a Knight limo was nothing new for Tiffany Knight obviously. She had driven in so many she had lost count. Tonight, was somewhat different though. People had been wishing her luck for the past month because she was rumored to win person of the year. Which is why it annoyed her to no end that the evening would be hurt by her sister.

"Well, are we all ready?" Cliff asked? The limo had parked on the far side of the hotel. They had no intention of making some sort of grand entrance. Cliff had never been one for them.

"I cannot believe you let Hannah move back in and didn't tell me." Hope said.

Cliff looked at his daughter. "She is your sister. It shouldn't be an issue." He reminded her. Cliff looked at Tiffany to back him up.

Tiffany was still thinking off into space when she reentered reality. "Oh, your father is right Hope. Hannah is your sister. It is time that the family be put back together." Tiffany really did believe that. She just had to convince Hannah that she really meant it. She had to convince everyone really.

The three of them got out of the limo. Hope was ahead of them and was quickly walking in heals towards a group that she was close to at the hospital. Cliff took Tiffany's hand, and she was trembling a little. He stopped them from walking any further. "Are you really that nervous to be around your sister?"

"Nervous? No… I'm definitely not nervous. I'm just not looking forward to whatever she has up her sleeves. This is a night for the doctors and nurses and everyone else on staff. Yes, Nial is her husband. That doesn't change my opinion though. Especially, considering we all know who Vivica would rather be with tonight.

This again… Cliff sighed. "Tiffany, I've been married to you for years. Vivica is a distant memory to me." He lied. Vivica was not a distant memory to him. He did love Tiffany though. He knew he loved Tiffany. Why else would he have stayed with her as long as he did? Really? Why else? "No, come on let's go in."

"Why didn't Hannah and Harry drive with us again?" Tiffany asked. She was trying to drag the conversation. The longer they stayed away from the event, the better she thought.

Cliff had no idea. He really didn't. Though he did notice Hannah's car. He would be personally selling it and replacing it with a current Knight model. She wanted money so badly made by herself; she was driving around in it. "Kids will be kids." He pointed out.

Kids would be kids? That is all he had to say? Tiffany needed just to calm herself down and let things be. They started walking again, and they made it to the entrance. There were local reporters taking photos and doing some interviews. It wasn't really that big of an event. Then Tiffany saw that channel seven was there. It had Vivica written all over it. This was a local hospital event. In the grand scheme of things, while Grosse Pointe was known for being a wealthy suburb, it was hardly newsworthy. Unless someone was caught embezzling or they had a secret sex dungeon.

A reporter walked up to the couple. She asked if she could take a few photos of the couple. Tiffany really wasn't eager to possibly be in the news, but Cliff insisted. The annoying thing is that regardless if she won the person of the year award, she would end up in the paper tomorrow morning. Her husband was after all the head of a major car company. Tiffany rarely ever put into consideration that Cliff was indeed Clifton Knight of Knight Motors. She only ever thought of him as her husband. Which she felt Vivica wouldn't have done. In Tiffany's mind, she felt that Vivica would have been more interested in being Vivica Knight than being Cliff's husband. Which was just another reason why Vivica shouldn't have ended up with Cliff. Tiffany pinched herself a little. She had to stop thinking about Vivica.

They entered the ballroom. It actually was stunning this evening. Clearly, they had taken the time to dress it up a little this year. In years past, it really just felt like a banquet. Though, the way it was dressed up was actually rather tasteful. Tiffany looked around scoping for some of her work colleagues. Instead, she noticed an all too familiar redhead. She then turned to look and saw Nial. Tiffany had no idea why, but she went too say hello to him. "Nial, how are you this evening?" She asked. Cliff was standing beside her. Cliff and Nial hated each other with a passion. As much as her sister and her didn't get along, very deep down there was an inkling of love. Nial and Cliff, on the other hand, shared no blood but bad blood.

"Tiffany. An honor as always." Nial kissed Tiffany on the hand. He looked at Tiffany. While he much preferred Vivica's body or at least did, Tiffany was a bombshell in her own right herself. "So, we are up against each other for person of the year I hear?"

"Well, yes. I just want you to know. I hope you win." Tiffany said. She honestly was a little shocked she did say it. She personally really did want to win.

Cliff squeezed Tiffany's hand. "Well, unfortunately for Nial he has no chance with you around." Cliff gave Nial a really dirty look.

"So, how has being a second-rate doctor been treating you?" Cliff asked out loud.

Nial chuckled. "Oh, just wonderful. Much better having earned my degree as opposed to being a victim of nepotism." Nial always scoffed over the fact that Cliff would call him out for being a doctor. Yet, Cliff himself was only in his position because his family owned the company. "I know getting a degree is not for everyone though."

The egotistical son of a bitch. No that wasn't right. Nadia Fitzpatrick didn't deserve that title. Cliff laughed. "Well, having mommy and daddy pay your way into a degree isn't much better I would say. Especially, for the patients." He could have gone on, but Tiffany was clearly not pleased by this conversation and a particular redhead was making her way over.

Vivica strutted across the room. She looked so flawless in her gown. Tiffany wanted to avoid her. "Cliff let's go find our seats."

"Well, I can assist you there. They are in the back row as usual. I didn't see the reason in giving you front row treatment. You can more easily duck out that way when you lose person of the year." Vivica tried holding on to Nial's shoulder, but instead, he walked away.

"Vivica, little sister... Not everyone cares about winning an award. Tonight, is a celebration of the hospital, town, and people in it. The award is almost an incidental thought." Tiffany sounded as if she had rehearsed that little bit. Which she did.

NIAL — 2018

The gala looked like shit he thought. This was where his family money had been invested? His wife was clearly not a good party planner. Five years in a row and this event looked worse than the year prior. Still, Vivica knew how to wear a dress. Which was one of the few reasons he chose to remain with her as long as he did. His plan was set into motion, and thankfully he had no regrets. It really mattered very little to him if he won person of the year that night. He would get his reward and Vivica would never see it coming. He noticed Austin walk in and go over to his girlfriend, Lucy. They seemed to be in love. Such a waste of time Nial rolled his eyes. He made his way over. "Austin, my good man. How are you this fine evening?"

"Oh, just fine." Austin couldn't believe he was talking to him here. He wasn't supposed to bring down the girl until right before person of the year was announced, which was at the end of the evening.

Lucy checked her watch. "I need to go discuss something with the hotel manager. I'll be back in a little bit." She walked off none the wiser.

"Change of plans kid. I want the task done sooner rather than later. Vivica is already pissing me off, and I've only been here ten minutes."

"I guess I can go and get her now. What about Lucy though?" Austin couldn't just leave her now that they had made contact. She would get suspicious.

This kid needed a reality check sometimes. It was clear he would never make it in the cut throat world of medicine. "The profit more than makes up for whatever excuse you have to make. Just do what I tell you and don't ask questions."

LANGLEY — 2018

The Grosse Pointe General Hospital gala was filled with the who's who of Grosse Pointe. The issue was that Langley knew not a single person. In New York, when Langley crashed a party, she could easily blend in. This wasn't the case in bumfuck Michigan. She didn't recognize a single person aside from her sister, her sister's fiancé Austin, and then, of course, Vivica Fitzpatrick who looked a lot older in person than she did when she was on TV or in magazines. Langley had been in more awkward situations though. She just strutted through the hotel banquet room until she found an empty table. There she spotted a cute but scrawny boy dressed impeccably well. "Mind if I have a seat?" She asked in a seductive tone. The boy didn't even look up. "Such, a boring event. Don't you agree?"

Harry didn't say anything to Langley. He was too focused on the black-mail emails from Todd. Harry was frustrated though and just slammed his phone down. He finally noticed the blonde girl sitting next to him at the table. She was tapping her fingers and looked as bored as he would be if he wasn't so internally freaked out. "Oh, sorry. I'm being so rude. I'm Harry... Harry Knight." He put out his hand for her to shake it.

It took everything for Langley not to snicker. Boys didn't introduce themselves as he did. So, formal. It was so adorable. "I'm Langley Kingsley."

"Do you go to Saint Agnes? I don't think I've ever seen you before." Harry said.

"I actually just moved here." Langley could slap herself. She shouldn't have said that. She knew that his next question would be why she was at the gala if she had only just moved here.

Harry nodded. "That's cool; I go to Saint Agnes. It seems like for forever to be honest." Harry sighed thinking about having to go back to school on

Monday. He was dreading the notion with all that was going on thanks to Todd Roberts.

There was definitely something off about this boy Langley thought. He was a little to well-polished for a teenage boy, his pants fit him a little too perfectly, his belt matched his shoes, his hair was clearly perfectly styled, and while he had a dreamy voice, it was spoken with a very slight lisp that one would have to listen carefully to catch. He also had not looked at her tits once. Most men ignored her face entirely and went straight for her tits. "So, is your girlfriend joining you this evening?"

He turned bright red. Not from embarrassment but because it seemed like everyone was asking about this girlfriend that he didn't have as of late. "No, I haven't dated any girls lately." Harry said.

"So, then will your boyfriend be joining you this evening?" Langley wondered. She decided it will be better to just be blunt about it. That was the sort of person that Langley was. Some called her a bitch, but Langley hated beating around the bush.

It took everything for Harry not to freak out with what Langley just asked him. "What? A boyfriend? But I'm not… Well, I mean not that there is anything wrong with… I don't understand what you mean. Why would I have a boyfriend?" He asked her.

This confirmed it for Langley. It was too bad. While he might have been a little thinner than she usually liked , he had great lips. "Oh, it's nothing she said. Not that there would be anything wrong with having a boyfriend or a girlfriend, just not both at the same time obviously." She laughed.

Normally, Harry would just laugh, but something about this girl was different than any he knew. "How did you know?" He asked.

"What exactly do you mean?" Langley said looking confused.

"How did you know I was gay?" He said so softly that there was no way anyone around them had heard.

Langley's eyes opened up widely. "Well, I mean it isn't that I knew. It was just a guess. You could have passed for one way or the other. Boys our age tend to dress a little better than in generations past. Though, it wasn't really by the way you dressed. More or less by the way you reacted to me asking if you had a girlfriend."

Somehow, that answer made Harry sigh with relief. It meant that he wasn't obvious about it. He just had to choose his words better going forward. "Look, I need you not to tell anyone."

"Well, I don't exactly know anyone here. So, it will be kind of pointless. I mean I have a lot of twitter followers but what would they care if I said, some boy named Harry Knight was gay?" Langley laughed but then realized the name she just said. "Wait, Knight? As in..."

Harry nodded. "As in, *Knight Motor Company*. My father is the CEO, and I'm the direct heir to the company."

Now things were making a little bit more sense. Only a little Langley thought though. "Well, I won't tell anyone. I'm not that much of a heartless bitch. Though, aren't your parents super liberal?"

The question asked by a thousand people in his head. Yes, his parents were liberal on paper, but the company wasn't. This was why he was still in the closet. While his parents donated so much money to charities involving minorities he never could tell how they felt about gay people. He also was unsure how his sisters would react. He didn't think that Hannah would care, but Hope probably would wait to see how their parents reacted and even then, she had such a fake personality that it would be hard to tell with her. Harry really wasn't close with either of his siblings though. "It's just complicated." He thought that was a simple enough answer.

"Hey, Harry." Brad said as he sat down at the table.

Harry jumped a little in his seat. His cousin Brad was the same age as he was, and they were only a month apart. They had been raised together as children, but Brad ended up going away to boarding school when they turned eleven and they sort of drifted apart. Brad was really the closest thing he had to a true sibling if he really thought about it. "Oh, um hey Brad." He looked at Langley who was staring down Brad like he was a billion dollars. Which in a way he technically was sort of? "This is Langley Kingsley." He said.

Brad smiled and waved. "Hey, nice to meet you." He looked at Langley in the eyes. Then he glanced down to her chest and smiled.

Well, this boy clearly was straight Langley thought. He was also downright cute. He was a totally cute boy with a short haircut. The way he was looking her up and down made it clear he was interested too. "So, how do you two know each other?" Langley asked. She needed to be certain that the two boys weren't secret lovers.

"Oh, Harry's my cousin." Brad said facing her directly.

This immediately made Langley put two and two together. If Harry was Harry Knight and Brad was his cousin that meant… "So, then that would make you Brad Fitzpatrick?" She wondered out loud.

Brad nodded, but the smile on his face quickly turned to a frown. "Yeah, my father is Nial, and my mother is the crazy redhead giving Harry's mother the stink eye over there." He pointed to Vivica who was currently going back and forth between yelling at Lucy and Holly while at the same time keeping her eyes on Tiffany and Cliff.

Langley took a glance but didn't want Lucy to see her, so she quickly turned back to the two attractive cousins. "Well, how about that. I crash a party and end up sitting with a Knight and a Fitzpatrick. Grosse Pointe might not be as bad as I thought it was going to be." She stated. Then she realized that she just admitted to crashing the gala…

The two cousins both snickered. "Why on earth would you want to crash a hospital gala? This is hardly the event of the year." Brad actually thought about that for a moment. "Well, no actually it is. If you are over forty that is."

"Well, to be honest, I needed to get out of the house. You see the blonde girl standing next to your mother?" Brad turned quickly and then turned back and nodded. "Well, that's my sister. She made this party sound so important like anyone who was anyone had to be here."

"So, you think you are someone?" Brad asked.

She snickered. "Duh… I'm Langley Kingsley."

The two cousins looked at each again, but both were a bit confused. Harry finally broke the silence. "I don't think either of us recognize the name Kingsley, to be honest."

She sighed. "Well, then clearly you two have not spent much time in Manhattan." As she said this someone shrieked from across the room. Langley and the two boys turned. Vivica and Tiffany were going on about something.

"Well, I better go stop my mother from getting in a fist fight with yours Harry." Brad walked off over to his mother.

That couldn't have been the end of their conversation. Langley needed to talk to that boy again. "So, Brad is your cousin?" Langley asked as if she didn't already know the answer.

Harry nodded to confirm. "Yeah, he is a great guy... Thanks for not telling him about me."

"Tell him what?" Langley asked confused yet again.

"You know... The fact that I'm... gay." He whispered.

Langley looked him deep in the eyes. "Look, I don't care if you are gay. I'm known for doing some pretty mean things to people, but I would never out someone."

This random girl was treating Harry more like a friend than anyone had in years. If he had come out to anyone at school, he was sure he would have been outed to the entire world by now. There was a total of three openly gay people that he knew of at Saint Agnes. Two of which were girls who apparently identified as bisexual. The other was a guy who Harry had never been very fond of for a variety of reasons. Things seemed to perfect for him when they were far from perfect for himself. "It's just weird for me to have someone be so friendly to me lately."

"Well, I don't understand why. You seem like a nice guy." Langley smiled at him.

TIFFANY – 2018

"Why do you always have to start a fight?" Tiffany spat at Vivica.

She didn't start this fight. She didn't even start this fight all those years ago. Tiffany did. Vivica was so sick of being the villain when she was looking at the real one. "Tiffany, I don't have time to argue." Vivica said. She was going to be the mature one.

"Hey, mom." Brad said as he walked over to his mother and aunt. "How have you been?"

It had been too long since she had seen Brad. "Bradly! Oh, I'm so happy to see you!" She hugged her child. "I want to hear all about your semester so far. Why don't we go sit down at the table? I'm sure your father will want to join us soon." Vivica took her son to the best table in the room, and they sat down.

Tiffany looked at Cliff. "Well, she is definitely up to something."

As much as he sided with Tiffany on everything he didn't work on this. Tiffany needed to just let this go. "Why don't we go and find our table? I'm sure that it is far back enough that Vivica won't bother us for most of the evening."

Was he not going to agree with her? He should agree with her right now, tiffany thought. As much as she knew Cliff loved her she always did wonder if he ever regretted marrying her instead of Vivica. "I just wish you would defend me more sometimes. You say you will, but then you don't." She grabbed his hand to find their seat. Cliff didn't move though. "Well, come on let's go find our seat."

Cliff looked at his wife. "Tiffany... I don't understand you sometimes. You started the fight with Vivica." He walked off to find his seat.

What did he mean by that? Was he talking about right now or was he talking about the overall history she shared with her sister? In which case, did Cliff really believe what he was saying?

VIVICA – 2018

Where was Nial? Vivica looked around the entire room and couldn't see him anywhere. The event had started, and people were seemingly having a good time. She had been trying to catch up with Brad, but he didn't really have anything to say to her. Vivica wished they were closer. She wished that Nial hadn't made him go to boarding school. Boarding school was great for some families, but Vivica could never see the appeal. In her opinion, the only reason that Nial himself went to a boarding school was that Brandon and Nadia couldn't believe that Nial had been their child. He was such the opposite of his two loving parents.

It had taken years for Vivica to be on good terms with both Brandon and Nadia, but she very much adored them at present. Even when she had been divorced to Nial, they still had a good relationship. They realized that Vivica was never the issue. It was their son that was the issue. Their children in general. Margot was never a catch herself. She was probably worse than Nial. Vivica stopped herself from calling Nial himself worse. Nial was a good person. He loved her after all. He wanted to be with her. She thought he did at least. Why would he have asked her to marry him again five years ago? Why did he?

Nial was five years younger than Vivica. He had always had a weird crush on her growing up. They had been step-cousins but had limited interaction. Nial had gone off to boarding school for so long that she honestly forgot about him as she had gotten older. Then she graduated from college after her breakup from Cliff and Nial reappears in town as a med student. He had definitely grown up, and he was definitely no longer the little perv that he had been when she had baby sat him once or twice when they were younger. That said, no one approved of their relationship.

It was almost hilarious. She had been dating a perfectly normal man, but no that wasn't good enough for anyone around her. Then she became reacquainted with Nial, and everyone from her mother to Cliff had freaked out. It was as if everyone was saying that Vivica had no right to be happy. She wasn't allowed to be with Cliff because her sister had married him. So, now she wasn't allowed to be with someone who wanted to be with her. Vivica hadn't cared and let Nial continue to pursue her anyway. They married the first time in an elaborate ceremony on a yacht. It had been so romantic. That marriage lasted four years. He cheated on her.

Their second marriage came after her being married to Luke Knight as well as an illegal marriage to Cliff. It had only been invalid because it turned out that Tiffany wasn't dead. She had a feeling that Cliff would have stayed with her, but Vivica reluctantly told him to go back to Tiffany if she didn't agree with it. So, the second marriage to Nial happened. It was a bittersweet run, but she had been involved with Luke at the same time, and Nial really wasn't into it at the time. The only reason they remarried was to claim money in a will. Then, Luke had left town at some point, and Nial had returned from out of state, and he seemed different. He was a changed man in a way. Vivica was more open to being with someone other than Cliff. It had been so many years. That brought them to the present.

Vivica looked around the room. She quickly glanced and saw Cliff and Tiffany who both seemed to be uncomfortable. Probably, her fault but she was trying to move past it. Then she noticed her nephew Harry sitting at one of the extra tables talking to a pretty blonde girl. Margot was apparently on her third cocktail and flirting with the mayor while his wife sits right next to them. Holly was on the phone on the right side of the stage. She was probably on the phone with her husband or children. Lucy was dealing with some last-minute things that probably weren't anywhere near as important since Vivica herself wasn't focused on them. Then she noticed her nieces Hope and Hannah arguing at the bar. She was shocked to see Hannah there. The two had had lunch together only a few weeks ago.

"Hello, darling." Nial sat down next to his wife. He smiled. "Bradly, my boy how are you doing?" He shook his sons' hand. He was not the type to hug his son even though his own father hugged him.

"Good." Brad said. Brad took out his phone and started texting.

This evening was starting to come together Vivica thought. It was actually going to go down without being too chaotic. "Oh, Nial I think I actually pulled it off this year!"

Nial looked at her in the eyes. "I want you to hold on to that feeling of achievement for as long as you can my dear." Nial had a malicious smile on his face.

What did Nial mean by that? Before she could ask though the lights went down, and everyone seemed to be sitting or at least quiet. Lucy was on stage…

"Good evening everyone. I would like to welcome our host for the evening to the stage to open the evening properly. Will Vivica Fitzpatrick please make her way to the stage?" Lucy asked to the audience. Lucy couldn't see much but she swore off to the side of the room she recognized a familiar blonde. She was going to have to deal with that…

Vivica stood, and the audience started clapping for her. It was humbling in a way. They had never clapped this loud before, or maybe they had. Vivica had really transformed herself in the last five years from the woman she had once been. She looked at the members of the audience. Colleagues of Nial and realistically Tiffany smiled and nodded at her. Mrs. Templeton gave her a wink as if she had done good. Anthony Costa and his wife Jackie were standing for her.

She walked to the stairs and made her way to the podium. Lucy walked no marched off stage. Vivica wasn't sure what that was about. Vivica silently cleared her throat and looked out to her audience. "Good evening. It is so kind of all of you to have come tonight…" She looked as Nial turned to Margot in the audience. He still had this unsettling look on his face. Margot was in a good mood it appeared. Too good a mood… "We all know how hard the doctors, nurses, and everyone on the staff at Grosse Pointe General Hospital work. The time and effort they put in for every patient. Doing, everything in their power to work miracles…" All of a sudden, the door opened. No one seemed to notice, but Vivica did. It was Austin Martin. Instead, of walking over to Lucy, however, he walked over to Nial. What was going on? "So, with that, we have the honor to celebrate the legacy of the hospital. The legacy of this great town really…" Austin whispered something in Nial's ear, and then

Austin quickly walked back out into the lobby. She looked over at Lucy who was whispering something into a blonde girl's ear. She clearly had not seen Austin walk in. "I think that we can all agree..." She looked back at her table and Brad was now sitting alone. Where was Nial? "I think we can all agree on that-..."

"I think we can all agree that you have done your hardest this year my dear sweet Vivica," Nial said.

Turning to her husband Vivica was confused. What was he doing up here?

"Why, let's all give Vivica one *last* round of applause..." Nial said.

The audience half started clapping. People were now whispering though. Lucy had stopped talking to the girl, and Holly had walked over. The two were now whispering in confusion looking at their notes for the evening. Brad had put his phone down. Cliff and Tiffany were both looking at one another just as confused as Vivica was herself. "What are you doing?" Vivica whispered to Nial.

"Ladies and gentlemen, you have all known me for years. You have all known my wife Vivica just as long it would seem. Some of you had the misfortune of going to St. Agnes with her. Some of you had the misfortune of being in a shop or restaurant with her while she threw a fit. Then there are those who had to deal with her cosmetic company or even worse that short-lived book club she hosted..." Nial looked at Vivica as if she were the scum of the earth. "Ladies and gentlemen, I think we all know the story of Vivica Weston. Why I believe it was Rodrick Knight himself who once publicly called her the *whore that came from Beverly Hills...* This was after going after his son and his fortune though. Yes, we all know the love that was, is, will never be Vivica and Cliff... People think they know the entire story of Vivica. The tabloids sure think they do."

Vivica was fighting back the tears. "Nial, why are you doing this?"

Nial turned to Vivica. "She wants to know why I am doing this. Why am I doing this? Oh, I don't know... Maybe because I deserved a wife who treated me well. A wife who actually loved me. Well, soon I will have that. A wife who loves me for me. Not my family's bank account. Oh, but first I thought I would introduce you all to my fiancé.

In walked a slutty twenty-something with a bitchy grin on her face. Clearly, not dressed for the evening.

Vivica was in complete shock. Why would Nial do this to her in public? She thought that he had some form of respect for her. Vivica looked at the audience who were all talking amongst one another. Vivica tried to form speech but she couldn't. Instead, she passed out...

VIVICA – 1986

Sunday's should be outlawed Vivica thought to herself as she looked for a dress that was appropriate to wear to Mass that day. It was ten in the morning. They would be going to the noon Mass at Saint Agnes. Cliff was going to be over in a little bit. They were going to drive him. DJ had already said yes on Friday night when he had come home. He thought it was a wonderful idea. It wasn't as if Vivica herself cared what he thought, but Cliff had felt the need to ask him permission.

If she were honest with herself, it did kind of make her stomach dance a little. The idea that Cliff was asking her step-father permission to attend something with them. It felt almost as if they were together. She knew that wasn't the case though as he was just being polite. Something, Vivica had little time for these days.

Someone knocked on the door. "May, I please come in dear?" Gale asked.

"If you really must, mother…" Vivica sighed.

The door opened, and Gale walked in fully dressed already. "Vivica, I thought we should talk for a little bit."

Vivica sighed. "What did I do this time?" Vivica asked aloud.

Gale sat down and gestured for her daughter to do the same. "Vivica I think we need to talk about your friendship with Cliff." She looked at her daughter who had instead of sitting next to her sat at her vanity. "Vivica, I understand you are getting older… I just want to make sure that you are rational with your choices."

She didn't turn around, but she did snicker. "What choices would those be? My sex life?" Vivica downright laughed at this.

"Your sex life? Vivica are you sexually active?" Gale asked standing up.

"How can you even ask that? Mother, I'm sixteen going on seventeen. I have some self-respect… That said, if and when I do choose to have sex you will never know. In fact, until I marry and become pregnant, you are to assume I am a virgin. You know what no. Actually, I want you to assume that any children I ever have are of immaculate conception…" Vivica stated as she worked on her make-up.

"Vivica, there is nothing wrong with talking to me about sex. I am your mother after all, and I am sure that there are questions you have." Gale explained.

This was starting to feel like a creepy after school special. Vivica had given up on those years ago and wished to do the same with this conversation. "Let's drop the subject of sex…" She started to put lipstick on and then turned to her mother. "What does my lack of a sex life have to do with my friendship with Cliff?"

Gale laughed innocently. "Well, Vivica I'm your mom. I can see the way you act around him. It is clear you have liked that young man for a while now."

If it was this obvious to her mother, she wondered how obvious it was to other people. Brianna was the only person who actually knew about her being in love with Cliff. At least she thought. If her mother of all people could figure out her crush, what about Cliff himself? If Cliff did know, what did that mean? She had been flirting with him for years so much that it just was natural to her to speak to him that way. Vivica would have entire conversations praising him. Yet, he would cluelessly respond to her. Stuff like *"Oh, thanks!"* or *"Gee, that's nice of you Vivica."* How many damn times was Vivica going to have to call Cliff hot or handsome before it got through to him that friends regardless of how close they were don't talk to each other like that?

"Knock, knock!" DJ walked in also fully dressed. "Vivica, Cliff is waiting for you downstairs."

She snapped back into reality. "He is?" She looked down at herself still not dressed. "Well, both of you leave. I need to get dressed. Tell him I will be down in like five minutes."

"Twenty minutes. Got it." DJ said. He and Gale both left the room.

***

After a dreadful car ride that took much longer than it should have Langley and Cliff were walking towards the church. They still had a while before Mass would start. "Sorry, about how long it took for me to get ready this morning," Langley explained.

"Oh, it was no problem. DJ kept me company. We were talking about the dealership." Cliff mumbled.

Vivica looked at him. "That must have been an awkward conversation." She said. Vivica was still not sure how DJ would react to him losing the Knight contract. She really did feel bad.

Cliff sighed. "I kept my mouth shut. I don't know how long I can though. It just isn't right that my father is doing this."

The two friends continued to walk around. They discussed school mainly. It was clear that Cliff didn't want to discuss his father or family in general. Which was always the case. Vivica knew it sounded bad but it honestly kind of annoyed her that Cliff didn't want to talk with her more about it. She knew it wasn't as if he spoke to Brianna at all about it or anyone else for that matter. Still, why was it so hard for him to just open up? She was willing to listen. She wanted to be there for him. She was willing to be there for him…

LUCY – 2018

"Come on Langley we are going to be late." Lucy marched up the front steps of Grosse Pointe West. She was still pissed off at Langley for crashing the gala on Friday night. Luckily, Nial's little charade shielded Vivica from noticing her there. That didn't stop a reporter from a local magazine noting that two of Alexander Kingsley's daughters were in attendance at the most shocking event of the year. Again, Vivica was too distraught to have noticed anything. Langley had spent all weekend dealing with the press and getting Vivica's affairs in order.

As soon as she was done here, Lucy had to get to Vivica's house. Not the Fitzpatrick mansion but the mansion that Vivica had inherited after her marriage to Luke Knight had ended. Nial had moved out of the house that Friday. Margot was moving back in. She had a heated argument with Austin on Saturday morning. She understood that Nial had been paying Austin well to give the woman extensive plastic surgery. This entire situation was now a conflict of interest. Austin was under Nial's pay, and Lucy still worked for Vivica. On Saturday afternoon, Lucy went to Vivica's office at her request to gather her things. Apparently, they were waiting for her in the lobby along with a contract from Margot herself to come work for her. Lucy would have accepted it a week ago, but Lucy was not a heartless woman. She would stay with Vivica for the time being. They had already spoken, and Vivica had every intention of keeping Lucy under her pay. Vivica had the money. Lucy had no clue if they were even still working for the party planning company though. Apparently, Nial bought it back from Margot and planned on giving it to Vivica as part of the divorce settlement.

Lucy learned rather quickly that this wasn't going to be a long drawn out divorce. The two had been married and divorced twice before. Each was going to get exactly what they wanted. Whatever they brought into the marriage they would take with them. Vivica would also receive upfront 1.5 million and ten grand a year for ten years regardless if she remarried or not. The one stipulation was if she were to marry Cliff. Which they both knew would never happen. Vivica would gain full-custody of Brad, which would probably be a plus for her. She missed being around her son and often talked about him. This would be her chance to get him away from boarding school.

"I'm not going here," Langley stated.

Lucy turned to her sister and looked her straight in her eyes. "Well, then you can go to juvenile hall for all I care. I'm sympathetic to what happened with dad, Langley but I'm not dad… I'm an actual grown up. You can stay out as late as you want, you don't have to work but don't expect more than twenty a week from me get a job. If Xander chooses to give you money that is his purgative. That said, you won't embarrass me, and you will go to school. Is that understood?"

"I guess…" Langley mumbled. Her sister just didn't understand what was going on in her life. Even if she did, Langley didn't care. She had every right to be mad at her sister.

The two sisters walked into the main office of the school. "We are here to enroll Langley Kingsley," Lucy said. She didn't even wait for the secretary to look up. Lucy had far too much to do today. They were handed a clipboard to fill out. Langley gave her sarcastic answers to the questions being asked. It took all of an hour. Langley's old school had luckily transferred over all the paperwork needed the Friday before. When they spoke with a poorly dressed counselor, they were informed that Langley would be placed in all AP classes to match with the curriculum of her old school. Apparently, while an average student at her old school Langley was considered accelerated here, Lucy had to admit she was impressed.

The older sister looked at her watch as they exited the main office. "Well, I have to go. Call me if you have any emergencies. Call, Xander for anything else. You should have Austin's number on your phone as well, but that needs to be a last resort. Ignore, the number I gave you for Vivica's main office. Just use the one for Holly if you need to reach me at work." She looked at her younger sister. Lucy sighed. "I do love you, and I do hope you have a decent day."

"Would you have been able to have gone here at my age? A public school?"

She thought about it. "There is a Catholic school in town. When Vivica is acting a little less crazy, I'll look into her getting you in. You have the grades. Obviously, we aren't Catholic, but Austin is. So, we could probably get you in at a discounted price. I just need you to go to school here until we can work that out. We don't need the press or the police finding out that Alexander Kingsley's daughter is not attending school for any number of reasons." Lucy patted Langley on the shoulder. She could sense a tiny grin on Langley's face. "Good luck, kid."

"Good luck with Vivica. I read that during her last divorce she went MIA for like six months." Langley honestly loved that she would be first to know all the information when it came to Vivica. Even if she had to do some snooping to get it.

TIFFANY – 2018

It was shockingly bright and sunny for January. Tiffany had been looking out her front window all morning. She watched as moving vans came and went and dropped off furniture and boxes across the street. It had always annoyed her that Vivica owned a home across the street. It wasn't directly across the street, but if the two were to happen to walk out the front door at the same time, they could indeed see one another. In the many years that Tiffany had lived at the Knight residence that had maybe happened twice. Vivica luckily hadn't lived there in five years. Now she was moving back.

Tiffany knew that Nial was the one in the wrong technically. She just didn't want to have to admit it. While Nial and Cliff hated one another with a passion, Nial had always been very nice to Tiffany herself, and he had always been good with her children even when he and Vivica had been divorced. She didn't expect that to change this time around. Tiffany just wasn't ready for what the bottom line of this entire situation would mean for her.

Every time Vivica divorced, she would go off the handle. Cliff would go and pick up the pieces. He never cheated on Tiffany as far as she knew, and she did believe he had always been faithful to her. That didn't stop the two ex-lovers from always caring about one another though. Cliff might not show up to calm Vivica down today or even in the next month or so but when he eventually did it would be an on-going event until Vivica attempted to cross the line. Then Cliff would distance himself from her yet again. This had been going on for years. Not even just during divorces.

The brunet doctor honestly had no idea what kind of a spell Vivica had over him. Yes, they had been high school sweethearts, but high school ended years ago and from what she knew, the college years had not been well for them. The nostalgia had gotten old years ago. When Tiffany married Cliff, there had been a small audience of people. Tiffany had seen photos of the invalid wedding between Vivica and Cliff; the church had been overpacked. Tiffany was Cliff's only wife and had been so for years. She was still looked at as the other woman.

"Tiffany, you have been standing there for over an hour." Cliff walked in and over to his wife. He looked out the window and rolled his eyes. The two of them had already argued about this long enough. He wasn't going to continue. "Why, don't we go and have an early lunch?"

She turned to her husband. "I guess that doesn't sound terrible, but I want to be there when she shows up."

As far as he knew, Vivica was already inside. Cliff had received a text from her the other day. He didn't tell Tiffany. It was dangerous to hide anything about Vivica from Tiffany; however, it was more dangerous to inform her of information about Vivica to Tiffany. It was a losing situation. Unless Vivica all of a sudden chose to join the homeowner's association they weren't likely to run into her though. They lived in an upper-class suburban town. You smiled, you waved, and in the likelihood, you did make small talk it would end with one party breaking out the checkbook to donate to some sort of event. Sure, gossip was always a possibility, but that would happen at the yacht club or on a golf course. Not, on their front lawn…

"I guess lunch doesn't sound like a bad idea. Sure, let's go to lunch. Let's go to that little diner you like so much. You almost never seem to let me go with you." Tiffany stated.

He was unsure if his wife was trying to pick a fight with him. She knew very well that the little dinner she was referring to had been his and Vivica's hangout throughout their childhood along with their friends. The owner still remembered them when they would go in. They never did together, but the owner would always mention that the other had come in earlier that day or the day before. He assumed Vivica was told the same thing. The few times that Tiffany had come in she was rude to the owners and wait staff. It was clear they didn't like her there very much themselves. He wasn't going to have them be rude to his wife, but at the same time, he wasn't going to stop going somewhere that he had always considered his home away from home. It was easier to separate the two things. "Sure, we can go." Cliff wasn't going to give her the satisfaction.

"Well, I guess we could just go to the club. I wouldn't mind a salad. You know the one that has some form of nutrients to it." Tiffany said in a bitchy tone.

"Tiffany, we can go anywhere you would like. If you want me to get the jet gassed up, we can go to France for all I care for lunch." Cliff stated.

She thought about it for a moment. "No, I have an evening surgery tonight. We don't have enough time for that. Let's just go to the club."

Cliff left the room without saying to grabbed his coat and wallet.

VIVICA – 2018

The bed in Vivica's mansion had always been a hundred times better than the bed at the Fitzpatrick estate. Vivica was trying her hardest not to flip out any more than she already had throughout the last two and a half days. Vivica wasn't going to give Nial, Margot, or Tiffany for that matter the satisfaction. Brad was staying with her. She was glad that he agreed to stay home a few extra days. They hadn't spoken about what would happen going forward.it is obvious that Vivica wanted Brad home. She suspected he wanted to be home, but she wasn't so sure he would want to leave his friends right now.

"Well, the press is just having a field day with this. It has gone international now. There was a damn article about your divorce in the Australian press." Holly told Vivica from a desk on the other side of the room. Holly knew how to handle Vivica during a crisis. She knew that hiding things or trying to cheer Vivica up did nothing for her. She was more likely to go manic if she didn't handle what was thrown at her right away. "Oh, you will love this that bitch Mrs. Templeton gave a statement… *I knew it was only a matter of time…* Say's the bitch who gets red wine drunk at every luncheon you have ever thrown and talked about all the affairs she has had. If it ever got out, she was fucking her yoga instructor I bet; she wouldn't be talking to the press. Not that anyone gives a damn about a do-nothing bitch like her."

It seemed that when Holly was angry, she grew the world's biggest mouth. That's what Vivica liked about Holly. It was what worked about their friendship. "Who is managing the movers right now?"

"Beats the fuck out of me… Probably one of the maids I hired yesterday. I'll go check on it when Lucy shows up." Holly was cross-checking articles and looking for any inaccuracies to give to Vivica's lawyers. "OH, I will have to go home tonight, just to let you know."

"Well, that is understandable. I'm sure your husband and children want to see you. I should be fine. Brad will be here, and Hannah said she wanted to come over after work today. So, if you want to cut out a little before three that should be fine." Vivica stated. It was no secret that Holly was her best friend in the world. Yes, she paid her, but she paid her to spend the day with her. If she were honest, she was worried that Holly wouldn't be friends with her if she didn't pay her. Vivica never intended to figure out if that was true.

Holly was grateful for everything Vivica had done over the past five years for her. Her husband constantly wondered why she didn't go and finish her degree. She only had a few classes left. Holly hated to admit it, but she would miss Vivica if she didn't get to see her every day.

Lucy walked in. "Sorry, I'm late. I swear my sister is going to drive me insane. I have about fifteen messages on my phone from different news outlets requesting statements. Also, Bridget Madwell wants you to have lunch with her in LA. I already told her it wasn't a good time." Lucy explained.

Bridget Madwell? She had been a friend of Vivica back in her modeling days. About ten years ago, she had taken over the Madwell Modeling Agency after her late husband passed away. Bridget had been trying to get Vivica to make a comeback for years. "Maybe, I should take the lunch," Vivica said out loud.

"Vivica, we have so much to deal with right now. A friendly lunch can wait a while." Lucy said.

"I have to agree with Lucy. You don't want to leave right now. It would give Nial the upper hand." Holly tried to point out.

Vivica honestly didn't care if Nial showed his five inches of manhood to the first lady right now. "I don't know; I sort of want to take this lunch. It might be exactly what I need right now. A little trip to LA." Vivica didn't have to take any offer that Bridget would make, but it is nice to know what they were offering. The last time Vivica had modeled it had been a complete disaster. Brad was ten, and she was in-between marriages.

Lucy and Holly looked at one another. "Vivica, I'm just going to ask… Are we still a party planning service? I mean what exactly did Nial do to get the company out from under the Fitzpatrick Group?"

"Yes, we are still open for business. We have that luncheon next month. I think we have a meeting at the end of the week to discuss the bulk of the arrangements for it. That said, I don't know how much longer I want to be an event planner. I mean I own the company, yes, but Margot retained a bulk of the employees. You technically are my lone employee right now. Unless we are counting Holly." Vivica had to admit that she didn't want to be an event planner anymore. Nial wanted to give her a company when they remarried as a way to show her that he wasn't going to let Margot be rude to her this time around. That lasted all of five minutes essentially. She knew that Lucy needed the money right now though and she also knew that with her father in prison, her last name was going to keep her from getting a decent job. So, she would keep the business going for the time being.

"Well, I guess I will keep scheduling meetings with potential clients," Lucy stated.

A ping went off on all their phones. "Nial Fitzpatrick announces his plans to marry Jazmine Sanchez." Read Vivica allowed. Vivica got out of bed, took her wedding ring off and threw it at the window so hard that the window broke. "Will, one of you please get someone to replace that window by the end of the day? Also, that was an heirloom. Some, great aunt or something. It's mine in the divorce, but Brad might want it someday, so tell whoever is downstairs right now that there is a cool five hundred for whoever finds it first... I'm going to take a shower. Someone book my flight for next week."

HARRY – 2018

Traffic had been terrible getting from Saint Agnes to Grosse Pointe West. One of his elective classes was only taught at this school, so he agreed to take it off campus. He was going to be late, and Harry hated being late so much. He wasn't paying attention to where he was going and boom… He bumped into someone knocking down both his books and her own. "I'm so sorry. I'm running late." Harry stated. He picked up both his and her books. When he looked up, he blinked. "Wait, don't I know you? Langley? Right?" He stood up and handed her the books.

"Oh, hey you're that cute gay guy I was talking to the other night," Langley said.

"You have to keep quiet! You don't know who might hear you!" Harry squeaked. "You never know who might be listening."

Langley snorted. "Oh, relax. There is no one around right now. I thought you went to a private school? What are you doing here?"

Harry explained the situation. The two spoke to one another for what seemed like an hour. When Harry looked at his watch for a second, he realized it had indeed been almost an hour. He was going to be in so much trouble if his actual school found out. "Oh no. No, this cannot be happening… They are going to suspend me, and it will go on my record. I can't have a bad record. What will happen when I apply for colleges?"

There was something about this boy that made Langley raise an eyebrow and yet she couldn't help but like him. Not in a romantic way. She knew better, but in a way that made him seem so much sincerer than most of the people she had known up until this point in her life. "I can forge a note for you. I'm really good at it. I already got out of the second half of my day today claiming I had a doctor's appointment. I maybe attended two weeks of school last semester, scattered throughout the entire time." Langley started laughing.

This was not amusing to Harry. Harry had missed a total of two days of school in his life. "I don't know… I mean yeah I just don't know…"

"Well, how is your cousin Brad doing?" Langley had to ask. Harry might be the only way to get to Brad. Lucy was not going to help her. At least not now.

"Brad? I don't know… Not great. His parents are getting a divorce for the second well third time technically. We had only just been born the first time they divorced. I've only texted with him a few times since then though. Why do you ask?" Harry put two and two together in his head almost immediately afterward. "Oh, you have a crush on him…"

Langley was confused by his tone. "Well, maybe a little one."

It wasn't the first time a girl had gone to Harry about a crush on Brad. He was used to it at this point though. It wasn't as if he was jealous that his cousin had all these girls wanting to date him. It was more he was jealous that there weren't guys going to Brad to ask if Harry was single. Though, Harry assumed that might be an awkward thing for Brad. Even if on the off-chance Brad did accept him. It still seemed strange. Which sort of made it a double standard. Sort of… Harry wasn't sure about that. "You seem like a cool person, so I'm going to warn you, unlike the other girls. Brad doesn't date."

"Well, I'm not necessarily looking to date him. I mean he is hot, but yeah dating isn't the only thing I'm interested in." Langley stated.

"I figured." He noticed Langley look at him sort of offended with this response. "I don't mean anything by that… It's just Brad sort of is a virgin."

"It wouldn't be the first time I was the more experienced person in bed," Langley said almost proudly.

Harry awkwardly laughed. "Brad doesn't plan on having sex anytime soon. I don't know why I'm telling you this." Brad had told him this in confidence when they were thirteen. A girl had offered to do things with him, and he declined. Harry was still sexually confused at the time but honestly was shocked. Brad knew even back then that both his parents had reputations for being sexually promiscuous. Vivica had been married more times than most and had dated many men. Nial was said to have slept with half the women in the state. He didn't want to be his parents even if he did love them. Brad tried his hardest to be the complete opposite.

No sex? This was an obstacle. Langley thought about it for a moment. She took the fact that Harry said anytime soon and not until marriage, to mean she could indeed get what she wanted. Langley would just have to get to know him, something she wasn't used to when it came to men and that one girl… Once. "Well, I'd be interested in getting to know him. I mean he seemed nice enough. I'd like to get to know you too. The idiots in my classes so far seem brain dead." Some girl in her physics class kept bragging about a designer scarf she supposedly owned. Langley could give a damn. It was clear the girl owned nothing that would go with the said scarf. Plus, there was more to life than shopping and even sex. Langley enjoyed a decent conversation. She had just yet to meet a man who could do both. Well, one that was straight. "What are you doing this afternoon?" Langley wondered.

"Nothing really. I have to study a bit. It's Monday though; we have school tomorrow morning." Harry pointed this out as if it meant that they would have to wait until Friday.

Langley blinked at him. "Your point being? We can still hang out. You can show me around town!"

Harry guessed he could do this. So, long as he was back by six, he would still be able to get a decent amount of studying in. "Well, alright. Yeah hanging out could be fine." Harry had to be honest Langley seemed like a cool girl. He was desperate for friends so, he didn't see the harm if he really thought about it.

HANNAH – 2018

She didn't even want to be here. The fact that the manager of the dealership felt the need to both kiss her ass and ride it at the same time for an hour and a half didn't help things at all. Hannah had worn a nice blue blouse and pleated navy skirt. She made the stupid mistake of wearing four-inch stilettos though because she didn't realize she would be on her feet as long as she was. Luckily, they finally gave her a desk. Selling cars was far from her dream job, but she would get a pretty nice commission from it. Hannah made sure she was starting off at the same rate as any other employee. The manager claimed she was, but she had a feeling it was still over the average amount a new employee would be making. She knew better than to ask anyone considering she could legit take the keys of any car at the dealership and never return it. Her family owned the dealership after all ...

This was temporary. At least that is what she kept telling herself. Well, no it was temporary. Hannah had a business degree. Why on earth would she want to sell cars for the rest of her life? Even if she didn't want to live off her family, even she had to admit that it be a strange life to be a car salesperson as her career.

The desk next to her had remained empty most of the day. She was filling out all this paperwork which she had to admit seemed pointless. It was becoming hard to remind herself that she had to pretend that her father didn't own the company. The less demeaning it would seem. As she filled out the paperwork, a blonde young man sat down. He had great eyes and nice bone structure. "Hi." She said quickly smiling before turning back to her paperwork. Hannah needed to stay focused.

"Hi, I'm Xander Kingsley!" The boy said, he held out his hand to shake hers.

Hannah looked back up and dropped the pen to shake his hand. He had an excellent grip and knew how to shake a woman's hand. Firm but not overpowering. The complete opposite of the manager of this place... "Hannah... Knight." She somewhat whispered her last name.

Xander smiled. "Oh, cool you have the same last name as the dealership. That must be an interesting conversation starter."

"It's actually my first day here. Also, fair warning my last name happens to be Knight because my family owns the company. My father is Cliff Knight." Hannah figured this would be where they turned into instant enemies.

He nodded, keeping his smile. "Nice. Starting from the bottom up. Yeah, I just moved to town. I actually want to be a police officer, but I had to put that on hold for a little bit." With his father in jail, the lawyers insisted that he stay on the down-low for a while. Xander wasn't happy about it but reluctantly agreed.

She thought about his name for a moment. "Xander Kingsley... Like the Wallstreet guy who was just arrested?"

"Yeah, my father. Alex Kingsley." Xander guessed everyone was going to recognize his name. It had become a large enough story.

Hannah could tell that he wasn't into talking about it. "Oh, don't worry I could care less about who your father is. On that note, pretend you don't care who my father is either."

Xander laughed a little "Yeah I think we can both agree on that."

"Plus, if it makes you feel any better people probably won't be talking about your father for long. At least not around here. My aunt's husband just left her, and that tends to get more press than it deserves usually." Hannah loved her aunt. She was an awesome person, but she had terrible taste in men. Nial was always kind of a sleazy person. Her uncle Luke was a man-child... Then there was her father. Hannah had to admit that a very small part of her wished that Cliff and Vivica were together. They clearly still had feelings for one another. As she had to keep telling herself, she did indeed love her mother, but Tiffany had never made much effort to have a relationship with Hannah. When Tiffany had returned from the kidnappers, she spent most of her time trying to validate that my father loved her. Most, people seemed disappointed to see Cliff go back to Tiffany. Even at her age back then she could tell he was only doing it because he felt he had to and not because he wanted to. It devastated Vivica, but not only because she had to leave someone who clearly, she thought of as her soulmate but because she clearly did love being a motherly figure to Hope, Harry, and herself. Especially, with how Laura had turned out. Hannah had realized over the years that Vivica had basically made her into the daughter she never got to raise.

When Brad was sent to boarding school, Vivica had been devastated. Brad had been her everything. Hannah tried her hardest to spend as much time as possible with her aunt. Which she knew upset her mother, but the older Hannah got, the less she honestly cared. Tiffany still had her favorite child with Hope. Hannah had no clue how her relationship with Harry was presently.

The paperwork was done. At least this round, she suspected there was going to be more. She sat back for a moment. It wouldn't kill her to keep sitting for a little bit. Her feet would probably be blistered by the end of the day. Her old car had like four pairs of more comfortable shoes scattered around it. Her new one was only a day old and was to clean for her taste. She looked at Xander who seemed to be struggling with the paperwork a bit. "Filling out your availability I see?"

He nodded. "Yeah, I mean I have availability, but I have my sister who is still in high school. My older sister has taken on the role of her guardian, but she works long hours."

"Your sister wouldn't happen to be Lucy, would she?" Hannah asked.

"Yeah. Do you know her?" Xander responded.

She shook her head yes. "I love Lucy! She works for my aunt. I assume you don't know anyone else around town then?"

Xander did not. He spent Friday and Saturday looking for jobs and then randomly got a call this morning to come in for an interview. Xander had never worked in sales before, but he jumped at the opportunity. He wasn't going to live of Lucy. It was one thing for Langley since she was still a teenager, but Xander had a bachelor's degree and was more than capable of working. "I actually know nobody. You wouldn't happen to know any decent tour guides, would you?"

Hannah smiled. "Well, I'm not exactly the welcome wagon, but a foreign exchange student once told me I was a great tour guide!" He was cute, and any excuse to stay away from the Knight mansion was good with her...

It felt hanging out with Langley. He talked about the celebrities he found cute. He discussed the music he liked but was too embarrassed to admit he was a fan of. Harry could be himself. "So, tell me more about yourself. Do you miss your friends back home?"

She honestly hadn't thought about her friends in a few days. They had not tried making contact with her at all. If anything, she had noticed her social media following had dropped rather suddenly after she left. It personally didn't bother her. Many of the people she spent time with were out of convenience. She would live if she never saw half of them again. "Not particularly. Friends are like clothes. You love them until you outgrow them, then you miss them for a little but find new ones."

Harry wasn't so sure if he agreed with that sentiment. Sure, he really hadn't had many friends, but he wanted to think that years from now there would be a group of people he was friends with. As far as Harry knew, his parents didn't have any lifelong friends. His mother left California in college and had some cheerleading friends she would make jokes with on social media, but that was about it. His father had a girl named Brianna Belle that would come to visit on the rare occasion. Then, there was his aunt, Vivica. That was about it though. He didn't want to think Langley was right, but could she be? "That's kind of a sad way to think if you say it out loud."

The blond shrugged. "Most of the people I knew in Manhattan were more about connections than genuine friendship. I honestly don't care about popularity. The people I associated with did though. Which I found incredibly stupid. I enjoy partying and having a good time. If it were possible to do that by yourself, I would. Well, it is, but then you are considered crazy." Saying this all out loud made Langley realize just how superficial if not artificial her life had been up until a few months ago. When he father had been arrested, she needed to turn to someone, anyone. She ended up having to stay with a family friend because none of her supposed friends would help her out. They didn't want to be there for her. It wasn't as if she had treated them bad either. They just didn't want to deal with the real world. They had no issues with hanging out during school, shopping, or partying but when it came to her father being arrested well no they didn't want to be there then.

The two just walked down the street in silence for a few minutes when a boy around their age came walking up to them. He was decent looking from a distance, but the closer you got to him, the more his obvious flaws became apparent. Which included the smell of cheap perfume? Yes, perfume not cologne. He had stylized curly hair that was honestly messier than styled. His eyes were dark brown, and he was dark skinned. "Harry! Long time no seen man!" The boy spoke in theatrics. "Why haven't you been responding to my text messages? I've been awfully worried."

Langley gave the boy a second glance. This was definitely not a friend of Harry's. When she turned to look at Harry, he had tensed up and looked both embarrassed and scared. "Who might you be?" Langley asked the boy. She could tell Harry needed someone to stand up for him. "Nice, shoes." She looked at his no-brand worth talking about sneakers.

The boy put out his hand to shake, but Langley clearly wasn't going to return the gesture. He put his hand down. "I'm Todd. I go to school with dear sweet Harry." He said with a bitchy smile.

"Well, he's never mentioned you," Langley said as if she had known Harry her entire life. "Then again, not everyone we meet is worth a mention in the cliff notes of our lives." She said disgustedly.

Todd looked at this girl. It was clear she didn't go to Saint Agnes. "Why aren't you a fierce one."

"Why aren't you a bitchy queen…" Langley said without changing her expression.

"Oh, sweetheart I'm bi." Todd explained.

What did it matter if he were bi? Langley knew a queen when she saw it. He could sleep with a thousand girls and enjoy it. It didn't change his personality. "Well good for you. I'm a blonde. Harry is tall. What other nonsensical things can we state about each other?"

This girl was too good to be hanging out with the likes of Harry Knight, Todd thought to himself. "Well, I'm a filmmaker you see." Harry's eyes widened. Todd liked that he got where he was going with this. "In fact, Harry made a little film for me a while back. I'd love to show you sometime."

"We can talk later Todd. I'll text you. I promise." Harry said.

Todd looked at his watch. "Well, alright but stop being a stranger Harry." Todd almost looked as if he was strutting a runway as he walked away.

"Who the fuck was that not so hot mess?" Langley asked. "Is he your ex-boyfriend or something?"

Harry looked disgusted at her. "Fuck no!" Harry looked down. "I just sort of hooked up with him a while back …" Harry hated admitting it out loud. He looked at Langley who had a blank expression on her face.

She shrugged. "Well, we have always had bad hookups."

"He was my first actually," Harry stated.

"Hookup?" She looked at him, and he shook his head no. "Time?" She looked a little more concerned. Langley wasn't going to lie. Sex just didn't mean the same thing to her as it did other people. She didn't know why but it didn't. "Well, I can imagine that he wasn't what you had in mind for your first time." Langley's first time had been when she was fourteen at a party. It was with a sixteen-year-old who honestly looked a year younger than she had been. It wasn't traumatic for her. It was more or less her getting on with something. She knew girls who had been experimenting when they were twelve. Langley personally thought that was too young. "Well, just think now you know what you like and don't like you can have better experiences going forward."

"The way it happened, I didn't get much out of it," Harry stated. Remembering, Todd whipping it out… Harry wanted to touch it, but he didn't know if he should. Part of him thought he was still too young. The other part of him knew that most of the people he knew had already had sex. He wished that he had the same restraint that Brad had.

"Look, I don't believe in destiny. I'm not much for being helpful, but I think the two of us can help each other out. We both need a friend to be there for us. I think we both are those friends for one another." Langley stated. She started laughing. "I'm sorry. That just sounded so much better in my head, but it came out so corny. You clearly need someone you can talk to about your life. Your real life, not the life you have to present to the rest of the world."

Harry nodded. He tried to withhold a smile. "Yeah, that would be cool." He didn't want to come off as too eager. Someone wanted to be his friend, and it wasn't because he was a Knight. "What do you get out of the friendship though?"

What did she get out of it? Langley had to think for a moment. "Someone other than my sainted brother and neurotic sister to talk to… Also, just saying if you wanted to invite your sexy as F cousin to hang out, I wouldn't object." Langley winked.

He could appreciate that Harry thought. "I think friendship could be something I would be interested in… Yeah, this does sound corny… Do people discuss their intent for friendship?"

VIVICA – 2018

After not leaving her house for a few days she realized that there was no food in her home. She imagined that Brad could go either way regarding take-out or home cooking, but Hannah was coming over later, and she didn't just want to have takeout to offer her. Plus, Vivica realized the lack of cheap wine laying around the house. Sure, she had good liquor, but she knew better than to take out her sorrow on a good bottle of wine. Vivica had wanted to drive into town herself to go grocery shopping, but Holly and Lucy protested it. Vivica had never been much of a driver. She had her license, but it was a shock to everyone including Vivica as to how she managed to get it. "I don't understand why you had to come along with me. If you don't think I'm a good driver wouldn't you have been safer staying at the house?"

Holly and Lucy had drawn straws as to who would be the one to go shopping with Vivica. Holly had offered to go on her own, but Vivica wanted her brands. Which of course she couldn't remember the name of any of them. It wasn't a smart idea for Vivica to be out in public so soon after. "Well, you have done a good enough job so far. Maybe next time, you can drive by yourself." That was a total lie. Vivica had almost ran over three squirrels and almost chased down some teenager who gave her the finger for going to slow. While Holly had no issue with telling people off in public, her husband was a cop. She didn't need to get arrested with Vivica. Again…

"Exactly. I'm doing a pretty good job." Vivica said. "So, what do you think about me going to LA next week?" Vivica wondered.

"Well, what exactly do you plan to get from the lunch meeting?" Holly asked. It was always hard to tell what Vivica planned to do exactly when she went about something.

She wasn't entirely sure. Vivica knew what the lunch would entail. There was some past account that wanted her back. Bridget would beg her, remind her of how much fun the two had with one another in the past and Vivica would more than likely decline. That is how it always went down. This time though? Vivica wasn't completely sure. It was different this time. In the past, it was Vivica who had left Nial because he was cheating on her. This time it happened he left her because he was of course cheating. Vivica didn't want to think about it, but she had to imagine that there was more than just *love* involved in his intentions of marrying this woman. Nial had pregnancy scares in the past. That is what ended their first marriage. He had another child from a fling that happened before them. Rod… A boy that probably would never know the love his father had for him. Just as Brad never would either. If her suspicions were true, she hoped it wasn't a son. Nial would just look at him as a competitor. Nial didn't get along with other men very well. He was great around women. Which was the problem.

Vivica's modeling career was something that had started when she was a teenager. She would model in local papers and do tiny runway shows for the local department stores. It would lead to her getting signed by a visiting agent from the *Madwell Modeling Agency*. She was flown out to New York. Which was where she had met Bridget. The two became very close friends in a world that took advantage of both children and women very quickly. They took care of each other. Vivica remembered that Cliff had just come back from a summer away. He was sad that she had left as soon as he had come back. He would say how proud he was of her, but she knew that he was secretly insecure about her being around other guys. Most, of which were gay or had reputations that turned Vivica off. Vivica never cheated on Cliff though. She told him back then that she loved him far too much to cheat.

The two of them had such a passionate romance when they were teenagers. They never could spend much time apart. Cliff ended up at a majority of her runway shows. Including, several that were out of the country. Vivica knew that Rodrick hated the amount of time the two spent with one another. Cliff's mother was basically out of the picture by the time they had become an official couple, but she had gotten along with her. It was Cliff's grandmother Delia who had always been her biggest supporter and fan.

"Why don't you come with me? It would be a great vacation." Vivica offered.

"I can't just leave my family like that. It's one thing when I have to spend all night with you. It is another thing if I have to leave the state. I'm your maid Vivica." Holly hated sounding like that, but not many maids were invited along on a trip to California.

Vivica needed someone to go with her. "Well, I guess Lucy will have to come then." She realized that wouldn't happen either. Lucy had to stay around to run the business while she was gone. Vivica made a left and noticed a boy who looked familiar. Was that Harry? He looked like he was talking to the same girl he had been at the gala. Was he dating her? All of a sudden Vivica slammed her head on the back of the seat as the airbags went out. "I don't want to hear a word out of you." The two of them had ran into a street light.

"Why couldn't you have just let me drive?" Holly sighed…

The two friends got out of the car. Vivica checked her hair in the side view mirror. "Well, the good news is I still look ok." She glanced across the way at Holly and looked at her. "Well, aside from the angry look on your face you look good too." Vivica continued to stare at her for a few moments. "Oh, come on! This is far from the worst car accident I've ever been in." She quickly thought about the car accident that resulted in the world thinking Tiffany was dead for several years "Ok, let's change the subject. We will go grocery shopping and then get Lucy to pick us up."

"Yeah, that isn't how this works. We have to get the car towed out of the way… Report it to the insurance company." Holly stated.

"If we must…" Vivica sighed. She leaned against the car as she noticed her nephew Harry and the blonde girl running from across the street.

"Aunt Vivica! Are you alright?" Harry wondered.

She once again sighed. "Oh yes, I'll be fine. Holly will be to once she wipes the dirty look off her face." Vivica noticed the blonde girl looking at her in awe. "So, who is your friend Harry?"

Langley looked at Vivica. It was THE Vivica Fitzpatrick. The legend in the flesh. "I'm like your biggest fan."

This girl had to have been Harry's age and yet she was her biggest fan? "How on earth do you know me?" Vivica asked.

"You were only the biggest American model of the 90's! Not to mention your social life since then has been legendary. I can't believe that piece of scum left you. You should have left him. I always thought you looked best with that Luke Knight guy... Harry is he related to you?" Langley looked at Harry. He nodded yes. "Oh, well yeah he looked the best. Though the love story of you and Clifton Knight is a legend of its own."

Again, this girl was Harry's same age. Yet, she knew of her career and personal life. It was both shocking and flattering that she had a fan base under the age of thirty-five. "Well, I don't know who you are, but Harry I approve of her," Vivica stated.

Langley put out her hand. "Langley Kingsley. My sister Lucy actually works for you." She told Vivica with a smile on her face.

LUCY – 2018

The Harper Inn was a diner on the edge of Grosse Pointe and Detroit. It was relatively close to where Lucy and Austin lived. The diner was far from five stars, but it had been a staple in the town for nearly three decades. When Lucy arrived in Michigan, it was where she ended up having her first meal. Vivica took her. It would also be where Austin first met her. Lucy and him argued as they both rushed to put in lunch orders. The Harper Inn would also be where the two would go on their first date. It only fitted it would be the same place they would go to discuss further the current situation they found themselves in.

"You look nice today," Austin said awkwardly. He had left the Fitzpatrick mansion only a little bit ago. He would be working a late night at the hospital.

Lucy tried smiling. It wasn't happening. "Why did you keep this a secret from me? I want to believe that you had no idea what Nial's intentions are. I just don't understand the secret keeping. I thought you were visiting your friends for heaven sake when you went out of town…"

He knew his girlfriend was hurt. He hated that she was. It didn't help that he was cheating on her, with Nial's fiancé. He didn't want to cheat, but he couldn't help himself. This was a constant when it came to him and other women. It had been a few years since he had cheated, but then again, up until not, Lucy was all he needed. The thrill was lost with Lucy. He wished that it could return. He loved Lucy. Other women were just that other women. A hole to stick in in for a half hour or so. "I had to sign a contract with Nial. I'll show it to you if you want. I'm not supposed too but I will. You have to understand that his fiancé is my patient, so I had to remain somewhat quiet about what was going on."

Was she angry because he kept the entire thing a secret or because of how it affected Vivica? Lucy was never really sure how she felt about Vivica in general. Was she her boss or her friend? Lucy had to admit that Vivica had always treated her very well. "You are working so close with Nial is what is hard for me to understand. Why did he choose you?" She realized what she said and how it came out. Lucy wished she hadn't said it.

Austin looked at her as if she just insulted his intelligence. "What, I'm not good enough to work for Nial like you work with Vivica Weston something – something-something? Is that what you are saying?"

It wasn't as if she was disputing that. Lucy very much knew that Vivica had a very colorful past, present, and more than likely future. The number of times the woman was married was enough of a red flag. The fact she owned an event planning business based on her soon to be ex-husband wanting to give her a gift had always been baffling. She also knew nothing about business, and most of their early parties where Vivica insisted on being in charge all felt so out of date. Lucy was unsure of how much Vivica personally took home with her from the business. She knew that she was being paid far too much for the role in which she took in the company even if the work she did went beyond the job title. "I'm not disputing your ability Austin. You know better than that. I've always been your biggest supporter." When she first moved to town, Austin had been a struggling med-student. His father had moved across country a few years earlier but allowed him to stay in their house. That didn't stop him from always being completely broke. Lucy was living off her savings at the time as her paychecks back then had been much smaller, and she wasn't living with him as of yet. She paid for many things regarding Austin's career. When he finally was considered an actual doctor only a year ago, she had to buy him work clothes. He didn't realize that doctors had to dress somewhat nicely... She out of anyone in his life believed in him. Austin had been a screw up as a teenager. Holly had gone to Saint Agnes with him. She told Lucy all about his past once. Lucy never confronted him about some of the things that Holly had said. She had no reason to not believe Holly but also wanted to give Austin the benefit of the doubt. "You know I love you Austin."

"I know you do." Which is why he felt so guilty. "I love you too." Which is why Austin was so conflicted. He knew that he wanted to marry Lucy and now more than ever was the right time. He couldn't pretend that he didn't have some feelings for Nial's fiancé though. It was more than sex. The more he got to know her, and all that she had gone through in life made it so much more real for him. She wasn't just some pretty face. "We should have a date night. Not tonight I have to work, but sometime this week when we both have a night free. I imagine right now you have a lot to deal with when it comes to Vivica."

"Understatement of the year… She wants to go to California next week. Holly and I are trying to talk her out of it. It isn't going very well." Lucy took a sip of her tea. She looked around the diner for a moment. She spotted two people in the corner of the room. "Don't look now, but I think Cliff and Tiffany Knight are here."

CLIFF – 2018

How on earth did they end up at the Harper Inn? They were two minutes away from the club when Tiffany changed her mind again. She decided all of a sudden it was going to be a cheat day. That didn't stop her from ordering water without lemon and a garden salad no dressing though… "Well, how is your salad?" Cliff asked his wife.

"I've had better but fine. They use a mix. You know the club hand tosses their mix." Tiffany reminded him for the third time since they had gotten there. She looked up and spotted Lucy and Austin. "What are they doing here?"

Cliff turned around. "Who?" He turned back.

Tiffany rolled her eyes. "Lucy Kingsley and Austin Martin. Why on earth are they here?"

If he didn't know any better, he would think that Tiffany was under the impression that Vivica had planted them here. Cliff rolled his eyes. "They come here all the time. It is a public place." Cliff wasn't sure why but as of late things with Tiffany just hadn't been great. He just wasn't realizing it until now. Cliff honestly wondered when it started to go downhill. He still loved her more than anything else in the world, but as time went on, he realized that he had nothing in common with her. Why was Cliff only realizing that now though? They had been married for a very long time.

Was he trapped? Cliff didn't think so. He knew he couldn't confront Tiffany with his issues though. If he did, she would automatically jump to the conclusion that Vivica was on his mind. She was but not because he wanted to rush back to her. Vivica was only on his mind because he was worried about her. Which Tiffany wasn't. Which did concern him a little. The two sisters had never gotten along but still…

In his opinion, Tiffany had no reason to be worried. At this point in his life, he had no desire to run to an ex-girlfriend because she happened to be single. The issue though was that it wasn't as if he ever did. When Tiffany had been presumed dead, he and Vivica had not instantly gotten together. It was only after Vivica had discovered how much of a mess he was that she stepped in to help take care of Hope, Hannah, and Harry. She wasn't living there. She went home at night, which just so happened to be across the street. There were some nights she would take the children with her because they wanted to spend time with their aunt, Vivica. He saw nothing wrong in that; she was Tiffany's sister. Plus, Harry and Brad had always been close.

Cliff was happy that when Tiffany did come back, she didn't get in the way of that friendship that bordered on two cousins practically being brothers. It was Nial who did that... He sent Brad to boarding school. Though, there was a lot more to that.

It was no secret that Cliff hated Nial with a passion. He wasn't a good person. Nial was about five years younger than he and Vivica. They hadn't grown up together. He was sent away very early to the same boarding school Brad went to. It wasn't because his parents didn't love him. It was because his parents couldn't control him as much as they tried and they did try... Cliff never really had an opinion of his sister Margot. She loved to judge Vivica even though she had been married fives time and not to the same person. Yet, Vivica remained the whore from Beverly Hills. He hated when people called her that. It had been his father who had coined the term years ago. He decked him in the face when he found out. Cliff to this day had no clue how the town found out. His only guess was an old maid they had must have overheard and told someone.

"Are you almost done? I have to go and get ready for work?" Tiffany asked Cliff.

He looked down at his plate. He hadn't eaten any of it. "Yeah, I'll get the bill."

CLIFF – 1986

Very rarely did Cliff have what he considered perfect days. Today was one of them. He got to witness what in his mind was a real family. Sure, Vivica resented her mother and found her step-father to be an annoyance. That is what made it real though. In Cliff's house, it was just chaos. His parents didn't get along; his grandmother was resentful of how his father had turned out, his step-grandfather and the only grandfather he had ever known was hated by his father. Cliff's mother spent as much time away from the family as possible. She was wife number three for Rodrick. Cliff happened to be Rodrick's first and only child. Which shocked everyone including Cliff himself considering all the affairs he had. Cliff knew he had an uncle somewhere in LA as well as a cousin that he had only met once. The stayed away for some reasons, but Rodrick was one of them. Which begged the question why Cliff was named after a said uncle.

North Pointe had been built in the early 1910's. His family had always been wealthy. It was heavily rumored that the Knight's had stolen their original car model from a competing car company that was no longer around. There was much proof in disputing that, but Cliff wouldn't have been shocked if it turned out to be true. Cliff was not sure where the family wealth came from previous to that though. It didn't matter to him. If he all of a sudden live in a house the size of Vivica's or Brianna's it would be fine with him. If it meant that he didn't have the best of the best he would move on rather quickly.

His grandmother was the only person who seemed to understand him. She was a nurse at the Grosse Pointe General Hospital. His father deeply disapproved of her being around poor sick people all day. Rodrick thought it was time she retires but she refused to.

Cliff walked into the foyer of his family home. Vivica had wanted him to spend more time with her. He said he would come back later that night, but he needed to get some studying done by himself. The library was closed on Sunday, and his father more than likely wouldn't be home. He was going to be out of town for most of the week if Cliff remembered correctly. So, if he hadn't left yet, he was probably with one of his mistresses or at the office.

Walking down the long narrow hallway it was clear that the family home had seen happier days. It wasn't that it was run down. It was that it just didn't feel lived in. Cliff looked at the family portrait that had been done of his great-grandfather, grandfather, grandmother, uncle, and father when they had been younger. He had always been afraid of it. None of them looked to be very happy in it. Delia had once mentioned to him that his uncle wasn't even really there that day. The artist had been instructed to insert him into it. Rodrick argued that was a lie. Cliff once again could have cared less. Cliff stopped looking at the painting and walked upstairs. He went into his room and sat down at his desk where his books had been left open from the night before.

He wanted to study but he couldn't. Vivica continued to be on his mind. He wasn't really sure why. It seemed weird as of late with her, as if there was more going on than friendship but he wasn't sure. Part of Cliff wanted to approach his friend with the question of her true feelings for him. The issue was that he wasn't sure about how he felt about her. Cliff couldn't lie to himself. He thought she was beautiful. He thought many women were beautiful though. Cliff had known Vivica so long that he wasn't sure if she was just being nice to him or if she meant more to the way she acted. He knew that regardless she truly did care about him.

Studying wasn't going to happen anytime soon. He knew that. He turned on his desk lamp and opened the drawer. He dug through it until he found a photo that Vivica had given him the year before. It was a school picture. He remembered her rambling on about how some of the administration thought her smile was a little to seductive. Cliff didn't know it was back then but looking at it now he did wonder. Her long red hair was sexy, and she had great eyes. While the picture didn't show it, she also had a great body. The more he thought about it, the more he started to feel differently towards Vivica in more ways than one. His face got warm, and his heart started pounding a little faster than it normally did. Cliff went towards the fly of his pants and slowly began to unzip it when the door to his bedroom swung open. He quickly dropped the photo and jumped up. Rodrick was standing at the door.

"Where the hell have you been you little shit?" Rodrick looked at his son.

Fuck. Cliff thought. "I was at church. You know that thing you don't do on Sunday." Cliff suspected that Rodrick was even a little afraid to walk in a church of fear lightning would strike.

"Why on earth did you go to church? You never go unless it is a holiday or mandatory for school." Rodrick crossed his arms.

"It was mandatory for school." Cliff lied. He knew that if his father found out he had been with Vivica and DJ, it wouldn't have ended well.

Rodrick sighed. "I'm going to be gone for the entire week. I want you to think of your actions while I'm gone. When I get back, I don't want any more lip from you. Do you get that boy?"

Cliff nodded. "Yes, sir." He whispered.

The father looked at the boy up and down and then at his desk. "For someone who is having a religious awakening you don't know what you are doing is looked down upon."

Cliff rolled his eyes. "Says the man who can't keep his dick in his pants," Cliff said under his breath.

Rodrick walked over Cliff and smacked him across the face. "Don't you ever talk to me like that again you little bastard." Rodrick walked out.

He stood there for a little bit. Did he just confront his father like that? For years he had ignored the fact his father cheated on his mother. Why did he feel the need to bring it up today? Cliff sat back down. He zipped his pants back up and put away the picture of Vivica. The mood he had been in was lost. Still, he didn't want to study. He reached for his phone and dialed. "Oh, hi Misses Brash. Is Vivica home?" He waited all of a minute before he heard another voice.

"Cliff?" Vivica asked sounding almost out of breath. "Sorry, I was just fixing my hair. Didn't mean to leave you holding for so long."

"Oh, no you're fine. I just wanted to thank you for letting me go to church with you today."

Vivica laughed on the other end. "Oh, that was no problem at all. We all enjoyed having you along. Did you still plan on coming over for dinner today?" Vivica wondered.

Cliff thought for a moment. "Yeah. When did you want me over?"

"Um, well anytime really. We probably won't eat until five though." Vivica explained.

"I'll tell you what; I'll come over around three. I just need to get a few things done around here." Cliff told his friend.

"Ok. I'll see you then." Vivica hung up.

Suddenly, Cliff felt the feeling he had earlier and took the picture back out…

"You rang?" Nial said sarcastically as he walked into his sister's office. "I have a million things to do today, so I don't have long. I'm meeting with my lawyer right after this."

Margot stood up from her desk and walked over to Nial. She crossed her arms. "You are going to get married again?" She said pissed off.

"Well, not immediately. This is her first time getting married. She wants to plan things out. Obviously, I could give a damn, but this is what she wants."

"You never learn..." Margot scoffed.

Coming from the serial bride herself Nial couldn't help but hold back a few chuckles. "You got what you wanted. So why the hell do you care about what happens next for me?"

This was true. Margot got back the family home and had Vivica out from under her company. Margot didn't like any of Nial's love interests though. It wasn't that she was protective. It was the fact that he was stupid when he was horny. Just because you enjoy putting it in some girl doesn't mean you have to give them pretty things. After her third husband, Margot learned always to make them sign an ironclad prenup. They got nothing if they divorced. Nial was still too stupid and had promised Vivica so many things in each divorce including this one. "Oh, little brother you are very smart on paper, but in real life, you are a pretty big idiot." Margot rolled her eyes.

HANNAH – PRESENT DATE

Hannah had to admit to herself, Xander was pretty cute. She usually doesn't fall for men who had their shit together or at least on the surface did. She knew about the Alexander Kingsley case and had followed it since the beginning. It was sort of surreal to be talking to the man's namesake. Yes, she knew that Lucy was also the child of Alexander, but that was sort of different. She had never really spoken to Lucy all that much.

The two co-workers were having coffee in a café in town. Hannah had ordered several shots of espresso and Xander a chai latte. "Are you sure it is safe to be drinking that much caffeine?" Xander questioned.

"If it weren't for boosts like this I would probably have fallen asleep in my car." Again ... Hannah had been clinically exhausted for over a year. Something she had shared with no one but her aunt. It all started when she had been forced to take a job at a Michigan based grocery chain. Hannah took some form of pride from being fired though; they didn't just fire anyone ... "The number of energy drinks I consume would shock you."

Xander laughed. "Well, if you say it ok. So, tell me about your family. I've told you all about my father and Langley..."

Her family? "I'm not that close to them to be completely honest. I mean I don't hate them. Well, I don't hate my father and brother, and deep down I don't hate my mother. My sister on the other hand. That is a different story."

"How come?" Xander pondered.

"We are identical twins and yet are just the complete opposites. Hope looks to please everyone but also makes sure that she always gets her way out of it. I personally, just want to live my life. I have a business degree and could probably be working higher up at the company. Definitely, for Knight, but I don't want to." Material items meant nothing to the girl.

The blonde boy nodded. "I am sort of like that too. I won't lie, I benefitted from being privileged. It's just that people with money can do so much more with it than hoard it and spend it on themselves. Which is why I want to be a police officer."

Clearly, this guy was different than the ones that she had known growing up. Even, the poor guys she had met in the past few years had trouble with grasping that money wasn't everything. "If you want to be a cop so badly, then why not go after it?"

"Well, had my father not been arrested I'd probably have gone to the academy. I probably could have stayed in New York, but it was just kind of a mess. The press wouldn't leave me alone, and Langley would have tried staying. It wasn't a good situation for either of us to be in." Xander knew that if Langley had her way she would be staying with one of her friends right now. The issue is that those supposed friends wouldn't have stuck around. Langley would have had to have transferred to a public school. They had little money left. Each child had a trust fund set in place by their late grandparents, but it didn't become available in full until they turned thirty. Lucy would be getting hers in a few years. They got some of it to pay for college when they turned eighteen but that it had to go towards education. "So, what about you and your brother? Do you get along well enough with him?"

Hannah shrugged. "I could have a better relationship with him. I don't honestly know if he even wants one with me though. It is so hard to tell if he is on my parent's side or his own. Which, I understand if he wants to be on theirs. He doesn't really know any better."

Xander took a sip of his latte "What do you mean by that?"

"Well, this is between us." She heard the irony in telling a stranger that. "I don't think my parents love each other. They are more or less in love with the idea of being with one another, but neither is going to admit it out loud. I don't think my mother even really knows what she wants." Hannah had noticed this after her mother had returned. She noticed that her father had been happy with her aunt. The pictures of their weddings were entirely different. Cliff and Vivica seemed like two people who were meant to be together. Cliff and Tiffany seemed happy but never like two people that should have married. Hannah never knew the full details as to why her aunt and father didn't get married when they were first engaged. As far as she knew it was just something that no one wanted to dwell on. "If my parents divorced I wouldn't be shocked or sad."

"It's kind of sad they don't have much love in their marriage," Xander stated with a look of sorrow on his face.

Hannah shrugged. "Well ok, maybe not loving each other is too strong. They love each other, but they are not in love with each other." If her aunt was not in the picture at all, then Hannah assumed that Cliff and Tiffany could easily live with one another forever in ignorant bliss. "What about your parents? What happened to your mother if you don't mind me asking?"

His mother? It had been years since he had thought about her. "She was like my father. Which was the issue. My parents were and are soulmates, but they are two very volatile individuals. I was pretty young when she left, but I do remember her. She loved the three of us, but she wasn't ready to be a mother, and I don't think she ever will be."

Hannah frowned herself. It was odd; she had many friends over the years with more fucked up parents than her own. Yet, Xander seemed to be the only person she had ever met who didn't seem to blame his parents for his issues. Which he didn't seem to have himself really. If he did, they didn't come out on the surface. Hannah looked down at her phone. "Oh, wow I have to get going. I'm supposed to meet up with my aunt. I can drop you off at your house if you want."

VIVICA – 2018

"I swear that insurance worker was an asshole for no reason," Vivica said out loud in her living room.

Holly sat down next to Vivica and shot her a dirty look. "I'm so glad you forgot to get your license renewed… It was so great calling up my husband to get the officer to look the other way."

While Vivica never thought about it. It was nice to know she had a police officer in her corner. Though she had a suspicion that Holly's husband wasn't very fond of her. "I said I would get it renewed."

The last thing that Vivica needed was to get her license renewed. "Will, you just let me do the driving from now on? You don't even like driving for crying out loud!" Holly buried her face into a pillow and screamed.

Lucy walked in. She had heard about the accident but knew better than to bring it up. "I booked your plane ticket. I still don't think this is a good idea." Lucy also heard all about how her sister had recognized Vivica, and that was part of why Vivica wanted to go to the meeting. She knew that deep down she couldn't blame Langley, but she wanted too. This was going to throw off their entire schedule, and Lucy would have to be in charge of everything. "Are you sure that I cannot talk you out of this?"

"I couldn't talk her out of driving. Do you think that you will get her to not go to her favorite place on earth?" Holly mumbled.

"The two of you need to relax. I am going to have lunch with a friend, see what is out there and then be back. The business will not suffer." Vivica stated as she got on her tablet. She was looking at different things to do while in Beverly Hills. "I should probably do my shopping while I'm out there. Well, at least my US-based shopping."

The doorbell rang. Holly reluctantly got up to open it. It was Hannah. Thank goodness, Holly thought. She could talk some sense into her aunt. "Hi, dear. Your aunt has been expecting you." The two walked back into the living room.

Hannah loved Vivica's house. It was a very warm feeling with wood paneling and dark red furniture. As opposed to the icy feeling of the Knight mansion. "Hi, aunt Vivica!" She smiled.

Vivica stood up and went to hug her favorite niece. "Darling, why on earth didn't you tell me you were moving back to town? You could have moved in here."

"Well, to be honest, I didn't know until last week that I was going to be," Hannah said still bitter. She looked at Lucy. "Oh, hey I met your brother today at work. He seems really nice. We just had coffee."

"Oh, great my brother is having coffee with you and my sister is parading around with your brother giving Vivica life advice..." Lucy screamed a little as she walked into the other room.

"What's going on?" Hannah asked. She looked at Holly for an answer, but the maid just shook her head as she walked back towards the foyer. "Aunt Vivica, are you doing ok?" The brunet asked.

Was she doing ok? Vivica thought for a moment. "Surprisingly yes I am doing great. The two lackeys are just mad that I'm going to Beverly Hills for a few days."

Hannah gave her aunt a look of worry. "Are you sure it is a good idea for you to be going to Beverly Hills?"

This was getting frustrating the red head thought to herself. "Oh, for goodness sakes yes! If you are so worried, you can come with me as well."

Beverly Hills? The weather was being obnoxious right now, Hannah thought. "Personally, I would love to go. I can't help though. I just started my job at the dealership. If I jump ship now, everyone is going to assume I just gave up." She knew that Hope would never let her live it down.

"I don't understand why you would go to your father when you know very well I would have given you a place to live and a job working for me," Vivica said as she crossed her arms. "Cliff means well, but selling cars?"

Hannah didn't want to explain why she did what she did for the third time in three days. She was going to stick with her gut on this. It wouldn't be for long. "Aunt Vivica if I had taken a job with you I would never have left. Obviously, I love the idea of working with you. It's just the idea of not being my boss, in the long run, goes against all my dreams and ambitions." Hannah admitted out loud. If it meant having to work at a car dealership for a few months even a year, then so be it. She would save her money and figure out a career for herself.

Vivica laughed. "You know who you sound like?"

"Don't even say it." Hannah half groaned, and half laughed.

"Your father when he was younger," Vivica remembered listening to Cliff for hours on end saying how he would be successful on his own. He had dreams of doing so much good in the world. Then everything changed when Tiffany came along… It was funny. Vivica was willing to live a middle-class life with Cliff forever based on the things that Cliff wanted. Then Tiffany came along, and Cliff did the complete opposite of what he always said he would do. Vivica to this day couldn't figure out if this were a good or bad thing. Considering, she was not the one with Cliff she guessed it didn't affect her. Vivica thought about it for a moment. She took her niece's hand. "Hannah darling, if you have dreams and ambitions you need to go after them. Just remember I will always be here to help you."

This was why she loved her aunt. Vivica always believed in her even when she clearly wasn't worth believing in. "Thank you. I promise that if push comes to shove, I will come to you."

The two hugged one another briefly. "Well, just remember it doesn't necessarily have to feel like a hand out from me. Just think of it as spending Nial's money…" She rolled her eyes. It was as if mentioning the man triggered something because Brad walked in. Vivica looked over. "Dear, where have you been?"

Brad waved at his cousin. "I was just at the gym."

"All day?" Vivica asked concerned. She stood up.

He shrugged. Brad didn't know what else to do. A lot of his local friends he had before boarding school had dropped him. The ones that were left were all at school obviously. "There isn't much else to do." Brad didn't know how to approach the subject, but he wanted to tell his mother that he wanted to permanently move back home. Boarding school was fun, but he missed being around his family. Even, if he didn't approve of the way his father acted.

Hannah looked at her phone to check the time. "You know, Harry should be home from school soon." She pointed out. "Maybe, the two of you could hang out. I'm sure he would love that."

"Oh, he is definitely off of school. I saw him a little while ago." Vivica smiled. She looked at Hannah. "You know how much I hate gossip, but I think Harry was on a date with Lucy's sister."

The two cousins both looked at Vivica in shock. "My brother was on a date with Langley Kingsley?" Hannah giggled. She had yet to meet the girl, but from what Xander had told her, she was a force to be reckoned with. "I didn't think he had it in him."

Was Harry on a date with that blonde girl they had met the other night? Brad was in disbelief. Things had changed. Harry had always been the shy one of the two cousins. Brad also had to admit that he kind of thought Langley was cute. "Maybe, I will call him up." Brad would respect that Harry was dating Langley. It wasn't as if Brad even knew the girl. He just wanted to talk to his cousin. There were so many things that he needed to discuss. "I'll see you guys later." Brad started to walk to the staircase to get to his room when Holly walked down. "Oh, hey Holly! How are you?" He asked.

"Ask your mother…" Holly said giving Vivica a dirty look.

Brad turned to his mom. "What's going on?" He asked.

Vivica rolled her eyes. "Oh, for crying out loud… I'll pay for your therapy out of pocket woman… Was driving with me really that traumatic?"

With that, Brad knew exactly why Holly was in a mood. "I'll let you guys deal with this." He sprinted up the staircase.

CLIFF – 1986

The teen boy stood outside the Brash household waiting to be let in. Cliff had stood at the doorstep over a thousand times it felt like. Yet, this was the first time he had ever been nervous. The door opened. "Oh, hey DJ!" He greeted one of his hosts. All of a sudden, he became a little less tense. DJ let him in, and he sat down without even being asked. Cliff had nothing to worry about. Just because he had realized he had feelings for Vivica didn't mean anything. Cliff wasn't even sure what he was going to do about these feelings.

Cliff had spent most of the afternoon considering what a relationship with Vivica would be like in his head. The first thing he thought about was how it would affect Brianna. He figured someone had to factor her in. She would become the third wheel. Then he considered what would happen if the two happened to break up. It would be awkward but also devastating. He couldn't imagine that Vivica would want to continue being his friend if they broke up. Would he want to be her friend after a breakup? Cliff then pondered on if he was even old enough to date? Which was silly. He had been on dates before. Vivica had gone on dates before as well. They were old enough. Cliff had to get out of his head. Gale walked in, and Cliff stood up to greet her. "Hey, Mrs. Brash!" He said.

"Hello, Cliff. Nice to see you again today. It's a good thing probably. DJ and I made enough food that we will be having leftovers for the next week. Don't tell Vivica though..." She giggled.

"Oh, trust me I won't." Cliff had to admit he always liked Gale and DJ.it is obvious they loved each other, unlike his parents. They also were always so nice to him. Which was another thing. What would happen if they did start dating though? Would they continue to treat him the same way? Cliff had to get out of his head. That's when she walked downstairs. Vivica looked beautiful he thought. She was wearing a black turtleneck with a gray skirt and black boots. Cliff was sure that she had warned the outfit at least a dozen times, but it was like the first time he had seen her in it in many ways. "Hey, Weston," Cliff said choked up.

The redhead smiled. "Hi." She giggled back. Vivica sniffed a little. "Cliff, are you wearing cologne?" She wondered.

He blushed. "Yeah. I mean just a tiny bit." He looked down at the floor.

DJ looked at Gale. The two parents smiled. "We are going to finish up dinner. We'll call you kids in when it is ready." Gale said. With that the left the room.

If Cliff were honest, he wished that they hadn't gone anywhere. He needed their awkward small talk to mask his own. He realized he had to say something. "So, how was the rest of your afternoon?"

"Oh, it was fine. I finished up my homework. Probably a bunch of B-work but that's good enough for me." Vivica admitted.

"Yeah, I still have some left too. I got kind of distracted this afternoon…"

Something was different about Cliff, Vivica thought. His hair looked a little bit more done, he smelt really good, and his clothes seemed a little less thrown together. Vivica also felt like the tone in his voice sounded even sexier than usual. She sat down on the couch and gestured for him to sit next to her. "I'm so not looking forward to this week. I can guarantee you it will be longer than it needs to be." Vivica rolled her eyes.

Cliff nodded his head pretending to listen. He just kept looking at her eyes. He was sitting a lot closer to her than usual. "Vivica can we talk about something?" He asked.

She shrugged. "Yeah. What about?" She asked. Vivica waited a minute, and he said nothing. Cliff had stopped looking at her, and it was getting confusing. "Cliff are you ok?" She pondered. "Cliff?" Finally, the boy looked back at her again and went straight in for a kiss. Vivica's eyes widened for a brief second, but then she closed them and got into the kiss. He knew what he was doing. Then he stopped. "What was that? I mean I don't get me wrong that was well amazing but… What was that?"

What was that? It was all the confirmation he needed. "Do you like me Vivica?"

Vivica looked at him straight in the eyes and for the first time in her life was at a total loss for words. Was this some sort of prank? Were her parents in on it? Was this why her mother had asked her about Cliff this morning?

"I… mean do you? I just kind of figured." What was he saying? Cliff felt so stupid. Why on earth would he ask her? "I have to be honest. I think I like you. You know, like more than just in a friendly way." He waited for a response, but she said nothing. Instead, she stood up and walked out the front door. DJ walked in.

"Dinner's done," DJ said. He looked around. "What happened to Vivica?"

Cliff shrugged. Then all of a sudden, the two heard a scream so loud that both were sure that all of Wayne County had heard. "I think I should go check on her. Keep our plates warm… This might be a while." DJ nodded in confusion. Cliff proceeded to walk outside without a coat on and walked over to Vivica. He looked back for a moment and saw that both DJ and Gale were looking from the window. He was about to tell Vivica when she grabbed his face and kissed him. It was a very passionate kiss, and he swore that he felt her tongue move around a little in his mouth.

Inside DJ looked at Gale. "Should we stop them?"

"If we value our sanity we should just go into the kitchen and pretend like we saw nothing." Gale pointed out.

DJ nodded. The two walked back towards the kitchen. "Oh, by the way, you owe me twenty dollars. I told you they would finally admit their feelings this year."

Back outside, the two teenagers continued to kiss one another. Neither was wearing a coat, and it was snowing now. "I'm not dreaming right?" Vivica asked as she broke from the kiss. Cliff pinched her. "Ok, that really hurt but I'm still here."

The two smiled at one another and continually going back and forth between kissing and smiling. Cliff didn't know what the future brought, but he knew that at that moment, Vivica and him were dating.

HARRY – 2018

This entire day had been surreal to Harry. A person was willingly spending time with him and treating him like he mattered. This had never really happened. Harry was so used to just talking with people at school. On occasion, they would text, but that was about it. His weekends were spent watching TV and internet videos. Today a Monday of all days was being spent with Langley Kingsley…

"Wow, you have some really interesting taste in music…" Langley said as she looked through his phone's playlist. It was mostly boybands and top twenty pop singers. "You need to listen to some rap."

"It's not my kind of music," Harry admitted as he sat down on his bed next to her. "I mean I have the *Hamilton* soundtrack saved somewhere," Harry said this as if it made up for his lack of rap.

Langley laughed. "Well, ok…" As she continued to scroll the phone started to vibrate and play a pop song. It was 2018, who on earth used a song for their ringtone anymore? She noticed the name. It was Brad. "Oh, look it's your hot cousin calling. Answer it!"

Harry awkwardly took the phone and hit answer. He hated talking on the phone with people. Even if it did happen to be Brad. "Hey, man what's up?" Harry was trying to speak a little more masculine than he normally did. It never felt authentic though.

"Harry, hey! You wanna hang out? I'm bored as f over here… Can I come over? I need to talk to you about something."

Harry looked at Langley, and it was clear she was trying to listen in. "Yeah, sure. That girl we met from the other night happens to be here just hanging out. Is that ok if she sticks around?"

"Yeah, man. I'll be over in like less than five minutes." He hung up.

"Brad is going to come over for a little bit. He said it was cool if you were here." Harry assumed she would want to stick around. It was kind of obvious that Langley had a thing for Brad. Not that he thought it was going to get her anywhere.

Langley smiled. "Sounds perfect. I can flirt with him and work my charm." She got out her phone and turned on the camera. She started to fix up her makeup a little bit when someone walked in the door. She immediately looked up, and it was Brad. "Lord, did you teleport here?"

The two cousins laughed at one another. "No, my mom's house is across the street." It was nice that Langley was oblivious to the goings on around town. Otherwise it might have seemed pathetic that his mother had a home right across the street from her childhood ex-boyfriend. Even though, it was her other ex-husband who happened to be a Knight himself who had bought the house for her in the first place.

Brad turned to Harry. "So, I think I want to move back permanently. What do you think about that?"

This day was shocking. First, he made a new friend with Langley and now he was possibly getting Brad back? If someone like Harry Styles or Timothée Chalamet walked into the room naked later on when he was alone then the day would truly be perfect. He wasn't that hopeful though. "I think that would be totally awesome!" He hugged his cousin and then realized it was kind of awkward.

So, Brad was moving back to town? Langley thought to herself. This was almost to perfect. She could actually have a real shot at being with the hot blonde. "Awe, it's so cute to see two cousins reunited."

The blond boy turned to Langley. "Yeah. I could leave if the two of you were trying to have some private time together…"

Langley and Harry both looked at each other with straight faces. "We are really just hanging out. I don't know anyone else in town yet. I guess now I have two new friends if you are sticking around. Though, I assume you will be going to Saint Agnes with Harry, not GPW?"

"Yeah. Sorry. It's too bad that you can't go there with us. I mean, I will pretty much be starting over. I haven't really stayed in contact with my old friends. I'm sure that Harry will be able to help catch me up with everyone."

Harry sighed a little. Well, yes, he could help reintroduce him to everyone at school. It would just mean that he and Brad wouldn't be hanging out as often as he just thought they would. Harry regularly checked in on Brad's social media accounts. He did so much with his friends at boarding school. Yet, Harry was a loner. It was fun spending time with Langley today, but he didn't see himself going to parties or anything like that. Sure, maybe with Brad back that would change. He was sure to push Harry in that direction, and if Langley wanted to hang out with him, then he was sure to end up coming out of his shell. Whether he wanted to or not it seemed.

"Totally I can." Harry sighed.

"We should exchange numbers." Langley looked at Brad. She was playing with her hair seductively. She handed him her phone. He instantly put his number in there. Langley took the phone back and looked at the contact. *Brad Fitzpatrick* along with his number sat there on her phone. This was to perfect. She looked up, and Brad was looking at her. So, was Harry awkwardly. "I already have Harry's number. So, now we can all hang out whenever." Brad was smiling. Langley knew she was close to scoring the deal with him.

VIVICA – 2018

A week had passed, and Vivica was all packed. She was waiting in her living room for the car she had ordered to take her to the airport. Holly had offered to take her, but Vivica was taking an early flight. She didn't want her to have to be here that early. Her husband already had issues with Vivica. While the red-head looked at her phone she couldn't help but check through her photos on her cloud. So, many pictures of her and Nial that she really should get around to deleting. She would keep the photos of Brad. That said it didn't mean she needed a majority. As she scrolled, she went far enough back to notice photos of her and Cliff with all the children back when they had been together. It was a very different time. Vivica sighed. Things were definitely different now. She had accepted that a long time ago.

A knock on the door somewhat startled Vivica. The driver was supposed to send her a text, not knock on the door. Nobody, else was here yet though so it was up to her to answer the door. She walked into the foyer and looked through the peephole. Vivica was somewhat shocked. She opened the door. "What on earth are you doing up so early?" She asked to Cliff.

"I was just on my morning jog and noticed that your lights were on. What are you doing up so early?" He wondered.

"Well, I'm going to Beverly Hills for a few days. I'm meeting with Bridget Madwell to discuss a few things."

Cliff sighed. He was not a fan of Bridget Madwell. Bridget had been there during the early days of Vivica's New York modeling days. She had always been a terrible influence. Cliff was aware that she was now the CEO of the modeling agency that the two girls had once modeled for though. He also knew that she had two children of her own so maybe she had grown. The

Madwell Agency had booked many of their models for the Knight Car Show in the past. "Well, hopefully, it is a brief business lunch."

Vivica laughed. "You still have an issue with Bridget, don't you?" She rolled her eyes. He had never been a fan of her friendship with Bridget. Even when they had been teenagers. Bridget was in her early twenties at the time though. "I guess some things never change?"

No, they really didn't. "Vivica don't go." Why did he just say that out loud? "Why can't I go?"

Why couldn't she go? There was no reason that he could give to stop her from going. It was actually probably for the best. If this was how he was acting around her then it was clear they needed separation. "I mean you can go… I'm just saying well you know…"

"You're just hoping that I would stick around. Well, I'll be back soon enough don't worry. I'm only catching up with an old friend." She lied. Vivica knew that she would more than likely be doing some sort of modeling job. It would probably be some silly anniversary issue for a magazine she posed for in the 90's. She didn't care. Vivica's confidence was higher than ever.

Cliff looked at his dear friend. "So, how have you been since Nial ambushed you?" He awkwardly asked.

She shrugged. "I sulked like I normally do after a bad breakup, but I've picked up the pieces. Nial can have his young piece of ass… She probably lacks a brain. Which is probably a plus for Nial. You know I'm shocked Hannah didn't mention I'd be going out of town."

"Well, Hannah and I are still on not so great speaking terms. I'm shocked she is even speaking with you."

Vivica smiled. "The two of us have always had a special bond I guess. I've always loved that girl like a daughter. Same with Harry as a son."

"What about Hope?"

"I love Hope very much. She just never needed me as much. Even when Tiffany was away. You know that very well."

He did. Cliff often wondered if Hannah and Harry's personalities were a result of Vivica's influence. Probably. Hope was very similar to Tiffany. "We should have lunch when you get back home."

She would love that but knew it wouldn't be practical. "If you can get her to behave for an hour maybe we can ..." Vivica smiled. Her phone pinged. "My car is here. I should get going."

LUCY – 2018

Monday mornings since Vivica had left for Beverly Hills had been rather hectic for her. It wasn't just Monday's Lucy had to admit to herself. It was basically every day that ended with Y. Xander had already left for work, but Langley still had not exited her bathroom. "Langley come on if you want a ride to school you have ten seconds to get downstairs. I have to rush to a meeting." Austin walked into the room; he didn't start his day until noon. What a lucky son of a bitch she thought. "Are we ever going to get a day just for the two of us?" Lucy asked as she went through files.

Austin shrugged. He was having too much fun with Nial's fiancé to worry about the lack of alone time they were having. "It's fine. You just need to calm down a little." Austin really meant hat.

"Langley get the hell down here already!"

Langley marched down the stairs wearing skin tight jeans with a sweater that showed way too much. "Alright, I'm ready to go."

Lucy looked at Austin who was apparently trying not to stare. "If you were trying to make a statement I don't even care. We don't have time for you to get dressed again." She opened the front door, and Langley sighed.

The two sisters got into the car and took off for work and school. Lucy realized she didn't say goodbye to Austin. She sort of felt bad but was so busy that she didn't have the time. "I need you to not skip out on your afternoon classes today."

"Who said, I was skipping out?" Langley pretended to play dumb.

"You do know they take attendance, daily right? I get a call informing me when you are not in class. Where on earth do you even go? You have no money!" Lucy screamed out.

Well, no shit she didn't have any money. "I just hang out with Harry and sometimes Brad." Never enough with Brad. He was always studying. It was odd. She knew that Brad liked her, yet he chose to stay distant from her for some reason. Harry claimed that Brad said nothing that made him suspect that he was turned off by her. It drove Langley crazy.

"I think it is great that you have friends, but I can't keep getting phone calls in the middle of the day. Eventually, a truancy officer is going to show up..." Lucy gave her sister a quick glance. It seemed like every time Langley would do something that a typical teenager would do; she had to stretch and manipulate it just to cause drama. Lucy remembered her own teenage years; her father was far from a perfect parent, but she had a set of rules that she was expected to abide by. Langley clearly didn't have that under their father.

Langley didn't want to listen to this nonsense. "You want me to have friends, but I don't get to be around them."

"I already told you that I would look into getting you into Saint Agnes. I just have been busy dealing with a lack of Vivica right now." Lucy really needed Vivica to return from her trip already.

The younger sister sighed. "I understand that you are dealing with things too. It's just, ugh I cannot believe I'm telling you this. I sort of kind of like Brad Fitzpatrick."

Lucy quickly looked at her sister. "You like Vivica's son?" This was not going to end well. "Langley, you hardly know him."

She didn't need reminding. "Well, I think he's hot."

"What about you and Harry Knight?"

Langley couldn't help but chuckle. "I mean Harry is an awesome guy, but I just don't think there is anything there." Langley was shocked by the number of people that thought she was dating Harry. Harry was an awesome friend, and he was definitely cute, but even if he weren't a hundred percent gay, she wouldn't fall for him. He was too much of an innocent little puppy. Yet, Brad was the pure one with no intention of having sex. Harry at least had experimented even if it was a traumatic experience for him.

The last thing she needed was for Langley to start dating Brad and then the two broke up. It would be awkward between her and Vivica for sure. Langley was just as much a drama queen as Vivica. They would both expect her to choose sides and the fact was that Vivica paid her and Langley was somewhat of a burden. She hated thinking that way about her sister. It wasn't the fact that she was living with her or that she had to pay for everything for her. Lucy could deal with that with ease. It was the fact that she just couldn't stay out of trouble to save her life. Langley wasn't going to school, she wasn't doing very well in school even though she received a 4.0 at her old school, and she would back talk everything. She was at her wits end. Her entire life she had wanted to be a mother of her own. Yet, since taking in Langley she had been put off by wanting to be a mother for at least another ten years.

"Oh, relax. I wouldn't let a potential relationship with Brad get in the way of your job. I'm not stupid or heartless." Langley's phone all of a sudden went off. It was Harry. He needed to see her right away. He was freaking out. "Can I maybe skip school this morning?"

Lucy turned to her sister yet again and looked annoyed. "Have you been listening to me at all?"

"Look, Harry needs me right now. I promise to you that this will be the absolute last time that I will skip out on school. I'm trying to be there for one of the only friends I currently have." Langley explained.

"I'll call your school and tell them that you are running late because of a doctor's appointment. You better be in school for the rest of the week. Do you understand me?" Lucy asked.

"You truly are the best sister ever."

"Unfortunately…" Lucy turned her car in the opposite direction. She really did need to get Langley enrolled at Saint Agnes. It was close enough that Langley would be able to walk to school.

Hannah – 2018

Working at a car dealership was not something that Hannah ever thought she would do. She had to admit though she was rather good at it. Hannah wasn't stupid. One of the reasons that she was good at it was because men wanted to talk to the pretty girl. Xander had done pretty well for himself as well. He was sincere which the customers seemed to like, and Hannah seemed to like a lot.

"Hey, stranger." Xander put his bag down on his desk.

"Good, morning Xander!"

"Ready for another day filled with fun?"

Was she ever! She planned on asking him to go to dinner with her on Friday. Things were moving fast with Xander, but she didn't care. She took things slow with other guys, and it always ended in regret.

Hannah logged into her computer when she started to notice she was seeing double in her reflection on the screen. Then she realized it wasn't her reflection… "Hope?" Hannah turned around.

"Well, how is my twin doing at her big girl job?" Hope asked her twin.

What on earth was Hope doing here? The two had little to no contact with one another ever since she had moved back to the house. Yet, here Hope was today for no apparent reason. "Hope, what are you doing here?"

Hope ignored her sister. She noticed the cute blond boy sitting on the other side of her desk. "Well now, who are you?" Hope inquired.

Xander stood up and put out his hand. "Xander Kingsley. Nice to meet you."

Hope put out her hand to shake his. He had a nice firm grip. "Aren't you the cutie." She thought for a moment as he blushed. "Kingsley? Are you related to the blonde girl who keeps hanging out with my brother?"

Her brother? Their brother... Why did Hope always have to take possession of everything. She wasn't even sure that Hope liked Harry all that much. "Hope, don't you have work?"

"Not until this evening." She looked over at Xander. "I'm in med school. I'm in a program with the hospital right now shadowing with different doctors."

"Wow, that's awesome." Xander enthusiastically said.

Was he falling for her? Hannah felt a knot form in her throat. "We really do need to get started for the day around here Hope. You should probably get leaving."

Her twin sister just rolled her eyes. "I doubt you will get in trouble Hannah dear. There is no one in the parking lot, and our family owns the dealership. I just wanted to spend a little time seeing what my favorite sister does all day."

Favorite sister? More like favorite victim.

"I actually have to go talk with our manager for a minute." Xander admitted. He walked away.

"Well now isn't he cute?" Hope stated.

"Hope leave him alone."

Hope giggled. "Oh, do you have feelings for him? If you have feelings just say so and I will totally leave him alone."

Hannah didn't believe her for a moment, and she didn't want Hope getting involved in her social life what so ever. "I think he is too nice for a timid bitch like you." Wrong choice of words.

"Well, I think he should really be the judge of that. I'm going to go ask him out." Hope stated.

If Hannah were a stronger person, she would stop her, but the reality was once Hope wanted something she got it. Hannah watched as Hope cornered Xander. They spoke only for a few minutes before Hope left and Xander walked back over.

"So, your sister just invited me over for dinner at your place on Saturday."

That was unexpected. Hope was clearly playing games. Saturday was Harry's birthday... "Well, I guess we will see each other on Saturday." Hannah mumbled.

VIVICA – 2018

"Don't look at the camera Vivica!"

She wasn't looking at the camera. They kept moving the camera into her line of vision, and the flash kept going off in her eyes. Who was this photographer? He had to be the worst that she had ever worked with. Vivica wouldn't have agreed to this shoot had she known it would be so unprofessional. "Can I please take five?" She didn't even wait for a response. Vivica got up from the chair she was sitting in and walked over to Bridget.

"So, how is it going? Doesn't it feel great to be back in front of the camera?"

Vivica didn't really know what she expected to happen when she agreed to do a series of shoots. Vivica was doing a campaign for nostalgia by reshooting many of her old photos. It was for some sort of multimedia campaign. "Bridget, I need to take some time for myself. This photographer is stressing me out."

"Alright. I'll rearrange a few things. Take the rest of the day off, and we will recoup in the morning." Bridget went over to the photographer to discuss the new arrangements.

Digging through her purse, Vivica went through her phone. Four missed calls from Lucy. She didn't understand why Lucy was freaking out so much. She did most of the work herself already. Holly had left a few crudely worded text messages. Which wasn't a shock. She had previously threatened to come get her three times. Brad had sent a daily check-in text. Then there was a photo from Margot of Nial and the bimbo he was marrying kissing each other. She deleted that one.

This was what she needed right now. Not everyone agreed with her on that, but it really was. Vivica needed to be away from her life right now. She wasn't living in the past even if that was the entire point of the campaign. She had moved on from her past a long time ago.

Her phone started to ring. It was from someone who really was a blast from her past. "Hello… I'll be there in twenty…"

***

Vivica sat down at a small restaurant somewhere in downtown Beverly Hills. She then saw her and immediately sprung back up. "Brianna Belle!"

"Vivica Weston!" Screamed Brianna as she ran over and hugged her long-time friend. "Oh my gosh, it has been far too long. I have been trying to get a hold of you since the moment I found out you were in California."

"Well, I was going to come visit you in San Francisco. I just had to get myself together first." The two sat back down. "So, tell me everything. How are Julie and the children doing?"

Brianna got out her phone and showed her a billion pictures. "Julie definitely wants you to come over for dinner. She is not taking no for an answer. The kids want to see their aunt Vivica!"

"Well, I definitely want to see them too. I hate that you moved out here after high school." If she had Brianna in her life during the college years and through the Tiffany fiasco she probably never would have ended up marrying Nial three times or even broken up with Cliff in the first place.

"You know I had to get away from home. Obviously, my parents and I are on much better terms now. I just needed to find a place where I could be me."

It shocked her to this day when Brianna came out as a lesbian. All those years of her thinking that Brianna was jealous of her. In reality, she was jealous of Cliff. "If only I were a lesbian. Things would have turned out so much simpler. I'd be married to a lawyer. Don't tell Julie I said that."

The dark-skinned beauty couldn't help but laugh. "I'm just glad that even with the distance we have remained friends after all these years. It's too bad that Cliff isn't here. The three musketeers would be reunited." Brianna quickly regretted saying that. "Sorry."

"Oh, it's fine. I gave up on longing for Cliff and me to get back together several years ago after Tiffany came back. I'll always love him, but I'm not interested in playing games anymore. I'll deny it if you ever tell anyone but I'm just too old to deal with a love triangle anymore." The two giggled together.

Langley ran over to Harry who was sitting in his car in the parking lot at Saint Agnes. "Harry, I got your text. What's wrong?"

The curly haired boy couldn't speak. He was too ashamed. "It just won't ever end. Todd won't stop threatening me. I'm not ready to come out, but I feel like I have no choice but to at this point."

Langley slid into the car and hugged Harry. "Did he threaten to release the video again?"

"No. He is starting to spread rumors. I don't think Brad has heard anything yet."

She thought about it for a moment. "Well, if he is only spreading rumors then let's prove to him that the rumors aren't true."

"How do I do that? I am gay Langley. The rumors are true."

"Yes, but what if you were dating a super sexy New York Socialite?" Langley looked at Harry.

He looked at her. "You want to pretend to date me? What about Brad though?"

"What about Brad? He sends mixed signals and is way to pure and innocent. I mean it isn't like we have to claim we are an item. Just that we are casually dating."

Harry still wasn't sure about this. It just seemed a little too easy. "Well, he still has the video. What happens if he releases the video?"

Langley had already been thinking about that in general. "Well, then he goes to jail Harry. You both are still underage. He would be distributing child porn. Unless he is truly sadistic then he won't release the video."

As much as Harry wanted this to go away, he just was reluctant. He knew that Langley liked Brad. Brad had admitted in confidence to him that he kind of had a thing for Langley. Plus, even though he wasn't ready to come out he didn't want to pretend to be something he wasn't. Staying single and not discussing his sexuality wasn't lying in his mind. It was just not talking about it one way or the other. Having a girlfriend would be lying. Harry just wanted this to go away though.

Before he could say anything about it, Langley was kissing him and snapping pictures. "I'm going to post these all-over social media. My followers will get it to spread fast enough that I'm dating Harry Knight. Well, I never thought I'd date a Knight. Though I did once date Kennedy. That family really knows how to make men."

"They really do…" Harry blushed.

"Alright. It's posted. You and I are officially dating. However, considering no one follows you on social media and it might take a while for the press to take wind of this, we need to do one more thing."

She got out of the car and gestured for Harry to get out as well. Harry grabbed his book bag and followed her. She yanked his hand as they walked to the front entrance of the school. Langley was walking rather seductively. There were countless people standing around before class started. She looked and noticed that Todd was standing up against the wall all by his lonesome. This was perfect. "Well, I have to get going to school Harry darling." She said a bit loudly. "I'll, be counting the minutes until school gets out for both of us." She looked at him in a way that said exactly what he needed to do. Harry caught on quickly and came in close for a kiss. They both closed their eyes. It felt so unnatural for Harry. Langley seemed to be doing all the work. It seemed to get rather quiet around them though. Then it was over. Langley backed away. "Bye, sweetie!" She strutted off.

Harry looked around. People had definitely been paying attention. Brad casually walked over sort of at a loss.

"Harry are you dating Langley?"

"Uh… Well, we are sort of seeing each other. I wouldn't say we are together, together though." He awkwardly told his cousin. Harry felt bad now.

Brad nodded. "That's cool man. I'm happy for you." He patted him on the shoulder for a quick second. "I kind of figured. You guys spend so much time with each other. I hope it works out."

The curly haired cousin could tell that Brad was not taking this revelation very well. It was a necessary evil though. Harry just needed to figure out the best way to come out as gay. He needed to wait a little bit. He didn't want to do it close to his birthday. He wanted it to be on a random day that he would be able to forget. Harry happened to be gay. He wasn't looking for that to be his personality. It wasn't something to celebrate. It wasn't something he wanted to be ashamed about either. It had to be on his terms though when he did come out though.

"So, did you finish your homework for history?" Harry asked his cousin.

"Yeah. I got it done. It's weird. I get so much more done now that I'm basically living alone." Brad stated. He hadn't seen his mother in like two weeks. His father had made little attempt to get to see him. His aunt Margot wanted to have lunch with him, but he was somewhat hesitant about that. Holly was there when he got up and when he got home, but she would leave after dinner was done. He saw Lucy the most out of everyone. She was in the home office at all hours of the day and night though she was still quiet.

"We should totally take advantage of that one of these days. Have a small party." Harry joked.

Brad nodded in agreement. "You know that wouldn't be a bad idea."

"Dude, I was joking. Your mother would kill you."

"My mother is in Beverly Hills modeling lingerie and swimsuits." Brad crossed his arms looking at his cousin.

Harry could see what he meant. "Well, maybe one day. Are you still going to come over on Saturday for my birthday dinner?" Harry preferred having his birthday dinner at home as opposed to going out. They went out to celebrate everything else it seemed, so he liked having a family dinner at home.

Brad smiled. "Totally, bro!"

TIFFANY – 2018

Looking at the cover of a magazine that had her sister on it was the last thing that Tiffany needed this morning. Cliff had left for a business meeting early that morning. He didn't even say goodbye to her. She could tell they were growing distant which was ripping her apart inside. Vivica wasn't even in the state, and she was still causing a mess for her marriage. She looked at the magazine again and ripped the cover off, crumbling the page into a tiny ball. She threw it towards the door as it opened. Nial walked in. He caught it.

"Having a good morning?" Nial smirked.

"I'm mad at you." Tiffany said.

Nial sat down on the edge of her desk. "Does it have to do with Vivica?"

Tiffany rolled her eyes. "She is going to go after him eventually."

"Well, she might. If she does then she loses out on a lot of money from our first divorce. So, it would be in her best interest to stay away from him." Nial pointed out.

Money wouldn't matter to Vivica. "As much as you don't want to hear this, Cliff has more money than you do."

The blonde doctor hadn't thought of that. "Good point. Are you accusing your sister of going after Cliff only for his money though?"

Was she? As much as Tiffany thought that Vivica was up to no good she wasn't sure she could accuse her sister of going after her money. Though, the fact that Vivica only seemed to go after wealthy men would make a lot more sense. "Why did you leave her? I mean aside from the young piece of ass."

"Well, you have met your sister. She isn't exactly the easiest person to live with. Plus, she never really loved me. Even if she never is with him again, Cliff will always be the love of her life."

Tiffany turned around and looked out the window. "He loves me though."

136

"I'm not saying doesn't. He had a second chance with her, and he still chose you." Nial pointed out. "Clearly, the man has some sense if he knew which sister made sense. I mean you have three children with him after all."

It was hard to tell when Nial was trying to be supportive and when he was just being an asshole. Yes, she had three children with Cliff. That didn't mean that it was the only reason that she and Cliff were still together. They made sense together. At least she thought they did. "Have fun with your little girlfriend, Nial. I really do hope she is everything that you wanted and more." Tiffany turned back around and headed for the door. "I have to get going."

The brunet doctor marched down the hallway of the hospital just trying to get the heck away from her idiot ex-brother-in-law. As she walked, she noticed Austin Martin talking with what appeared to be Nial's fiancé. She knew that he had been seeing her as a patient, so she didn't make anything of it and just kept going. Austin was engaged to Lucy and Lucy worked for Vivica. It seemed everyone in this town knew one another, and that drove her up a wall.

"Mom, there you are!" Hope shouted from across the hall. She quickly walked over. "I've been looking all over for you."

"You knew I had surgery this morning." Tiffany reminded her.

Hope seemed to ignore this. "Well, I just wanted to let you know I invited a guy over for dinner on Saturday."

Tiffany looked at her daughter in confusion. "You're inviting a random man to your brother's birthday dinner? You know he likes to keep this a family event."

"Well, Brad is going to be there so is it really a family event?"

"Brad is your cousin." Tiffany reminded her. Tiffany was unsure of how to react to Hope throwing her first cousin out of the loop as family.

The med student sighed. She needed to get her way. "Well, what if I can get Harry to say yes to it?"

The surgeon shrugged. "I guess I wouldn't have an issue with it. I can't imagine your father would either. Do you think this boy has staying power in your life though?" Tiffany worried about Hope's love life sometimes. She always seemed to serial date men who she didn't seem to think were right for her daughter.

"Oh, I definitely think he will stick around." So, long as it annoyed Hannah, Hope would go after Xander. It helped that Xander happened to be extremely hot. Still, she was mainly just trying to mess with her twin.

Hope looked at her watch. "I have to get to class. I'll see you later." She blew her mother a kiss as she walked away.

It always amazed her how different all her children were. Tiffany was happy that they were individuals. She just wished she understood the reason that Hannah and Harry had for doing certain things.

LUCY – 2018

"You want to have a white party?" Lucy asked Mrs. Templeton in total confusion. "It's March…"

Mrs. Templeton was your average old as a dinosaur middle American socialite. She got most of her ideas from lifestyle magazines. Lucy had to assume she was reading a three-year-old late August edition though. Vivica would know how to talk her out of this. Mrs. Templeton was sure to be made a laughing stock if she actually went through with this party plan for her birthday. Lucy wasn't even sure why she was planning her own party. Then she realized, no one in town liked Mrs. Templeton.

"I want a white party!" Mrs. Templeton demanded.

Lucy sighed and made a few notes. "Alright then. I'll look into a few different concepts for the White Party and get back to you by the end of the week." Lucy walked Mrs. Templeton out of Vivica's living room and into her foyer where Holly was pretending to dust. Lucy could tell that she was obviously just listening in. Lucy opened the door for Mrs. Templeton, and neither said a word to one another as Lucy quickly closed the door behind her. "That woman is infuriating."

"Well, no one is going to disagree with you on that one. Mrs. Templeton has to be a hundred years old. I've seen old pictures at Saint Agnes of her back when Sister Mary Newman was in her twenties, and Mrs. Templeton looked her current age. She walked up to me once when I was in the choir to tell me that I should stand in the back. Not because of my voice but because I was outshining the as she put it *pretty white girls.*

The blonde assistant dropped her jaw in shock. "What on earth?" Lucy thought for a moment. She really hoped that Mrs. Templeton didn't really mean plantation style party. "It's weird to think sometimes that you grew up with Austin."

Holly walked into the living room and sat down. Lucy followed her. "Well, we went to the same school. I wouldn't really say we grew up together though. Austin was kind of a troublemaker. I was a theater geek. A friend that I lost touch with years ago dated him for a while." Holly often felt that she needed to warn Lucy of Austin's past. Though she knew that it really wasn't her place. She didn't even know if she considered Lucy, a friend. They just happened to work for the same woman but not under the same capacity.

"You know we should hang out more outside of Vivica's house." Lucy suggested.

"Well, sure." Holly smiled. She was trying to be nice. She really didn't think they had much in common. While Holly didn't grow up poor she definitely didn't grow up in the same lifestyle that Lucy had. It was why she got along with Vivica so well. While sure Vivica ended up marrying into wealth, she grew up in a middle-class environment. Plus, she had no clue what Lucy even saw in Austin. He was still the same guy he was back then. It just happened he got a medical degree in the process.

"Hey dear." Austin walked in and kissed Lucy on the forehead. "I thought I'd surprise you with lunch." He looked at Holly and gave her a casual nod.

The blonde turned around in her seat and hugged Austin. "Well, this is unexpected." She stood up. "Why don't we all have lunch together?" She turned to Holly.

The maid looked at Austin who was rolling his eyes. "Oh, I wouldn't want to intrude on some quality time between you too. You are engaged after all." She just wanted to remind Austin unless he had forgotten. She did hope that he hadn't.

Austin stiffened up a bit. He never understood why Holly disliked him so much. She claimed they went to school together, but for the life of him, he couldn't remember. It didn't really bother him one way or the other that he didn't remember. He just didn't understand her obvious problem with him. "Nonsense Holly. You should totally eat with us." Austin wasn't going to come off as a jerk with her.

"Should we eat in or order out?" Lucy asked.

"Why don't I whip up some leftovers. It will give you two lovebirds some time to talk." Holly walked into the kitchen as quickly as she possibly could.

Austin sat down on a couch next to Lucy. He looked at his fiancé. Lucy was definitely beautiful and the type of woman he was meant to marry. Austin just wasn't sure he wanted to marry someone like her. He just knew that he had to to get his inheritance.

"So, you won't believe this, but Langley somehow convinced me into letting her skip her first period this morning. She promised she wouldn't skip anymore school. I don't know if I believe her though."

"Well, you can give her the benefit of the doubt." Austin said shrugging it off. "It's odd how your siblings ended up getting so involved with the Knight and Fitzpatrick families though."

Lucy had thought about this as well. Langley had asked a lot of questions about Brad, but then she managed to spend all her time with Harry. Lucy had already warned her against playing the two cousins against one another. The last thing she needed was for Vivica to be upset because her son was being played by Langley. Then again, Lucy had no clue what Vivica was doing. "You didn't grow up with the Knights or Fitzpatrick's, right?"

"I was Vivica and Luke's pool boy for a few summers. That was about it. I knew Nial's other son briefly, but he was several years older than me. He was pretty messed up, which I guess is expected considering how screwed up Nial himself is." Austin reminisced.

"It's weird, Brandon and Nadia are touted as being this amazing couple. Yet, their children are not such great people. I mean Margot is not terrible, but she is definitely an odd character herself. I have never been a fan of Nial. I don't know how you can work with him." Lucy said.

"He pays me well. It doesn't mean I like the guy. Well, he isn't as bad as I think people want him to be. You have to understand, but Vivica isn't exactly known as the saint of Grosse Pointe herself."

Lucy knew all about the term that people called her by. Margot would use it all the time in conversation. "Why on earth do people call her the Whore from Beverly Hills? Sure, she has been married multiple times, but did she cheat on someone or something?"

"It's an urban legend. No one even really knows at this point. Supposedly, Rodrick Knight coined the term. Though, I've heard the story of Margot Fitzpatrick also being the first to use it." He found Vivica to be annoying. It drove him crazy that the town was known for being wealthy and the place where Vivica Fitzpatrick lived.

VIVICA – 1986

Easter Sunday was admittedly Vivica's favorite holiday. She loved pastel colors and springtime. She just wished that there were fewer floral dresses. Lord did she hate floral dresses.

She walked out of DJ's car with Cliff following her. They were semi-officially dating. Vivica wasn't exactly sure. They never really made things official, but they were going on official dates. Things seemed to be going great, even Cliff's grandmother seemed to approve of them. Vivica did wonder about his mother but Cliff never really spoke about his mother as of late.

The Fitzpatrick Mansion has been built in the 1940's but was only purchased by the Fitzpatrick family in the mid-70's once they had struck it big. It was often hard to believe that the Fitzpatrick family had humble beginnings. Vivica only ever went to the Fitzpatrick Mansion during holiday events. They were only related by means of DJ and Nadia Fitzpatrick being siblings. Vivica could tell that Nadia was not very fond of her mother. When Vivica had tried confronting Gale about it, she just shrugged it off. She was only worried about what DJ thought about her. Which never made sense to her…

"Are we staying all day?" Vivica wondered. They had gone from Mass straight here. "I have to get up early tomorrow for that thing…"

"It will be so cool to see you in the fashion show tomorrow!" Cliff said giving her a peck on the cheek.

"You've seen me model before. Plus, it isn't even that big of a deal." Vivica really meant that. The red head was not being humble. The only reason that Vivica was even going to the fashion show was that she needed money. If Vivica had any desire to get a real job, she wouldn't be doing this. Sure, Cliff always offered to pay for everything. There were other things she needed and wanted that she didn't want Cliff buying her. If only Gale would let her use the money that her father put in an account for her. Gale insisted that be put towards college though.

The four walked up to the front door, and DJ rang the doorbell. In her opinion, the Knight Manor was the more impressive home. This was sure to be a day filled with dullness. Nadia and Brandon were two of the cheeriest people on the planet. She couldn't stand their daughter either but for completely different reasons.

The door opened. "Hey, Nial, little man!" DJ said to his nephew.

Nial looked at them and just rolled his eyes. He had been away at an in-state boarding school for the last semester. Vivica was shocked he returned. If she had gone to a boarding school, she probably wouldn't have left even for the holidays. They all walked inside, Nial had grown since the last time they saw each other. He whispered into Vivica's ear. "You know technically we aren't related." Vivica smacked him.

"No mother he isn't coming." Margot screamed at Nadia in the next room.

"I was just wondering dear. Your father and I did remember to set a space for him at the table." Nadia explained to her daughter. Nadia was a light olive-skinned woman with brown hair she normally kept in a bun. Vivica assumed that she was very pretty in her youth. Not so much anymore in her opinion.

"He is on business in Aspen." Margot screamed yet again.

Nadia turned around and noticed that there guests had arrived. She quickly walked over to DJ. "How is my little brother doing?" She hugged him. Nadia ignored Gale but did hug Vivica. "So, wonderful to see all of you." The way she said that made it clear she was only happy to see DJ and was alright with seeing Vivica. Vivica was unsure of how she felt about seeing her mother though.

"I hope it is alright, but I brought Cliff along today." Vivica mentioned.

Nadia nodded. "I see." She made a slight smile.

The Knight's and the Fitzpatrick's hated each other. DJ and Gale had no issue with her bringing Cliff along. However, they all knew that it would be an awkward day because of the long going feud between the two families. Vivica was sort of shocked that Nadia seemed to take part in that feud. She seemed to be a lot more level-headed than the rest of the two families even if she herself had issues with Gale.

Brandon walked in. He was a pretty good-looking man with red hair and blue eyes. For a man in his late forties, he was in really good shape. He immediately looked at Cliff. "Well, it would appear we have a Knight joining us today." He walked over to Cliff and shook his hand. "Welcome."

"Thank you for having me today, sir." Cliff responded. The handshake lasted longer than most.

Vivica took Cliff's hand afterward, and the two went into the living room where they were alone. "We can leave if this is awkward for you."

"No. Are you kidding me? This is normal in comparison to my family."

This was true. Vivica still had vivid memories of the Knight Christmas party from when she was 12. So, many broken bottles of champagne. "I'm just glad that we get to spend the day together."

Cliff smiled at her. "I am too. I'm also serious; I'm so excited to go and watch you model tomorrow."

The redhead shrugged. "If you want to come you can. I know that Brianna will be there too. I keep telling you both that it isn't worth going to see."

"Vivica, what brand of shirt am I wearing?"

She looked. "You're wearing an *Hermès* sweater."

"See you know that stuff. I don't. I could care less about fashion. I only want to go so that I can watch you. If you were in a pie eating contest, I would go and cheer you on."

"If, I'm in a pie eating contest I want you to smack me until I come to my senses." Vivica stated.

The curly haired boy laughed. "You know what I mean."

She did. Vivica really did, and she loved him for it.

CLIFF - 2018

It seemed the older he got, the shorter days had become for Cliff. Yet, since Vivica left town, the days seemed to drag. They had exchanged a few emails since she had left, but that was about it. The only positive about Vivica leaving was that Tiffany had been less on edge. As he was thinking this, Tiffany walked into his office.

"Well, Harry's birthday party keeps getting larger." She stated as she kissed her husband. "Apparently, two out of the three Kingsley children will be in attendance."

"Kingsley as in Alexander Kingsley? The Wallstreet guy?" Cliff asked confused.

Tiffany nodded. "Well, you knew that Lucy Kingsley was Vivica's PA or whatever. Apparently, the two siblings moved in with her after their father was carted off to jail."

Cliff looked at his wife still confused. "So, why are they going to be at Harry's birthday dinner?"

"Hope is apparently dating the son and get this, but well Harry is dating the younger sister." Tiffany smiled

This was sort of shocking. Cliff felt sort of bad; he should have been paying more attention to his son. He was always so busy. "Well good for Harry. Hope as well…"

The brunet doctor shrugged. "Langley. That's the girl's name. She posted a picture of her and Harry this morning on social media. The shirt she was wearing looked like it was painted on. Do we really want him dating someone like her?"

He knew what she was actually saying. Did they really want him dating someone who could potentially be identical to Vivica? "I think that he will be fine. He is young. This has to be his first girlfriend."

"I guess that is true. I'm not sure what the Xander boy looks like. I'm just hoping he isn't anything like his father. You know they are Republicans." Tiffany pointed out.

"The horror." Cliff joked. He got up and went to open the blinds of his office. It was too dark. "I think that we will survive." Cliff really never cared about politics himself. His own father was about as red as you could get when it came to politics. Which is probably the only reason he continued to vote democrat for everything.

Cliff was still shocked that Harry was dating. It felt like only a few weeks ago; Harry was ten years old. Yet, now he was a teenager with a girlfriend. Time really is moving fast he thought.

VIVICA – 2018

"Holly, will you calm down? I will be home in a week or so." Vivica said over the phone.

"Vivica, you need to come home now. Lucy is driving me crazy." Holly stated.

"How is she driving you crazy?" Vivica asked.

"Well, she won't stop talking to me." Holly admitted.

Vivica rolled her eyes. She loved Holly, but the girl was not a people person. She was about to respond when he walked in… "Oh good lord. Holly, I will call you back in a little bit." She hung up the phone and quickly walked towards the back of the bookstore she was in. Why was he here? Vivica thought to herself. She buried her head in a book, but after a few minutes, he made his way back to the store.

"Hello, Vivica." Luke smiled at her.

"I'm not talking to you." Vivica said. She wanted to walk away, but her legs weren't letting her move.

Luke was still smiling. He had such a great smile. "I heard you were in town. I figured we would bump into one another eventually."

This was all too coincidental in her opinion. "How did you know I was here?"

Still smiling Luke sighed. "Well, it's a funny thing. When you post your location on social media, it tends to make it easy for stalkers and admirers to find you."

"Well, which are you?" Vivica asked.

"That's up for you to decide." He winked at her.

She couldn't help but smile at that. Luke always knew exactly what to say to her. She hated that. Cliff was the one that got away. Nial was the one who wouldn't leave. Luke was different in so many ways. "Aren't you engaged?" Vivica asked.

Luke stopped smiling. "We ended things. On good terms mind you, but now I'm no longer engaged."

The red head frowned. "Oh, I'm sorry. I didn't know." Vivica felt awkward now.

"I heard about you and Nial." He blurted out.

"People in Australia heard about Nial and me…" Vivica rolled her eyes. "Do you honestly want to talk about Nial Fitzpatrick of all people?"

This was true. He hated Nial. "Well, it's good to see you aren't pining after my dear cousin."

If Vivica had one more person inquire if she wanted to go back to Cliff, she was going to cause a public scene. "He is married to my sister." Vivica spat out. Did that stop her from having feelings for him? No. Why should she? He had been hers first. She wasn't a homewrecker though. Well, not anymore.

Luke nodded. "Would you like to get lunch?"

She looked at her watch. "I really shouldn't." Vivica was not ready to rebound. Notably, not with Luke. If the paparazzi saw them together, everyone and their grandmothers would know about it. Nial would see and put his two cents in. Cliff would throw a fit and probably show up in Beverly Hills just to punch his cousin in the nose.

"We work well together, and you know we do."

"I'm not going to deny that we do Luke. That doesn't change certain facts…" Vivica reminded him.

The dark-skinned hunk crossed his arms. "I want you to admit the reason we couldn't work as a couple again? You're single."

It was obvious that Luke wasn't going to let this go until she said it out loud. "I'm in love with your cousin. I'm in love with Clifton Knight the Second. I've been in love with him since I was twelve years old. I'm not going to go after my feelings though because he is supposedly happily married to my bitch of a surgeon sister." Vivica didn't take a single breath while saying that and was now breathing very heavily. She looked at Luke and started crying. She hugged him, and he held her tightly. "Let's get lunch."

***

The two sat in the back corner of a small restaurant outside of Beverly Hills. Vivica looked at the menu and then at Luke. She hated him, but she loved him. She just didn't love him in the same way that she loved Cliff. "Why can't I move on? I'm a pathetic old hag…"

"Darling, you are far from a pathetic old hag." Luke assured her. "Let's be realistic, in an alternate reality where we met first we would be a power couple."

"I'm pretty sure that history will already put us down as one regardless." Vivica stated.

Luke laughed. "Good."

Vivica thought for a moment about nothing in particular. "I need to just go away and find a life away from Grosse Pointe and Beverly Hills. Maybe in New Zealand?"

"Why New Zealand?" Luke asked.

"Australia won't leave me alone." Vivica started to giggle.

Luke looked at her confused. "Why won't they leave you alone?"

The redhead shrugged. "I don't know. My maid Holly keeps trying to get their press to leave me be. It hasn't worked really well."

"When are you going back to Grosse Pointe?" Luke inquired.

Once again, she shrugged. "I don't know. It figures that the moment that I get Brad back from boarding school, I go and fuck things up by going into hiding."

"Is it really hiding? You've been campaigning a modeling return for the past month." He pointed out.

It was sort of true she guessed. "Wrong choice of words maybe. So, how is the west coast division of Knight holding up?"

Luke looked at his phone. "It's doing fine. I've got a few European meetings coming up." He put his phone down. "You're welcome to join me."

LANGLEY – 2018

The rest of the day had gone pretty smoothly for Langley. She managed to go to all her classes, some of her teachers claimed they had not met her. Which she rolled her eyes at. They apparently had since they kept reporting her as absent when she wasn't there. She saw Harry for a little bit when he came for his afternoon class. Then at the end of the day, she got a text from Lucy to meet her at Vivica's house. She did just that.

Vivica's front door had been open. The blonde realized that it probably would have been best to knock, but she knew that Vivica was out of town and Lucy was primarily just using the house as an office. As she walked into the foyer, she was shocked at how welcoming it felt. Langley had always imagined that someone as famous as Vivica would have some kind of modern feeling home. That wasn't the case though. It had warm colors with hardwood floors. The penthouse that she had lived in her entire life back in Manhattan was very modern and very cold. It was as if people didn't actually live in it. Her father, Alexander Kingsley had a crew of people there day and night making sure the house looked perfect. Langley never understood why. Her father had been one of the messiest people on earth. She once asked her brother if he found it odd. Xander had explained to her that their father thought that money meant he could be as dirty as possible. He had the money for other people to clean it up.

She walked to the kitchen where Lucy sat at a table typing on her laptop while she looked over at a tablet. It was weird seeing her sister work. Langley knew that her sister had always been a hard worker, but it was still weird. Langley herself never really believed in working hard, she agreed with her father's views. When you have money why work hard when the people around you can do it for you.

Lucy looked up from her laptop. "Good you are here. Have a seat we need to talk."

The younger sister sat down. She was confused about what this conversation was going to be about. "Did I do something wrong?"

"I'm sure you have, but I'm too busy planning three different events to get involved." Lucy closed her laptop. "We need to talk about you and Harry."

Langley gave her sister a look of confusion. "If this is the sex talk, I hate to burst your bubble, but that ship sailed a while ago."

The older sister closed her eyes and rubbed her forehead. "Good lord... No this is not about sex. This is about who you have gotten involved with."

"I don't follow." Langley stated.

"The Knights are well the Knight's. We might be old money, but they are older money. It doesn't help that our father is in prison and our mother once posed for an erotic magazine. Regardless, we aren't on the same level as them."

"Our mother posed for an erotic magazine?"

Lucy shook her head. "Not the point. I'm all for you dating someone. I'm just saying that you need to be very careful. It took me five years to establish myself in this town. Our family cannot deal with another scandal."

It took a moment to process, but Langley realized what she was saying. "So, you think I'm going to embarrass you?"

"No, Langley I don't think you are going to embarrass me. I think that you are a perfect split down the middle of our parents. Which is a dangerous combination. If you do anything to hurt Harry, they could very well come after us. Do you remember Jerry Sanford?" Lucy asked.

"The boy you dated in high school?" Langley sort of remembered him. She remembered him being cute. That was about it though.

Lucy nodded her head. "Yes. We dated for a few years, and then he ended up doing a few jerk things to me. Nothing that terrible looking back. Well, dad got involved, and now Jerry works as the manager of a grocery store."

"I'm sort of at a loss at why you are telling me this." Langley admitted.

"Let me repeat... We are old money. The Knights are very old money and own an international auto company. You piss them off; you're going to end up sandwich artist in Kansas for the rest of your life." Lucy explained.

Langley didn't really know how to respond to this. Her phone made a ping nose, and it was a text from Brad. She was sort of confused but also super excited. He wanted to meet at his house. She texted back that she was already there. "Where is Brad's room? He wants to talk."

The older blonde blinked her eyes in confusion. "Oh, for the love of all things right in this world you better not be doing what I think you are doing."

"If you are referring to talking with someone then yes I am." Langley confirmed.

"Langley, you cannot date two boys at once. You cannot date two cousins at once. You definitely cannot date a Knight and a Fitzpatrick at once... You snuck into the gala. You saw how Nial tried destroying Vivica on that stage. She didn't even do anything, and he did that to her. Do you honestly think this is a good idea?"

Thinking about it for a moment she considered what her sister was saying. She then remembered that she wasn't really dating Harry. She was helping him. She also felt like pointing out to her sister that all Brad wanted to do was talk... Langley considered telling Lucy that she was only pretending to date, Harry. Langley suspected that Lucy would understand and approve, but it wasn't her right to tell Lucy about Harry's sexuality. Even if it now did sort of affect her.

"You go back to your conspiracy theories. I'm going to go and talk with a friend. Remember what I said. Friend." Langley rolled her eyes as she got up from the table.

***

It was sort of bothering her that Lucy that had jumped to so many conclusions. Lucy had no right to jump at her all of a sudden. She never bothered getting involved before. Why was she all of a sudden?

Langley knocked on Brad's door. He had texted her which one it was. "It's Langley." She said loud enough so that he could hear.

The door opened. "Hey." Brad said.

She couldn't help but gulp a little. Langley thought that Brad had the most amazing eyes she had ever seen, and his body was perfect. She felt her body shaking a little, so she looked down. "You wanted to talk?" She said while looking at his shoes; this wasn't working though. Langley started to admire his muscular legs.

"Yeah, I just wanted to talk about you and Harry." He had both his shoulders behind his neck. "You can come in if you want."

The blonde girl walked in and sat down on the bed before she was even offered a seat. The room smelled like some sort of cologne and teenage boy. It definitely was turning her on. "So, what do you want to talk about regarding Harry and me?"

"This is kind of awkward..." He looked away for a second but immediately turned back. "I just want you to know that I want us all to be friends."

"Well, I sort of thought we all were."

"Oh, yeah totally we are. It's just I mean now that you and Harry are dating. I just didn't want you to think that you couldn't also be friends with me."

This conversation was more confusing than the one she just had with Lucy. "Well, I can't imagine that Harry wouldn't want us all to hang out. He admires you so much. You really are his brother in his mind." Langley wondered if that had been something Harry had told her in confidence. She couldn't imagine that Harry would mind.

Brad cleared his throat. "He's my brother too. I mean I have an older brother, but we have definitely never been close. Harry and I grew up together though. It was so hard having to say goodbye to him when I went to boarding school. I always tried to get him to come up on the weekends, but he really never did."

"It must be great to be able to reconnect with him now then."

"Definitely. I just you know don't want to be the third wheel."

Third wheel? Langley couldn't help but laugh. "I sort of feel like I'm the third wheel, to be honest. Brad, you might have gone away for five years, but I'm brand new. You and Harry share a history together. One that I hope to be a part of for a long time to come."

The blonde boy smiled. "I definitely hope that happens too."

HARRY – 2018

The library at Saint Agnes was filled with forty-year-old books falling apart. The school insisted that students could always request new books and they would be bought. The issue was that most students at Saint Agnes had access to tablets. Harry was no different. That didn't stop the curly haired boy from spending hours in the library.

When he had been in grade school, he was always eager for library day. He would read his books as soon as he checked them out. Harry would often beg Tiffany to take him after school to check out new books in place as he couldn't wait an entire week to get new books. His mother always pointed out that she would happily buy him any book he wanted or even get him a library card at the public library. Harry insisted on the school library. There was just something about it. As he grew older, the library had become a second home for him to hide from the real world.

"Thank you, Sister." Harry said as he took a book from Sister Mary Newman. "I'm just going to browse it in my regular spot."

"Oh, take your time Harry. I'll just be at my desk going over some things for Mass this week."

Sister Mary Newman had been a staple at Saint Agnes for what seemed like forever. Apparently, his grandfather knew her when he was a student here. She was a frail old woman but probably had the most life in her out of anyone Harry knew.

Harry took the book and went to the back corner of the library. It was a large library. There were a few students around studying. Harry just ignored them as he was about to start reading when someone grabbed the book from him. "Hey, what are you doing?" Harry looked up and realized who it was.

"So, you are dating that slutty public-school girl now?" Todd asked.

"Why do you care?" Harry asked as he avoided eye contact.

Todd shrugged. "I don't, but don't think it changes anything between us. Where is my money by the way?"

Harry sighed. He took out his wallet. He had taken a hundred dollars out of the bank for spending money. If it kept Todd quiet though then he could take it. He shoved it at Todd. "Happy now?"

The tall boy rolled his eyes. "This is hardly the amount we agreed on. It will do for now though."

"You know that you would technically go to jail if you ever posted that video." Harry reminded him.

"Do you really think I would be stupid enough to get caught? Trust me; if the video ever does see the light of day, I'll make sure no one knows it was me." Todd said with glee.

"You're in the video though." Harry pointed out.

Todd laughed. "You never see my face, and while what you can see of me is impressive no one is going to be demanding to see it in a courtroom."

The curly hair boy cringed at the image. Harry was not sure what he had seen in Todd initially. "I don't believe you." Harry stated. He stood up and grabbed his bag. Todd stopped him.

"You aren't going to win. I'm stronger, and I'm definitely bigger…"

"Will you let me in already!" Vivica said under her breath as she continued banging on the door. Finally, it opened. Brianna stood there confused on the other side.

"Vivica? What on earth are you doing here?" Brianna asked.

Vivica walked in without saying anything right away. She had never visited Brianna while she had lived in this house. It was interesting looking, to say the least. "I slept with Luke."

Brianna gave her a look of confusion. "You went to see Luke?"

The red head shook her head. "No, he found me. I slept with him though. Oh, this is not going to end well. Cliff is going to find out." Vivica slurred her words. She had been drinking since she left Luke's house. Brianna took her into the living room and got her to sit down. "Why do men have to be so terrible? Why couldn't I have been a lesbian like you?"

"Vivica please don't make me answer that. It took years of therapy for me to except that you weren't a lesbian." Brianna rubbed her head.

"I was such a terrible friend to you. I thought you wanted Cliff." Vivica started sobbing

Brianna started to rub her back. "I know you did. I know…" She mumbled.

"I should call Cliff. He is the only man I've ever truly loved. Don't tell Nial. He'll just punch Cliff in the nose again if he finds that out. Oh wait, I'm not married to that cheating son of a bitch anymore. Why did I marry that son of a bitch three times? Why am I calling Nadia a bitch? She is the nicest woman ever. Even if she wasn't fond of me until after DJ died." Vivica started sobbing even more at the thought of DJ. "Why was I so terrible to DJ? He was a good man. Better than my father, who hasn't even returned my calls since I've been in town."

There was so much for Brianna to dissect from Vivica's ramblings. "Sweet heart you need to calm down."

Could she calm down? Vivica wasn't even sure anymore. She had been trying so hard for months to be strong. Why was it that she wasn't allowed to just break down when things fell apart? "I should call Cliff." Vivica took out her phone and dialed his number. She knew it by heart even if it was saved to her phone already.

"Hello?" Cliff said from a video call. "Vivica is that you? It's late." He said from his office.

"Hi, Cliff! Look Brianna is here with me." Vivica shoved the phone in Brianna's face. "Say hi to Cliff Brianna! Don't worry Cliff; she doesn't have a crush on you. She is a lesbian and married to a woman!"

Brianna yanked the phone out of her hand. "It's so nice to see you. Obviously, we are going to have to catch up very soon. Right now, probably isn't the best time. Give the kids hugs from me. Love you always… Bye." She hung up the call without waiting for him to respond. "Should I call someone for you? Brad maybe?"

"No, I don't want him seeing me like this. Call Holly." Vivica screeched.

Brianna looked through her contacts and found the only Holly in there. "Hello. No, this isn't Vivica. No. I'm Brianna, her childhood best friend. Who are you exactly? Her maid? Ok… Well, I think you might need to come take her home."

The day of the fashion show was something that Cliff was actually looking forward to. His mother had been a no-show the entire day on Easter Sunday, and his grandparents went out of town. Cliff was unsure if his father had been home at all during the day because he made sure not to return until it was late enough that Rodrick would either be asleep or too drunk to talk.

Cliff sat down next to Brianna. "This is going to be fun." Cliff said. He had noticed that as of late Brianna had gotten a little cold towards him. He wasn't sure of why. Vivica had insisted that she was fine with the two of them seeing each other. Yet, her personality completely shifted towards him.

"Yes. Totally." Brianna said looking down at the floor.

"Brianna are you upset at me for some reason?" Cliff asked.

Brianna shrugged. "I'm not upset at you. Myself more than anything. It's silly really."

The tall boy looked at her confused. "Why would you be upset at yourself? You're such a good person."

His friend took a deep breath. "Cliff, can you keep a secret?"

"Definitely." Cliff responded.

"Well, I'm just a little jealous of you being with Vivica." Brianna admitted.

Cliff tensed up a little. "Oh, wow. I didn't realize that you felt that way... about me." Cliff admitted. He really didn't. He honestly thought of Brianna as one of his best friends and nothing else. She never gave off any hints of having a crush of any sort.

Brianna laughed. "Cliff, I didn't have a crush on you."

It took him a moment to realize what she was saying. "Oh." Cliff looked at Brianna. She looked somewhere between uncomfortable and happy. "Does Vivica know?"

She shook her head no. "Not yet. I mean what is the point in telling her that I like her?" She sighed. "I know that realistically we couldn't have gotten together. Still, though she has just always been such a great friend. It was hard not to fall for her even just a little."

"I get what you mean a little bit. You do plan to tell her that you like girls, though right?"

"I suppose I will eventually. How do you feel about me liking girls?" Brianna asked.

"Well, I don't think it really changes anything. I mean I don't have any issues with gay people." Cliff explained.

"How many gay people have you even known Cliff?"

Cliff had to think about it for a moment. "None. Well, I mean you now. Still, it's cool. I don't have an issue. Who cares what you like? I've known you since forever. There is nothing different with you than anyone else I know." He hugged Brianna. It was like clockwork, Vivica walked over in a bathrobe. He stopped hugging her. "Hey, Vivica." Cliff smiled.

"I just threw out half my make-up. The other models thought that I was inclined to share because I put my bag down. I'm never going to replace like half of that stuff." Vivica crossed her arms.

Cliff stood up. "I think you will be fine. You don't need make-up."

"Dear, you have never seen me without make-up on. Nor will you ever." Vivica stated. She looked over at Brianna. "Do you have any lipstick on you?"

Brianna looked through her bag. "I do, but Vivica it really isn't your color. We have completely different skin tones."

She didn't care. Vivica grabbed the lipstick out of her hands. "It doesn't matter. Every other damn model is wearing my old shade. I almost threw up at the thought of putting that near my mouth again. You're a life saver." Vivica said. She ran off.

"That's our best friend right there." Brianna chuckled.

"Yeah and my girlfriend…" The two burst out into laughter.

Brianna pulled herself together. "Cliff, you should go wish her luck. She seems a little nervous."

***

Cliff waited backstage as one of the handlers went and got Vivica. This building was so old. He couldn't imagine it ever being torn down. Then a redhead walked out of the dressing room. It wasn't Vivica though. It was Margot Fitzpatrick. He had seen her on Easter and only said a few words in passing. She didn't seem to be a very pleasant woman in his opinion. Vivica didn't seem to like her very much either. Vivica didn't really seem to be that impressed with the Fitzpatrick family. Cliff told her constantly that his families feud didn't mean she had to hate them. She seemed to dislike them on her own though.

The teenage boy looked at Margot and gave a slight smile. "Hi."

"Your girlfriend is a piece of work…" She rolled her eyes and stormed off.

Vivica walked out from the dressing room. "Where is that bitch?" Vivica screamed.

"Do you mean Margot? She just walked down the hall."

"I swear one day I am going to put Margret Fitzpatrick in her place. I've seen her room before. It's filled with those plastic pony toys that little girls play with. That's probably why her husband left her. He probably got freaked out by all the creepy little ponies!" Vivica once again screamed loud enough for other people to hear.

Cliff put his hand on Vivica's shoulder. "You don't have to worry about Margot or anyone else. You're the hottest girl here today. Heck, you are the most beautiful girl in all of Grosse Pointe!"

Vivica smiled. "Cliff, we are in Detroit though."

"All of Michigan then!" Cliff stated. "Margot isn't a very good person. You are. People know that. That's all that is important." He kissed Vivica.

Hannah – 2018

"I'm obviously coming to Harry's dinner, mom. Why wouldn't I? Well, I live at home this year." Hannah rolled her eyes as she spoke to her mother on the phone. She sat at her desk at work. It wasn't even nine AM yet. Hannah questioned why her mother would be calling her this early. "I'm at work… I have to go." Xander sat down at his desk and waved at her. "Bye." Hannah hung up and slammed her phone down. "I hate my mother."

Xander smiled. "What were you talking about with her?"

"She wanted to make sure that I was indeed coming to Harry's birthday dinner tomorrow night. You know the one at the house. Why wouldn't I be there?"

"What exactly should I wear to the dinner?" Xander asked suddenly.

Hannah had forgotten he was going to be there. "Oh, um something nice but not too dressy I guess. I don't know… Harry likes when people dress up. You never know what he will wear himself though. So, you either end up looking over or underdressed in compared to him." She looked at him; he was nodding and texting at the same time. "So, who are you texting?"

"Your sister. She wants to meet up for lunch. You should come with us." Xander offered.

She couldn't help but laugh. "I'm definitely not invited."

"Hope really doesn't seem as bad as you say she is. I mean she does complain about you a lot herself, but you guys really should try to reconcile." Xander stated.

If Xander could just realize all the things that Hope had done to Hannah over the years, he wouldn't be saying that. The list was far too long to get into though. "I'm good. So, your sister will be at this dinner too. Apparently, our siblings are dating now? I honestly am shocked to see Harry with your sister. She's so… pretty."

The blonde boy shrugged. "Yeah, I'm a little concerned about the whole dating situation. Not because of Harry. It's more, I'm worried about Langley treating Harry badly. From, what I've heard about Harry from you and Hope… Well, I mean…"

"She's going to whip him. There is no doubt about it. He is a very quiet and sheltered person. I'm honestly not that worried. I've known girls like Langley. I was a girl like Langley." If she had to, she knew exactly how to go after her. "Things seem to be moving fast with you and Hope."

Xander looked confused. 'I wouldn't really say so. We just talk on the phone a lot. She really likes to talk about med school. Which is cool. I was looking into the law enforcement program that the GPPD offered last night. It seems to be a reasonable force."

Why did he have to like her sister? Hannah honestly had to wonder. They were legit identical twins. If he had a physical attraction to Hope, then he would more than likely like her as well? She had a better personality than Hope. The twin knew the game her sister was playing though. She wanted to mess with her head. That way she could play victim once Hannah did put her move on him. Then she would go crying to her parents, and she would get chastised yet again.

"Well, I think you will make a great police officer. You clearly really believe in doing the right thing." Hannah said. She looked at her watch. "I should go make the rounds see if I can snag an early morning customer."

Hannah looked at Xander who was smiling at her. "We should hang out sometime outside of work again." Xander said. He stood up too. "Like, just the two of us."

"What about Hope?"

"She's a nice friend. So, are you though." Xander smiled.

Hannah was unsure of how to take this. She wanted to say yes though.

"Excuse me. Girl, I'd like to buy this car." Mrs. Templeton screamed. Hannah snapped out of whatever she was thinking about and went to deal with the crazy woman.

HARRY – 2018

"You know you don't have to come to my birthday dinner if you don't want to." Harry explained to Langley. They were walking to his car after school. Langley had walked all the way from West Grosse Pointe just so that they could drive home together.

"Why on earth wouldn't I want to go to your birthday dinner?" She inquired. Langley sat down in the passenger seat.

Harry shrugged. He had never had a non-relative at one of these dinners. The curly haired boy struggled to remember if he had ever asked a friend to celebrate his birthday with him though. "I just wanted you to know it wasn't that important. You know if you had anything more important to do or something."

Langley rolled her eyes. "You're my best friend in the state of Michigan. I'm of course coming. That said, I'm also your girlfriend as far as the world knows. It will be strange if I didn't go." She looked at Harry and smiled. "We need to get you some Xanax. I swear sometimes you just need to take a deep breath."

"So, Todd confronted me the other day at the library. He wasn't pleased that we are dating…" Harry mumbled as he put his seatbelt on.

"Well, it doesn't shock me that he is jealous. I mean who wouldn't be jealous of me?" She looked over at Harry who didn't seem to laugh. "I was joking just so you know. I'm not that vain." Langley claimed as she looked at herself in the mirror.

Harry shrugged. "Sorry, I'm just tired of all of this." He wanted to just be himself. He was sick of relatives talking about all the pretty girls that must have liked him. He was sick of other guys trying to relate with him when a girl who was supposedly attractive walked by. Yet, he didn't want to be thought of as a walking stereotype. "Why can't I be gay without being gay?"

The blonde girl turned to him confused. "What like Metrosexual? Harry, those men are annoying."

"What? No... No. I mean like, why can't I just like guys without having to go through with all the activities like the parades and what have you. I don't have issues with guys who are all into that. I just don't want to be part of that."

"You don't have to be. I realize that in the Midwest, people have all these assumptions about gay people, but being gay doesn't automatically make you a drag queen or force you to dye your hair rainbow colors." Langley looked at Harry's hair. "Plus, your hair is so curly that you would look like a clown..." Harry chuckled at that. "Well, there we go."

The curly haired boy took a deep breath. "I'm going to tell my family tomorrow at dinner."

"I thought you didn't want your coming out to be during a big event?"

"Well, I don't. Though knowing my family, I'm the only one who will remember the actual date of my coming out. If I don't do it now than when am I going to?"

Langley hugged him. Brad got into the back seat. "Hey, guys. Do you need me to walk home?"

The brown-haired cousin looked into the back seat. "No. We were just um... Well yeah." They broke the hug. "So, what took you so long?"

Brad shrugged. "It's nothing. I just was talking with someone about something."

"That's fine." Harry said as he looked through his book bag. "Shoot... I have to go back in for a second. Sorry." He ran out of the car, closing the door behind him.

The two blonde teenagers were left alone in the car. Langley looked back at Brad. "So, are you excited about Harry's birthday dinner? He is very nervous for a multitude of reasons it seems."

"It should be nice. I'm glad that I'm back this year. I don't know if you have realized this, but Harry is kind of a shy and nervous guy. He doesn't really like to rock the boat with people. Which is why I'm glad he has met you." Brad looked out the window. "Has he mentioned being picked on to you?"

"Um... What do you mean picked on?" Langley inquired.

Brad sighed. "The person I was talking with… It was this guy, Todd Roberts. He seems to have a real hard on against Harry."

The choice of words… "Well, he has mentioned not liking Todd before. That's about it really." She lied. "What did Todd say?"

"It's not really important." Brad didn't want to talk with Harry's girlfriend of all people about this. It would be awkward. It might be the right thing to do though. He didn't want to worry Harry about this, and he needed to talk to someone… Harry got back to the car though…

"Sorry, I forgot my math notebook. I have a test tomorrow and need to get in some last-minute cramming."

VIVICA — 2018

Holly walked up to a strange porch in San Francisco. It took all day to arrange a flight. Her husband was far from happy that she was leaving the state randomly. It didn't matter to Holly though; she needed to get Vivica back to Michigan and quickly. This charade had lasted far too long, and Holly hated admitting it, but she missed Vivica.

She knocked on the door. "Vivica are you in there? She started screaming." The door opened.

"You must be Holly. Brianna said with a smile on her face. Thank you so much for coming to pick her up. She came over last night and while she is always welcome she just didn't seem herself."

The maid said nothing and walked in. She had never met Brianna before. Holly had heard her mentioned once or twice, but that was it. So, to receive a call from her definitely felt surreal in a way. "Vivica, come on let's go." She screamed as she walked into the foyer. "Where is she? She then turned to her right and saw the living room. Vivica was lying on the couch. "You look terrible."

"It's nice to see you too." Vivica said. She looked around. "Did Cliff tag along?"

Holly rolled her eyes. "You are a piece of work. You know, that right?" She grabbed hold of Vivica's hand. "Come on; we have imposed on your friend long enough." It didn't take much to get Vivica to get up.

***

The two friends sat in first class on their way back home. Holly crossed her arms and turned to Vivica. "So, do we talk about it now or when we get back to your house?" She looked Vivica directly in the eye.

167

The redhead wasn't sure what needed to be said and what didn't. Vivica realized that at the end of the day, no she shouldn't have slept with Luke. Yet, she didn't regret it. Yet, she did. "You are just going to yell at me." Vivica took out her phone. There were no messages from Luke. That bothered her a little.

"Why did you stay away so long? I don't know how to tell you this, but you were needed. Brad's in love with your assistant's sister, who is dating you nephew. Then you have your assistant planning a racist as hell party for that see you next Tuesday, Mrs. Templeton. Oh, and the niece you like is fighting for a man with her sister. Doesn't that sound familiar? On, top of all that…" Holly took Vivica's hand and looked at her directly in the eye. "I missed you."

Vivica put her phone down and hugged Holly. "I missed you too." She then thought about everything else that had just been told to her. "I have a lot of nonsense that needs to be fixed, don't I?"

Holly nodded. "More or less."

"It's Harry's birthday tomorrow. We need to stop at the store and get him something." Vivica always remembered her nieces and nephews' birthdays. She suspects that Tiffany only remembered Hope's. Which was pathetic considering that Hannah was born on the same day, two minutes earlier.

Holly turned to Vivica. "You don't plan on going to his birthday dinner?"

"Why shouldn't I? I'm his aunt!" Vivica said a little louder than her usual tone.

"I know you always get him gifts, but you have skipped out on the dinners since I've known you." Holly pointed out. "Was it a bad idea for me to bring you back home? Vivica you aren't planning on going after Cliff, again are you?"

The redhead smiled. "Holly, I have no idea what you are talking about."

Yet, another day of dealing with Mrs. Templeton, an angry Brad, and the overly jealous maid. Lucy couldn't wait. She couldn't wait so much that she just sat in bed while she contemplated just taking a sick day. It wasn't as if she had to clock in and out. Vivica would never know.

Lucy thought it was time for a day off. She wondered if maybe she could get Austin to do the same. He was taking a shower. The blonde knew she shouldn't, but she wanted to check out what his schedule included for the day. She reached over to the other side of the bed and checked his phone, where a copy of his schedule was sure to be. When she unlocked the screen though, there was a text message open. It was an unlisted number, but there was a message from a girl standing topless. She read the corresponding text message. *"I just can't stop admiring your work. I know you can't either. Come over, Nial's gone for the day.* Lucy dropped the phone. Her heart was beating like a loud drum. This couldn't be happening. They had been together for three years. They were engaged.

The shower stopped in the next room. Lucy didn't know what to do. She couldn't confront him though. She grabbed whatever she was wearing yesterday from off the ground and a pair of shoes. Lucy marched downstairs and yanked Langley off the couch. She said nothing on the way to driving Langley to school. Then the car stopped. "We might be moving soon."

"Thank God. That room is so small…"

"Well, have a good day." Lucy didn't even turn to look at Langley. She needed to get to work. The blonde would do anything to stay away from her fiancé. Was he even still her fiancé?

Langley got out of the car, but before she closed the door, she looked at her sister. "Are you alright?"

Was she alright? Now all of a sudden Langley cared? It was so nice of her to pick right now to notice her emotions. "I'll be fine. I just need to get on my way to work. Please close the door." Her sister did so, and Lucy started driving again.

Why were all the men in her life such scum? Well, Xander wasn't. That was about it. She thought about Vivica and Nial for a moment. What a screwed-up situation that was. She married that man three times. Each time it was clear neither of them was madly in love. Then there was Tiffany and Cliff. She never really cared for Tiffany after the countless stories she had heard about her but was Cliff really a good man himself? Was Tiffany the issue in the never-ending feud or as it the man in the middle?

Where would she go? She had money, but not enough to afford a place in Grosse Pointe. Langley threw a fit over going to a nice public school. If they had to move somewhere a little less upscale, she would never get the girl to leave the house.

Would Austin even fight for her? Would he be relieved that he didn't have to go through with breaking up with her? Was Austin a coward? Did he even love her anymore?

Lucy was sick to her stomach. She had to stop thinking about this. The blonde parked her car in Vivica's driveway. She looked at herself in the vanity mirror. It would be an alright day. She knew that it would. Lucy had been through worse. As she walked into the house, she heard a familiar voice. A voice that she honestly thought she was going to be glad for once not to listen. Vivica was home…

"Lucy, good you are here. We have some major damage control to take care of." Vivica stated from the living room couch. "Mrs. Templeton? Oh goodness no. That woman made Hitler look like a saint. I also swear she has been the same age for the last thirty years. She is like a vampire."

"You're finally home?" Lucy said with a fake smile. "It's so nice to have you home." She actually meant that.

The redhead got up and hugged Lucy. "I know I screwed up a little. It happens every time I divorce. I'm not sure why."

"Well, we should get to work. Are we dropping Mrs. Templeton then?" Lucy wondered.

Holly put her hands on her hips. 'If you don't then you will both be labeled racists…"

Vivica nodded. "That crackpot can leave us a bad review for all I care. We need to focus on rebranding anyway. As of right now, we aren't taking any new clients. Lucy, I want you as my partner in this. No more you being my assistant. Are you on board? There would be a raise of course."

This was all too much. "Yes, I mean… I don't know… I think I have to leave Austin." She ran into the kitchen and started to throw water on her face in the sink. She turned around, and Holly was standing at the door.

"So, what did he do to you?"

"I'd rather not talk about it. Especially, with you."

"I've known Austin Martin since we were grade school. He was a punk when he was a child, and I never liked him as an adult." Holly admitted.

Lucy looked at Holly and frowned. "Well, you don't seem to like me either so why are we even talking?"

Holly sighed and crossed her arms. She walked over to Lucy. "It's not that I dislike you. It's that I dislike Austin and I'm an extremely jealous person when it comes to Vivica." She sat down at the kitchen table. Lucy followed suit. "We both came into Vivica's inner circle around the same time. She both gave us a chance when others wouldn't."

"I thought Austin was the one. He was just so different than other men I dated. At least around me. I have no idea what he was like in high school. Part of what made me like him was the fact we didn't talk about our pasts. If I were in Manhattan right now, I'd be a laughing stock among my social circle for not knowing about his affair."

"Luckily, you aren't in Manhattan. You're in the suburbs. I don't know if that is better or worse."

The two laughed. Lucy's eyed then widened. "Oh, good lord, It's Saturday, and I dragged Langley off to school…" The blonde shrugged. "She will find her way home…"

Vivica walked in. "Cliff has not responded to any of my text messages since our plane landed. I guess I don't need to ask permission to go to Harry's party. Right? I'm his aunt after all. Yeah, I shouldn't have to worry about that" Vivica put her phone down on the table.

The curly haired auto mogul spent the morning searching for his phone. It apparently had gone missing. He had already alerted the staff of North Pointe to search the estate, but no one could seem to find it. He would just have to make a trip to the store later. It was his family and friend phone; he still had his business one on him.

Cliff walked into the kitchen where Tiffany and Hope were eating breakfast. "Did Hannah go to work already?"

"Yes." Hope said without looking up from her eggs.

"I hope she at least wished Harry a happy birthday." Cliff stated.

"She did." Harry said as he walked downstairs still wearing his pajamas.

Cliff along with Tiffany and Hope all said Happy Birthday to him. "How are you doing son?"

Harry shrugged. "Fine, I guess. Nervous about tonight."

Tiffany laughed. "Oh, honey I'm sure we will all love your little girlfriend."

The curly haired teen looked confused for a moment. "Yeah, that's the reason I'm nervous..."

Cliff looked down at his breakfast. "Tiffany, did you cook this morning?" The eggs looked both over and undercooked at the same time.

"Our cook had the morning off." She explained.

Harry sat down at the table. "Oh, Brad texted me this morning. I guess aunt Vivica is back in town."

The room went dead silent. They all looked at him. "Well, I'm shocked you didn't know about this Cliff." Tiffany turned her attention to Cliff.

"My phone has been missing all morning." Cliff admitted.

Tiffany rolled her eyes. "This is all we need."

Hope shrugged. "Maybe, if we are lucky she has decided to become a nun."

"I very much doubt that would ever happen." Cliff said staring out into nowhere.

Harry looked down at his phone. "I have to go. Langley needs a ride. I guess her sister dragged her to school."

"It's Saturday. Why on earth would her sister have forced her to school on a Saturday?" Hope asked.

Harry shrugged. "I don't know." He got up from the table and walked upstairs. No one wished him happy birthday again.

"She, of course, had to pick Harry's birthday to come waltzing back into our lives. It's so typical of Vivica." Tiffany spat out.

Cliff looked around the table. "Where did Harry go?"

"He just mentioned having to go pick up his girlfriend." Hope said. She looked at her phone. "I've got to go and get ready for my shift at the hospital. Then I have a study group. I'll see you both tonight at dinner." She went upstairs.

Cliff and Tiffany were left alone at the table. Cliff realized the conversation that was coming. "So, what do you have to say about this?"

"I'm not going to say anything. She has left us alone for several months. She didn't waltz over here this morning. Maybe, she will leave us alone for a few days before resurfacing." Tiffany stated.

That was a very mature thing for Tiffany to say. She never was that mature when it came to Vivica. "Well, I'm glad you feel that way."

The brunet doctor smiled. "We have had a good marriage for a long time. We don't have anything to worry about."

Cliff really hoped so…

HARRY – 2018

Pulling into the parking lot of Grosse Pointe West, he immediately found Langley. She was sitting on a bench looking at her phone. He pulled over on the curve and went to sit down next to her. "Was your sister drunk or something this morning?"

Langley turned to look at him. "I don't know. It's always a possibility. I guess we are moving. I'm not sure where though." She looked back at her phone.

Was she going to be moving? Harry's heart skipped a beat. She was his first real friend aside from Brad. Yet, she was leaving now. This was totally something that would only happen on his birthday. "We will stay in touch, right?" He hoped they would at least.

"I think we will be staying in town." She put her phone down on the bench. "I honestly don't know what we are doing. Lucy was just sort of rambling this morning…" She blinked and came to a sudden realization. "Happy birthday, Harry!" She screamed as she gave him a tight hug.

Harry took a sigh of relief. "Thank you." He smiled. "So, what do you want to do today?"

She shrugged. "Don't you have to prepare for your party tonight? Or possibly spend time with your family?"

"The chef preps the dinner. We just all show up and get dressed properly. I don't think we have had a proper sit-down dinner together since my last birthday and Hannah wasn't at that one." Harry took another sigh of relief. It was kind of awesome he thought. Hannah was home; Brad was home. He had Langley in his life. Nothing could be wrong; he knew it was the right time to come out.

CLIFF – 1986

The kitchen of North Pointe was the heart of the home. It always had been and still would be. At least according to Cliff's grandmother Delia. Cliff sat at the table studying. Vivica was on her way over. The cook had stepped out to buy a few items for that nights requested dinner.

Cliff sighed. "This math is not getting any easier."

"Just keep trying dear. I know you can do it." Delia said as she straightened her nurse's hat. She walked over to Cliff and sat down next to him. "I'm shocked you are home tonight. It's been ages since I have seen you."

"Grandmother you just saw me this morning." Delia sighed herself. "You know what I mean. It's just a pity the one night you are here that I have a shift at the hospital."

The curly haired teen sighed. He knew he had spent a lot of time away. There were many factors to that though. Factors that Delia was well aware of. "Well, maybe tomorrow you and I could go to breakfast?"

Delia smiled. "I'd like that. Your parents will be out of town until next week you know. So, if you want to have any of your little friends over such as Vivica, it is fine with me."

"Well, you know she is coming over tonight right?"

"Oh, yes I know." Delia brushed her hair back. She had the same blue eyes as Cliff. She smiled as she looked at the boy. Delia was so proud of the young man that Cliff had turned into. "I don't know how you turned out so well." As much she didn't fault Cliff's mother Brenda for being spacey with a husband like her son. She didn't think that Brenda had been a very good mother. It was obvious that Rodrick had not been a good father. "Your grandfather would have been so proud."

Cliff put his pencil down. "Grandmother, why do you never mention grandfather? Father always talks so highly of him. Yet, you never seem to."

Benton Knight... Delia's first husband. She shuttered to think of the name. "Well, Benton had his good qualities. I fell in love with him. We had your uncle Clifton who you were named after when we were both still in college. It was a different time. My family had expectations. Your great-grand-parents had high expectations of Benton himself. He never really got over his own mother's death."

"That doesn't really answer the question though." Cliff pointed out.

"You're right. I suppose it doesn't. I really don't know how to explain Benton. I'm happy your father looks at the good in him. I don't regret marrying him." Delia didn't.

Cliff nodded as he heard a noise at the door. He assumed it was Vivica and stood up. "Hey, Weston." He said, but it wasn't Vivica.

"What on earth are you talking about boy?" Rodrick spat out.

Cliff and Delia looked at each other in confusion. "Father, what are you doing home?"

"Your bitch of a mother has lost her mind. I left her in Paris she can come home when she wants. Meanwhile, there is a business to handle here. I'm just going to change then I'm heading into the office."

"It's six at night." Delia pointed out.

Rodrick groaned. "Mother really... The workday never ends."

Bitch of a mother? Cliff hated when his father would talk down to his mother or grandmother or just about any woman. There was nothing he could do about it. Nothing that anyone would let him do at least.

"Hi, everyone." Vivica walked in. She immediately saw Rodrick. "One of the maids let me in. They told me you were in here Cliff."

"It's nice to see you Vivica." Delia admitted.

Vivica smiled. "It's nice to see you as well Mrs. Knight."

"It's Surry." Rodrick intercepted. "My mother has not been a Knight since she married that sorry excuse of a gold digger. Yet, it's her house." He crossed his arms.

Delia rolled her eyes. "Rodrick, your father left the house to me to give to you and your brother when the time was right. I live in the guest house. It isn't like I interrupt your affairs." She bit her tongue at that, knowing that Cliff was in the room.

Cliff looked at Vivica. He could see she seemed as uncomfortable as he felt. "Vivica and I are going to go into the drawing room." He walked over to Vivica and grabbed her hand.

The older Knight man looked at his son. "Where do you think you are going?"

"He just told you, Rodrick. The drawing room." Delia pointed out.

Rodrick turned to his mother. "Was I talking to you?" He turned back to Cliff. "Where do you think you are going?"

The young Knight man looked at his father. "I said I was going to the drawing room with Vivica. We are going to study for a little bit before dinner."

"I didn't invite your friend over for dinner Cliff."

Cliff looked at both Vivica and his father at the same time. "You weren't home. Grandmother already said it was ok."

Rodrick laughed. "Well, if your crazy grandmother said it was ok, then it must have been ok. You know better than to have people over when I am not home."

"When has that ever been a rule?" Cliff asked.

"Cliff, I can leave. It's fine. We can spend time together another time." Vivica told him.

Delia walked over to Vivica. "Dear, I don't think that you need to leave. As Rodrick already pointed out. This is my house. Not his. He has no authority over who I allow as guests. So, if you wish to stay, you may for as long as you want."

Vivica looked at Cliff unsure of how to respond. "Well, thank you ..." She said hesitantly.

Rodrick looked at all of them and shook his head. He walked upstairs away from all the nonsense around him.

"I'm really sorry Vivica. I didn't think he was going to be home. He should be leaving soon." Cliff explained.

The redhead shrugged. "Tonight, might not be the best time Cliff. I can come back another time. We can always hang out tomorrow or something at my house. I'd invite you there tonight, but it's my mother's book club. They are reading some Jackie Collins novel or something. Sister Mary Newman picked it out ..."

Delia looked at her watch. "I have to get going. You call me if you need anything, Cliff." She kissed him on the forehead. Delia grabbed her purse off the counter and left through the patio door.

The two teenagers were left alone to look at each other awkwardly. "This was supposed to be a good night for us. We never get to spend time at my house. It's always your house ... Not that there is anything wrong with that."

"Oh, no I totally get it. Your house is awesome. I love all the different rooms. I haven't been to your room in a while ..." Vivica admitted.

The curly haired boy started to blush. "Well, I mean it's the same I guess. Or well, I had it painted an off-white as opposed to the blue it was. Dad said that blue made it feel like a child's room."

"You will have to show me sometime." Vivica said. She held her right arm with her left one. She looked toward the kitchen door. "I should get going before he comes back."

Cliff thought quickly. "Come back in two hours. Grandmother will be working, and there is no way that my dad will be back tonight. I'm sure he will be with his mistress. I could show you what my room looks like now ..."

Vivica looked straight into his eyes. "Oh... Um, ok." Vivica couldn't believe she just said that.

Cliff hoped that Vivica got the gist of what he was implying. He wasn't so sure that he could say it out loud. He wasn't so sure he knew what he was even involving himself ...

LUCY – 2018

After talking with Vivica and Holly, Lucy was able to come up with a game plan. She was going to leave Austin. She wasn't going to let him explain himself. Lucy had no interest in staying with a man who was a cheater.

It was her lunch break. She decided it was best to come see Austin at work and then go and pack at home. She already texted both her siblings to meet her in an hour. They would be temporarily moving into Vivica's house. She was concerned about how Langley would react to living across the street from her boyfriend and in the same house as Brad. At the same time though it was the best option all around on such short notice.

Lucy walked down the hall at Grosse Pointe General Hospital. She walked past Tiffany Knight talking with Nial Fitzpatrick and right to the cafeteria. She found Austin sitting alone looking at his phone. "Hi."

"Oh, hey babe. What are you doing here?" Austin asked surprised.

"We need to talk." Lucy explained. She was unsure if she should sit or stand. The blonde decided to stand. "I know you have been having an affair." She noticed that Nial had walked into the cafeteria and was heading this way. It didn't stop her from continuing. "I'm leaving you. Xander, Langley, and I are moving in with Vivica short term. Good luck with your life but we are done."

Austin stood up. "What do you mean we are through? We have been together for like what eight years?"

Lucy rolled her eyes. "We have been together five…"

"Lucy, you can't leave me. We go well together. I mean we are engaged after all. You have my grandmother's ring." Austin pointed out.

She looked down at her finger. She took it off and slammed it on the table. "Here you go. Maybe, your mistress will enjoy it?" Lucy turned around and was ready to walk away.

"Lucy, you are the one for me. I just made one mistake. It was only one." Austin said. He didn't move though.

She turned around. "Austin, I'm not sixteen years old anymore. I'm not looking for excuses. Hopefully, the girl you gave the implants to enjoys them." Lucy stormed off.

***

It wasn't hard to get a moving van. Vivica offered up movers, but Lucy realized that they did't really own all that many things. Most of the furniture in Austin's house had been there before she moved in. Holly had helped arrange things as well. Having Holly on her side for once was weird. She liked that they were finally seeing eye to eye though.

"Can I please have a room next to Brad's?" Langley asked.

Lucy looked at her sister in shock. Harry was standing right next to her. "You will go to whatever room Mrs. Fitzpatrick has set up for you."

Vivica walked out wearing high heeled shoes. "I have you at the end of the south hall, Lucy. Xander is set up in the downstairs guest room. I hope Langley is fine with the room adjacent to Brad's though."

The blonde older sister rubbed her forehead. "Well, I guess that answers that." She looked at Harry. "Thank you so much for helping us out on such short notice. I know it is your birthday after all."

"Oh, it's not an issue at all." Harry explained.

"Can we take a break already?" Langley moaned.

"Let's just hurry through this and then we can all get back to our days." Xander instructed his younger sister.

It shocked Lucy that Xander was able to tell Langley what to do sometime. She wished that she could do the same.

A car pulled up to the driveway. It was Brad. "Hey, guys." He said with a smile on his face.

Vivica's eyes widened. "Where on earth did you get that car?"

"Dad called about an hour ago. He asked if I wanted to go to lunch. He surprised me with a car."

Lucy noticed the brand. It was European… In a block that was almost exclusively *Knight*. It stood out. Especially, when you considered that the Knight estate was almost directly across the street. "Hi, Brad. Thank you so much for saying it was alright for the three of us to move in on such short notice. I promise that we won't be here for long."

Brad shrugged. "It's no problem. Stay as long as you want. The Kingsley family is always welcome as far as I'm concerned."

"Just look at it this was Lucy. We will be able to work night and day on the rebranding and relaunch." Vivica pointed out.

As nice as that sounded, Lucy already knew that her moving in meant that she was going to get less work done than before. "Well, thank you both."

"Brad, why did your father buy you a car without asking me?" Vivica wondered out loud.

The blonde-haired Fitzpatrick boy shrugged. "Not really sure. He asked if you were doing alright though."

Vivica took a deep breath. "I need to go out for a little bit. I will be back." She grabbed Brad's keys and got into the car.

"Well, there goes my car…" Brad stated.

Langley put her head on Brad's shoulders. "You don't think she will make your father return it. Do you?"

Harry walked over to the two of them oblivious that Langley was very close to Brad. "Oh, she doesn't care about the car. There is just no way that car is coming back in one piece…"

VIVICA – 2018

She barely made it to the Fitzpatrick mansion in one piece, but she got there. Vivica marched out of the car and up to the front door. It was strange to be banging on the door as opposed to just opening it. Vivica suspected that all the locks had probably been changed the moment that she moved out though. The door opened. It was Margot herself…

"What do you want whore?" Margot crossed her arms.

Vivica didn't even wait to be asked in. She knew she wouldn't be. "Where is my husband… I mean Nial. Where is Nial?"

"How on earth am I going to know?" Margot asked. "He is a grown man, and I'm his sister not caretaker. I could care less… Probably with his much younger fiancé."

The two redheads stared each other down. "You are hardly Miss March yourself, Margret."

Margot rolled her eyes. "My name for the last time is Margot. I know being the whore from Beverly Hills is a full-time job though. So, you have little time to remember such details."

"Margot, Margret, Marge, Margie, Mary Mae Ward… I don't give a damn what your name is. Now tell me where he is or I march up to the pony room and start plucking hairs from your plastic little friends…"

Margot's eyes lit with fire. "You wouldn't dare."

Vivica wasn't in the mood to play around with her ex-sister-in-law anymore. She started toward the staircase. Margot ran after her. She yanked Vivica from going up the stairs, but Vivica managed to make it up a few steps. Margot continued to grab on to her. "Let go of me you cow!" Vivica screamed. Margot wasn't letting go. Vivica turned to her and slapped her across the face. Margot quickly slapped her back. Vivica put her hands-on Margot's shoulder and attempted to push her down the stairs. Instead, Margot grabbed at Vivica's waste.

The two enemies quickly fell down the stairs together. Margot got on top of Vivica. She started to yank at her hair. "Whore!" Margot screamed.

"I've been married to two men. How many men have you married? Margret Fitzpatrick- Sherman- Lance – Fields – Roe – Johns…" Vivica managed to get on top. The two women rolled around on the floor of the foyer for five minutes struggling with one another.

"When I go after a man Vivica I at least make sure I'm legally married to him. Can't say the same about you and Cliffy. Now can we?" Margot smiled.

Vivica slapped Margot again. "I'm going to ki—"

The front door opened. Nial walked in. He was holding the mail in his hand sorting through it. He looked up and noticed his ex-wife and sister on the ground. "I wish I could say that this shocked me." Nial rolled his eyes. "Will the two of you get up? Two grown women and you are still fighting like you are in your twenties."

The two stood up. Not helping one another. They didn't look at each other. "We need to talk." Vivica said looking at Nial.

"I agree. We do." Nial said.

"I will not have this whore in my house." Margot stated.

Vivica rolled her eyes. "Perfect Margot. You said the word whore at least three times. It's now officially your word. How fitting…"

Margot went to slap Vivica again, but Nial grabbed her hand. "Enough! Margot, Vivica and I are going into the library. Please, leave us be." Nial begged of his sister. He took Vivica by the shoulder and walked her into the library off to the left side of the foyer. He closed the door behind him. "We need to talk."

"Why on earth did you buy our son a car without consulting with me?" Vivica asked.

"I realize that as of late I've been kind of an ass." Nial said out loud. "It is possible I might have gone too far in leaving you at the gala."

It took Vivica only a second to realize what was happening. "I'm not coming back to you Nial." Vivica sat down on the couch. "Let me guess, the little slut you cheated on you with was faking her pregnancy?"

Nial sat down next to Vivica. "She was never pregnant. I just told you that to piss you off more." He took her hands and looked into her eye. "We have children together. There is something that always draws us closer together. Vivica you and I deserve to be happy."

The redhead couldn't help but laugh. "You expect me to jump back into your arms, don't you? I'm going to become Vivica Weston-Fitzpatrick – Knight – Fitzpatrick – Fitzpatrick – Fitzpatrick.

"The likelihood that you will be Vivica Weston – Fitzpatrick – Knight – Fitzpatrick – Fitzpatrick – Knight is even less likely. So, why don't you just accept the inevitable and come back to me?"

Vivica stood up. She looked at Nial. He was dressed for work. She couldn't deny her attraction to the man. He was walking sex as far as she was concerned, even if he wasn't the most well-equipped man on the planet. It didn't matter though. "Nial, it will be a cold day in hell before I go back to you. I just thought that I'd let you know in person."

Her ex-husband stood up next to her and put his hands on her shoulders. "We know each other so well. You knew that I had broken up with my girl-friend almost immediately."

"I knew that you couldn't be a good father without there being an ulterior motive. Lord knows your other son gets the same love that Brad gets. Which might just be for the best." Vivica stated.

"How's Laura by the way?" Nial asked Vivica in a sarcastic tone.

"This is exactly why we can't be together. You can't even leave Laura out of this…" Vivica walked towards the door, but Nial stopped her.

"Just think about it Viv. We might be toxic, but we are also the best thing for one another."

HANNAH – 2018

The day was just never-ending. She spent the morning dealing with Mrs. Templeton returning a car. Apparently, the car she had sold the old bigot was not white enough. How racist could the nut be? She didn't even bother parking in the back. She just got out of her car in the front driveway of North Pointe. Hannah looked across the street; she needed to talk with her aunt. Only her aunt was not who she saw. Instead, she saw Xander mowing the lawn shirtless. She dropped her purse and slowly walked across the street.

"What on earth are you doing mowing my aunt's lawn?" She asked.

Xander turned off the mower. "Oh, hey. I guess you didn't hear yet. Lucy and her fiancé Austin broke up. Your aunt was nice enough to let us move in with her temporarily. I guess we are neighbors now. Well for a little bit at least."

Hannah smiled. "Well, that's cool. It makes carpooling easy in the mornings." Hannah laughed like an idiot.

The front door opened, and Langley walked out. "Xander, I need to borrow money, and I need you to drive me to the store." She screamed as she walked over to the two twenty-somethings.

"Hi, you must be Langley. I'm Hannah. You are dating my brother."

Langley looked at the brunet girl in confusion… "I thought your name was Hope." She turned to Xander. "I need the money and the ride. I have nothing to wear for tonight."

Xander turned to his younger sister. "Langley, I'm sure Harry doesn't care what you wear."

"I'll be dining with the Knight family. You will be as well. We can't be caught in last year's outfits." Langley pointed out.

"Oh, trust me whatever you wear will be fine. It's just a small family dinner." Hannah admitted.

The teen blonde laughed. "You say that now and then I show up underdressed."

The older brother gave his younger sister a look of disapproval. "Langley, we are in Grosse Pointe, Michigan. Your overly judgmental friends from Manhattan are not going to find out that you wore a dress from a year ago."

"Well, they will see once I post a photo of my evening outfit on social media." Langley pointed out.

"Then don't post it on social media." Xander crossed his arms getting annoyed.

Langley just stormed back inside. It was apparent she wasn't going to win this. She slammed the door behind her.

Hannah cleared her throat. "She seems nice."

Xander put his hands behind his shoulders. "Sorry... She is something else sometimes. I gotta love her though."

Hannah couldn't help but look at Xander's perfect body. This boy clearly went to the gym every chance he got. She wanted to compliment him somehow, but they were once again interrupted...

"Xander! I just got your message as I was getting off work. This is so exciting." Hope said as she rushed over. She looked at Hannah. "You should move your car. I'm blocked..."

"I'll see you tonight I guess." Hannah said.

VIVICA – 2018

"Incoming!" Vivica screamed as she threw a framed photo of Nial from the second story of her mansion. She marched downstairs to pick it up.

Holly ran in from the other room. "What on earth are you doing?" She screamed.

"Guess who wants me back?" Vivica shouted.

"No. You are not going back to him."

"I never said I was." Vivica looked offended. "I have standards. I will not be Mrs. Nial Fitzpatrick for the fourth time."

Brad walked down the staircase and looked at the photo. "I see you spoke with dad. So, um do I get to keep the car?"

It took Vivica a moment to realize what he was talking about. "Oh, well... I might have slammed it into a fire hydrant in front of your father's house. We can pick you out a new car tomorrow. From *Knight.*"

"Why were you driving a car?" Holly demanded to know.

"Oh relax. I told him I was not interested." Vivica assured her.

Brad looked at his mother. "Does dad want to get back together with you?"

The red headed mother rubbed her forehead. "It doesn't matter. I'm not interested. How many times am I going to have to say that today?"

Holly looked at her watch. "I should be cleaning something..." She walked out of the room.

Vivica sat on the staircase. She gestured for Brad to sit next to her. "I know I've been absent since your return home. I feel so bad about that."

"It's fine. I get it. You needed time to move past how dad treated you." Brad said unsure of himself.

"You and your sister have always been the true loves of my life. Forget any of the men that have come and gone." Vivica looked at Brad. She could tell he was upset or confused or both. "I don't want you to think that you can't love your father. I want you to have a relationship with him whatever that relationship might be."

Brad smiled at his mother. "I know you do. I just don't want you to think that I don't realize some of the bad things he does."

When Vivica was a teenager, she never imagined that she would have a child one day that would be as wise as Brad himself was. "You are really a good kid." She kissed Brad on the forehead.

"Brad!" Langley screamed as she ran in from the living room. "I need your help. I have no clue what I am going to wear tonight." She yanked Brad off the staircase and took him upstairs.

"You can come back in." Vivica said as she stood and crossed her arms.

Holly walked back in with a broom and dustpan. "You can really be a good mother when you want to be."

Vivica smiled. "Well thank you. You are still a terrible maid though." She shot Holly a playful look. "You're still my best friend in the world."

"Oh, but what about Brianna Belle?" Holly said in a mocking tone.

"Brianna will always be my childhood best friend. I love seeing her when I can, but her friendship feels like a different lifetime now. We aren't the same people we were when we were teenagers." Vivica admitted.

The maid put her hands on her hips. "What about Cliff?"

"What about Cliff?" Vivica looked directly into Holly's eyes. "He will always be the one Holly. It's hard to explain to someone who wasn't there the first time we were together. Still, though, he is married. I might not like Tiffany, but she is his wife. I have to respect that to some extent."

CLIFF − 2018

Cliff promised himself that he would be home as early as he could before dinner started. He actually made it out of the office with time to spare. Tiffany wasn't even home from the hospital as of yet which shocked him to no end.

The curly haired man walked into North Pointe's dining room. The table was set. He heard footsteps coming from down the hallway. Harry walked in. "Happy Birthday, son!" Cliff called out to his child from across the room.

Harry almost blushed. "Thanks, dad."

Cliff walked over to his youngest child. "You know growing up in this house can be hard. Trust me I know. I'm just happy that you got to have your mother in your life longer than mine was in my own." He still thought about whatever happened to his mother. Did she want him, did his father force her to stay away? There were so many unanswered questions.

"Well, I'm just glad that everyone will be here tonight. Including, aunt Vivica." Harry stated out loud.

"What do you mean Vivica is going to be here? Harry, did you invite your aunt?" Cliff almost demanded to know the answer.

The curly haired son looked at his father in confusion. "Well, she asked if I was having a birthday dinner like normal earlier. I said yes. I invited her to come since Brad was already coming. It would have been rude not to invite her. Plus, aunt Vivica was the one who first started throwing me my birthday dinners when I was younger."

He had almost forgotten… It was Vivica who started this tradition when Harry was younger. Cliff himself had wanted to invite everyone from Harry and Brad's class over for a birthday celebration. Vivica had realized very quickly that Harry wasn't that social, and it would have been a lackluster day for him. She suggested a birthday dinner with just the family, and it stuck with them over the years. "Well, it is your day. If you want your aunt here, I have no issue." He didn't. It was Tiffany that would.

"I'm glad that you are ok with it. I think it will be nice to have the entire family here tonight." Harry got a text message. He looked at it and quickly left the room without saying anything.

"Harry? Where are you going?" Cliff called after him. He started to run towards his son, but the doorbell rang. He went to answer it. He noticed the family portrait of his grandparents, great-grandfather, uncle, and father that hung in the foyer. It still had an unnerving effect on him even as an adult. Cliff ignored it and opened the door. It was her… "Hello, Weston."

"Hello, Cliff."

Cliff was about to say more when a young blonde girl pushed Vivica aside from outside. "I need to see Harry…" Langley said as she marched down the foyer and up the staircase.

"Who on earth was that?" Cliff asked.

HARRY – 2018

The birthday boy sat on his bed and looked out the window. He had no clue what he was going to do next. He had extra Xanax pills from a previous prescription. He was unsure if they would do anything for him right now though. Harry's options rushed through his head.

The door swung open. "As God as my witness, we will get back at this Todd. I will use whatever connections I have left in Manhattan to make that little boy's life hell. He won't get away with this."

Harry looked at Langley. Tears down his cheeks. "Langley he already has."

"Oh, Harry a sex tape is hardly the worst thing in the world in this day and age. You are young, attractive, from a very well-known family. Cable networks are going to get into literal fist fights over who gets the rights for a reality show." Langley said.

"Langley you aren't in Manhattan anymore." Harry sat down on his bed and laid his head down. "I could get kicked out of my Catholic school. I probably will… Meanwhile, my parents will probably disown me."

Langley looked down at her phone. "It's yet to start trending. As of right now, we are the only people to know what is going on. We have time to think this one through."

Time was the one thing they didn't have. It was his birthday, and it might as well have been his funeral. "I can't do this…" Harry started to shake. Langley got on the bed with him.

"It will be fine." Langley tried assuring him.

Someone knocked on the door. It was Brad. "Hey, man!" Brad said with a smile on his face. He quickly realized that something was wrong. "What's going on?"

Harry wiped the tears from his eyes. "Um, nothing…" He sat up in the bed. He walked into his bathroom. "I'll be out in a second."

The two blonde teenagers were left to look at each other awkwardly. "Langley, what on earth is going on?"

"It's not important. If Harry says he will be fine, then he will be fine." Langley claimed.

"Langley, you need to tell me what is going on. I've seen Harry get like this before. It never ends well." Brad took a deep breath. "Growing up, Harry would get overly anxious and start having panic attacks. His parents never grasped what was going on, so it will be up to me to make sure he isn't pushed over the edge."

Harry walked out from the bathroom. "I'll be fine Brad." He had heard what Brad said. "Let's just go and enjoy my birthday dinner. I'm so happy you are going to be here this year." Brad walked over and hugged Harry. "You're my brother. I don't know how many times I have to tell you that. I'll always be here for you no matter what."

***

Harry sat at the head of the table. Langley was at the left side, and Brad was at his right. Hope and Xander sat next to Langley. Vivica and Hannah sat next to Brad. His father was at the opposite end of the table and his mother on the left side of Cliff. He couldn't help but shake.

The maid served the salads. He took a bite. There was light conversation throughout the table. No one's phone went off.

"It's just so nice to be back home with my family." Vivica said.

"It must be nice to have a broad definition of home…" Tiffany rolled her eyes without looking up from her salad.

Xander looked at Hope who seemed unfazed by what her mother said. He could tell that Hannah was not happy though. "Thank you all for having me tonight." He said. None of the Knight's or Fitzpatrick's seemed to notice.

Harry checked his phone again. He checked every social media site that he could think of. He checked the porn website that the video had been posted to. It had views but not many. There were no comments. He had sent an email

to the website to get it removed. It was the weekend and night time though…
The doorbell rang. Harry jumped. Langley grabbed hold of his hand. She gave
him a look as if to say it would all be alright.

The maid walked in. "Mr. Knight is here." She stepped back out. Thunder
and lightning struck the moment she left. In her place, a pale gray-haired man
walked in.

"Well, don't all stand to greet me at once. I swear you ungrateful bas-
tards…" Rodrick Knight said.

Cliff dropped his fork. He looked at Vivica who had turned white. "Father?
What on earth are you doing here?"

"I'm moving back into my house. Didn't you get my message this morning?" Rodrick asked. "I'm sure you didn't. You always screen my calls and probably delete the messages before you listen to them." Rodrick looked around
the room. "Is someone going to offer me a seat at the head of the table?" He
looked at Harry. "Boy stand up."

Vivica immediately stood up. "Don't talk to my nephew that way. It's his
birthday. I don't care if you did grow up in this house. It has never been yours.
We both know very well that Delia left it to Clifton, Cliff, and Luke. She wants
you nowhere near it."

Rodrick laughed. "If I didn't listen to that broad when I was a child, what
makes you think I would listen to her as an adult? She isn't a true Knight and
hasn't been for years. I'm the rightful heir."

"Well, that might be so in your small-minded little head. It doesn't change
the fact that it is your grandson's birthday. You can either stay and celebrate, or
you can get the hell out." Vivica screamed at him.

Rodrick took a seat next to Tiffany. "I see the little Whore from Beverly
Hills still thinks anyone gives a damn what she says."

"That's enough father." Cliff scolded Rodrick. "Vivica is right. We are here
to celebrate my son's birthday." He looked at Tiffany who looked offended
that Cliff would say that Vivica was right.

The night had taken a turn for the worse. Harry couldn't believe that he
was going to come out as gay only a few hours earlier. That wasn't going to
happen tonight. Then he heard a ping. He looked over at Hope.

"Oh, sorry." She took her phone out of her pocket. Her facial expression quickly dropped. "What on earth?"

Tiffany turned and looked at her daughter leaning over from Rodrick. "What's wrong Hope?"

Hope immediately looked at Harry. "How could you?" She sounded disgusted. Hope said as she rushed out of the room. She left her phone.

Rodrick picked the phone up. He looked at the screen. He looked at Harry. "This is unacceptable." He slammed the phone down in front of Cliff. "Do you think this is how a Knight man behaves in public boy?" Rodrick asked looking directly at Harry. "We don't allow faggots in this family."

Harry didn't even stay to see what happened next. He ran out of the room and out of the house. Langley ran after him.

***

Langley chased Harry across the street into Vivica's backyard. There was a guesthouse on the property. Harry was hiding in it and shaking uncontrollably. "My life is over. No one is ever going to like me ever again. What am I going to do? What the fuck am I going to do?" Harry whispered.

"Harry, please calm down. I promise you that once we explain the situation, things are going to be fine." Langley tried to calm him. They were sitting on a bed. The teenage boy was shaking uncontrollably. He kept whispering things, and it was to no one in particular that he said them to. Langley knew she had to do something and then it just snapped inside her… She kissed him. Not a peck on the cheek. She was passionately kissing him.

The blonde teenager got on top of Harry on the bed and started kissing him all over. It took a minute or so, but Harry began to kiss her back. She took his shirt off and continued to kiss his body…

VIVICA – 1986

This was something that Vivica had thought about many times over the past few years. It was just that though. Something she thought about but honestly never put much thought into actually happening. She spent hours deciding if she was actually ready. The more she thought about it, the more she realized that she was.

Vivica jumped a little bit as she waited at the front door. She swore she heard someone in the side bushes. The redhead contemplated going to investigate, but the door opened. Cliff opened it of course. He was dressed up and smelt of a really good cologne. Vivica smiled.

"Hey, Weston."

"Hello, Cliff." Vivica said back. She walked in. She looked at him unsure of what they would do next. "So, do we just..."

Cliff gulped. "Oh, well... I mean I guess we can go to my room." He took her hand. They walked down the foyer towards the staircase.

Vivica looked at the Knight family portrait and the unsettling expression on Rodrick's young face. It was as if to say he knew what they were planning to do. She got that out of her head very quickly as they made their way to the second story. They walked into his bedroom. It looked as it usually did. It was a different color as he mentioned. There also happened to be a large candle on his desk. It seemed sort of old. It was still a nice touch she thought. She decided it was best if she just sat on the bed first. It was clear that Cliff was unsure of what to do next himself. "Well, sit down." Vivica giggled. Cliff sat next to her. He looked at her in the eyes, and they started to kiss one another...

HARRY – 2018

Harry's eyes were wide open. He sat up in the bed. Langley was on her stomach texting. They were both naked. "I cannot believe we just did that. How did this even happen? Why did this even happen?"

"Oh, relax Harry. I got you to calm down. You are far from the first gay man I've slept with. Hopefully, you aren't the last." Langley went back to her phone. "Now, I've already done some damage control for you online. Not much, but the faster we get the video down the better."

The curly haired teen just stared out into nothingness. "I don't feel well." He was gay. The reason behind his panic attack was because of that reason precisely. Yet, he just had sex. Sex with a woman.

Langley shrugged. "You still need to calm down a little bit. Trust me this is far from the worst scandal I've ever seen."

"No… I'm not talking about the scandal. Well, ok I am but no… We just had sex." Harry said freaking out.

"It was nice I guess. I did most of the work, but it was cool." Langley shrugged again.

Harry didn't think that Langley really grasped what just happened. It was as if what they did meant nothing to her. It meant everything to Harry, but it shouldn't have. He was confused. It felt good, but it didn't feel right to him. "Langley… I need to be by myself for a little bit."

The blonde girl got up not covering anything up. "Harry, I don't want to leave you alone right now. I'm worried."

There was a knock at the door. "Thank God, I found you… Oh my God!" Brad screamed as he looked at his cousin and Langley.

Langley took a deep breath. She got up and gathered her clothes off the ground and quickly put them on. "Alright, I think you two should do a bit of talking. Harry text me, or I'm texting you. I mean it." She walked out.

"I don't know what just happened…" Harry said confused.

Brad's mind was going a million miles per hour. "What even was that? Harry, what on earth was that video? I'm confused. Are you bi?"

"No… I don't know why I just had sex with Langley. I don't really think it was my choice… I mean I didn't say no… I mean… Langley is an interesting girl. Anyway… I'm gay." Harry closed his eyes. He waited for Brad to either call him a faggot or punch him. He just wanted this to be over as quickly as possible. Instead, he started to feel to arms wrap around him. He opened his eyes, and Brad was hugging him. "Why are you hugging me? You realize I'm naked right?"

"Yeah…" Brad slowly stopped hugging him at the realization that his cousin was indeed naked. "If you think I care if you are gay or straight you are stupid though. Why didn't you tell me?"

The curly haired cousin shrugged. "I didn't know how you would handle it. I mean you have always been kind of conservative."

Brad laughed. "Conservative? Since when?"

"Well, your views on sex and stuff…" Harry pointed out.

"Just because I don't want to be like my parents doesn't mean I'm a conservative. Even so, you're my brother and best friend on the planet. I could never stop loving you." Brad hit him playfully on the head. "Thanks for thinking so highly of me man."

Harry felt terrible that he thought that Brad would react badly. "How pissed off are my parents?"

The blonde cousin shrugged. "I honestly don't know. Your father didn't really seem mad. Neither did my mom. She kept screaming at your grandfather after you ran out. Hope came back looking for you. Hannah was screaming at someone on the phone."

"What about my mom?" Harry asked.

Brad looked away. "Harry, who sent the video out?"

"Todd Roberts... He claims to be bisexual or whatever. He has been blackmailing me since it happened. I didn't know he was recording me." Harry admitted.

"I'll make him pay. First with my fist then in court. Don't worry about that." Brad promised his cousin.

Harry shrugged. "I mean I don't know what is going to happen now."

Brad put his hand on his cousin's shoulder. Then he realized that his cousin was still naked. "The only change that is going to happen is that you won't be hiding who you are. If anyone has a problem with that, they get to deal with me." He stood up. "Why don't you get dressed. You can spend the night at my house tonight. It is probably for the best."

VIVICA – 1986

"That was… Wow." Vivica said looking straight at the ceiling of Cliff's room."

Cliff looked directly at Vivica. "You were amazing."

The redhead turned and looked at him. "You were too." Vivica wasn't sure how to feel, but she didn't feel regret. That's when the door opened…

"What the hell is going on in here? I keep hearing thumping!" Rodrick screamed wearing a bathrobe. He struck a smile. "Well, there you go… Come look at this dear…" Margot Fitzpatrick appeared at the door.

"Oh my God… Rodrick, why would you show me this?" She was holding back laughter. "I think that girl is supposed to be my cousin or something…" She burst out into laughter and walked away.

Cliff sat up in his bed. "Why is she with you? Why are you even here?"

Rodrick rolled his eyes. "Oh relax. I'm just celebrating. Celebrating the fact that your cow of a mother is forever out of our lives. I got the call just as I was leaving work. I see you were celebrating as well. The Whore from Beverly Hills. I didn't think you had it in your son. How much did you have to pay her?"

"Oh my gosh… Stop Rodrick. That is just too perfect. I'm going to have to use that one." Margot screamed from the hallway.

Rodrick slammed the door shut.

Vivica looked at the wall. She didn't say anything.

"Vivica don't listen to him. You know that isn't even sort of true." Cliff said as the realization that his mother had abandoned him sunk in itself. The phone started to ring. Cliff looked at Vivica as she said nothing. He got up and answered it. He had his own personal line; he wondered who it could have been at this time of the night. "Mrs. Brash?" Vivica stopped looking at the wall and turned to look at Cliff. "I will get her there right away." He hung the phone up. "Vivica we need to get to the site of the new *Knight* dealership. DJ has been in an accident."

CLIFF – 2018

It was as if everything came crashing at once. First, his father, then his son… The night was indeed ruined. Cliff got out of his car. He had been looking up and down streets with Vivica for the last hour. "It's nice that Brad only just texted us that Harry was safe." He started to walk across the street towards Vivica's mansion. She stopped him though.

"Cliff, let the boy have the night to himself. Things are about to get very difficult for him." Vivica pointed out.

"Nothing is changing as far as I'm concerned." Cliff said. "Who Harry falls in love with is not my business. He is my son."

Vivica smiled. "Well, I never doubted that. You were the one who had to remind me that Brianna wasn't any different all those years ago. That said, she did have that crush on me. So, that definitely took some getting used to for a minute." They both laughed.

Cliff looked at North Pointe. The lights were on in various rooms. "I don't know what I'm going to do with Rodrick."

"I know some wonderful mercenaries. You remember from that time Nial, and I went on our second honeymoon?" Vivica had almost forgotten that Nial wanted her back again. "Oh, by the way, Nial is single again."

Cliff turned to her immediately. "Vivica don't go back to him."

The redhead sighed. "I'm not Cliff. I have no desire to be with him for the fourth time."

"I need to get a hold of my business lawyer regarding Rodrick, my personal lawyer to represent Harry, and possibly a family lawyer…" Cliff mumbled that last part.

"Why do you need a family lawyer?" Vivica asked.

He realized what he said and cleared his throat. "I don't know..." He looked at Vivica once more. "If you happen to see Harry tonight or even tomorrow just tell him I love him. I need to go deal with the cast of *Soap*... If only we had a Benson to make all this nonsense funny."

"You can borrow Holly if you want..." Vivica wasn't sure if that was offensive or not.

***

He somehow managed to miss out on his father and got directly to his bedroom where Tiffany was sitting on the couch near the window. She was reading something on a tablet. "Harry's at Vivica's."

"It's probably for the best. He isn't exactly welcome here tonight." Tiffany said.

Cliff looked at her. "Why wouldn't he be welcome here?"

Tiffany put down her tablet and looked at him. "Our son has a gay sex tape on the internet... I'm not exactly jumping with joy."

"Yes, our son has a sex tape. I'm sure that if we looked hard enough, we would find my father's sex tapes and filthy photos of all his old mistresses. We might be Knight's, but that is just it. We are Knight's. Old money is filled with dirty little secrets. We have no room to judge Harry. Especially, without knowing what the hell happened." Cliff sat down next to his wife.

The brunet doctor groaned. "It's not that he is gay. It's the sex tape. You do realize that. I don't have an issue with our son being a gay." Tiffany said.

Cliff nodded unsure of how to analyze what she just said. "Well, I spoke with Hannah a little bit ago. She wants to spend some time with Harry in the morning. I think that is for the best. Do we have any idea where Hope is?"

"I think she is just trying to get over the shock herself. I don't blame her. Who could? This is a big embarrassment to us." Tiffany said like a broken record.

Cliff was about to respond when the opened. "I've just been informed by our lawyers that the video has gone viral. They are looking for a response from the CEO of *Knight Motors*. As of right now, that is still you." Rodrick told his son.

"It's close to eleven at night. I've briefly spoken with my personal law-yer, and as of right now, the best thing to do is wait until Monday." Cliff told his father.

Rodrick laughed disturbingly. "Boy, you are not very bright. We need to get on this right away. The best thing for the company is for you to step down."

Cliff rose to his feet and got in his father's face. "You would like that wouldn't you?"

"It's not a matter of what I want. It's a matter of what is best for the legacy of my father, my grandfather, my brother, your uncle, his child, and your two daughters."

"What about my son?" Cliff asked.

The old man crossed his arms. "If I were you, I would send him off to boarding school and keep him there. He will never see a cent of the Knight fortune. I'll see to that."

Tiffany now got up and stood by her husband. "I think you might be over-thinking this Rodrick."

Cliff was happy that his wife was on his side. He was worried for a second.

"Harry needs to be here for the court case." Tiffany stated.

Cliff waited for her to say something else. She couldn't possibly be this against her own son. Cliff started to feel sick in his stomach for some reason. "You two discuss what you would like. I'll be seeing you." He turned back to his father one last time before leaving, "I'll be informing the security team that you are not to be allowed at *Knight* tomorrow." He then slammed the door and left.

***

Vivica opened her front door. "Cliff, what are you doing here?"

"Can I sleep on your couch for the night? I'm looking to piss off Tiffany as much as she is pissing me off right now." Cliff explained.

Vivica said nothing and opened the door wide open for him.

HANNAH – 2018

Sunday morning was interesting. She had spent half the night trying to find Harry with Xander. She was shocked that he went with her instead of going to check on Hope. Once they found out that her brother was fine, they spent the next few hours just talking in a parking lot somewhere. They really got to know each other even better. She learned that he had several friends who were not straight in Manhattan. He expressed his concern from a legal standpoint as well. He really was a good guy.

She woke up in one of her aunt's guest rooms. It happened to be the same one that Xander was staying in. It also happened that Xander was in bed next to her and that neither of them was wearing any clothes. She quickly realized what happened and turned to wake the blonde boy up. "Xander... Are you awake?" She asked him.

The blonde boy yawned and slowly started to wake up. "Hannah? What are you doing in my room?" His eyes quickly widened. "Oh wow..."

Hannah had forgotten the small detail that they might have decided to start drinking. She didn't remember at what point but she knew that Xander had joined in. The later events of the evening started to become visual... "Oh, yeah this apparently happened." She was sort of pissed off because she didn't remember if it was good sex or bad sex. She was still here though...

"I don't normally do these sort of things..." Xander explained.

Hannah couldn't help but laugh. "I don't either, but it sounds like you are trying to tell me you are sorry." She really hoped he would play along and say that he wasn't. It, unfortunately, didn't seem to be the case.

Xander sat up. His abs were revealed, and Hannah couldn't help but squirm a little in excitement. "I just wish I remembered what lead us here..." Someone knocked on the door. The two looked at each other.

Not having much time, the brunet twin grabbed a sheet and went to hide in the bathroom. She threw Xander's briefs at him. "Xander, I'm coming in. I need to talk with someone and Lucy would probably just scream at me." Langley screamed as she walked in. "I slept with Harry last night."

"As in Harry Knight?" Xander looked confused at his sister. "Langley, why did you sleep with a gay guy knowing he was gay?"

"Oh, like it was the first out gay guy I ever slept with…" Langley rolled her eyes.

Xander looked at his younger sister in a state of confusion. "Well, why are you even telling me this? I'd honestly prefer not knowing these kinds of things as your brother."

"Brad found us after the fact. I think I like Brad or at least I want to sleep with him. I'm not sure yet. Regardless, I'm not sure how he has reacted to this…" Langley admitted.

"Once, again please don't talk about your sex life for the love of all that is good… Wait, did you know that Harry was gay?"

Langley shrugged. "Well, yes. I've known since the day I met him. I only pretended to date him so that the idiot that posted the video would maybe back off. Lord knows it didn't work out that way though…" She looked down at her phone. "Brad wants to talk with me. This is not going to end well…" She walked towards the door but looked back. "Thanks for talking me through that." She walked out and closed the door.

Hannah walked out from the bathroom. "What even… Your sister makes no sense. She knew my brother was gay then sleeps with him after he is outed? Oh, and she likes my cousin?"

"I don't know what goes through her mind, to be honest. I think she meant well."

The brunet twin sat on the bed. "No, I think she meant well in some bizarre way as well. A very bizarre way." Hannah knew that Harry lacked friends. It was nice to finally see someone actively hanging out with him, who wanted to be around him. Even if said person was a tad over the top.

"So, obviously we will keep this between the two of us?" Xander asked.

"Oh, well of course." Hannah responded. She didn't know what to make of what was being said to her. Did he mean that he wanted to just feel this whole incident under wraps or did he not want Hope to find out specifically? Hannah was still in shock that they actually slept together. "I'm never drinking again!" She accidentally said out loud. Regardless, she meant it. Had it been it bad sex she would have remembered it.

HARRY – 2018

"I don't want to look at my phone. Just tell me if it is as bad, I think." The curly haired cousin told the blond one.

Brad had purposely avoided his phone. He had over a hundred text messages, from friends and acquaintances all looking for dirt on his cousin. He looked on social media and Harry was indeed trending in one way or another. "Harry give me your phone." He instructed his cousin.

Harry did so reluctantly. "Well, my life is over." He said as he got off the floor of his cousins' room. He had slept on the ground, even though Brad had insisted that he take the bed, or they share it. Harry was insistent though on not being any more of a burden then he felt he was.

"You have to look on the bright side of things, dude. The world isn't over. This might not have been the way that you wanted to come out, but at least you finally are…" Brad knew that wasn't a very good answer.

The curly haired boy sighed. He knew Brad was trying to help, but it wasn't helping at all. "I don't know if I should just curl in a ball and die or go into hiding." Harry stated.

"Knock, knock…" Langley said as she entered the room. "Oh, good you are both decent. So, what are we doing today?"

"Well, I should probably speak with my parents about this." Harry said rationally.

"Your father slept on the couch last night. Though, I don't think you are ready for that. Considering you are shaking and all…" Langley pointed out.

Harry looked confused. "Why is my father sleeping on the couch?" He had a bad feeling that his parents got into a fight. If they did, then he knew it had to have been because of this mess that was all his fault. 'I should go talk to him." He started towards the door. Brad grabbed him by the shoulder. Harry turned around. "I can do this." He lied.

***

Harry walked down the living room stairs where his father was sitting on the couch wearing the outfit, he wore the night before. Harry started to feel guilty. The boy thought it was best to maybe run back upstairs, but his father spotted him. He had an expressionless look on his face. "Hi…" Harry whispered.

"Come sit down." Cliff told him. He took a deep breath.

The son did as he was told. Though it didn't come off as a demand but an offer. Harry sat down at one of the armchairs adjacent to the couch. "I assume you hate me?"

Cliff looked at his son. "Why on earth would I hate you?" He asked.

"Well, any number of reasons after last night." Harry said out loud.

"Harry, I don't care if you like men, women, or trees. Now, that said if you were into couches then we would have to have a serious discussion. I mean if it was a really sexy couch then maybe I could understand." Harry sort of laughed at this. Cliff took that as a sign his son wasn't going to have a panic attack. "That all said, I'm concerned about why there is a video of you doing things with someone else. Though, I would be just as concerned if it was with a girl."

The curly haired boy nodded his head. He understood what his father was saying. "Well, I didn't know how to tell you about the blackmail… I just wasn't ready to tell people about myself in general."

Cliff's eyes widened. "You were being blackmailed? Harry, that's the exact reason that you should have come to me or your mother. Even your aunt for crying out loud. Why were you so afraid to come out to me? Do, I come off as homophobic?"

At that moment Harry didn't know how to answer. He really wasn't sure. Harry knew that his father had a lesbian friend that seldom visited, but that was about it. "I know you love me."

"Yes, I do love you. That isn't what I asked though."

208

"I guess I don't think you are homophobic if I really thought about it. That said, it wasn't really a matter of you liking gay people or not. It was a matter of it never being the right time. I didn't need people saying things like good for you, or congratulations. You don't have people doing that when you are straight. Why do I have to do that when I'm gay? It seems like being gay just comes with this entire set of rules. I like guys. I don't like girls. I can promise you of that." Harry thought of last night, and a cold shiver ran down his back.

Cliff nodded. "Well, there is a lot to unpack there, but I think I get what you are saying. I think at least."

"How is mom doing with this?" Harry asked.

Cliff looked away from his son. "Your mother is still shocked… About the video. Hannah was anxious about you though." He looked back at his son. "I've been on the phone all morning. We are going to be meeting with a lawyer."

"You have ten seconds to get that video link off your website, or I will have Vivica Fitzpatrick posting how your site endorses child pornography." Holly said as she walked in from the foyer and towards the kitchen. "Don't you make excuses…"

Vivica walked in after her. "I've been in talks with multiple people since this morning. From a social media standpoint, I've been making sure that the video is being removed. Holly is probably banned from using several social media sites and a few porno websites, but I think we are getting our message across." She walked over to her nephew and hugged him. She looked him in the eyes, and she held him by the shoulders. "I've always loved you and I always will." She kissed him on the forehead. There was a knock at the door, and Vivica went to get it.

Cliff smiled at Harry. "See, two more supporters just like that."

"Cliff, I need to speak with you now!" Tiffany screamed as she marched into the living room. She looked at Harry in complete disgust.

CLIFF — 2018

"Tiffany get the hell out of my living room!" Vivica screamed as she made her way back into the room.

Cliff looked at Vivica. "Could I just have a minute alone with Tiffany?" He asked Vivica.

Vivica looked pissed off. "I'll be in the kitchen with Holly and Lucy. I think the cook is making breakfast if anyone wants any." She looked at Tiffany. "I'm sure the kennel has prepared your daily meal." With that, she walked out.

"Harry, if you wouldn't mind… I need to speak with your mother alone." Cliff told his son very sympathetically.

The Knight son got up from the armchair and nodded his head. He looked to be confused. Cliff felt terrible about this. He said nothing though as he walked up the stairs.

"What do you want Tiffany?"

"I've been trying to get ahold of you all night. I didn't think I needed to use the tracking device on your phone, but here we are…"

Cliff rolled his eyes. "Oh, yes as you can see, I slept on the couch. Our son is staying here, our one daughter drunkenly walked in at some point during the night and is probably staying here, on top of our nephew, and three strangers, two of which are dating our children it would seem. So, I definitely came over here in the heat of the moment to sleep with Vivica."

The brunet doctor's eyes widened. "Who said anything about sleeping with Vivica?" Tiffany said defensively.

"Well, why else would I possibly be here? It has nothing to do with your reaction to our son." Cliff screamed at her.

"Cliff I could give a damn if our son is gay. If you think I'm some sort of homophobe, you are wrong." Tiffany screamed back.

He honestly didn't know what to think. "That's wonderful, but I'm not going to send my son off to some European boarding school and allow him to be disinherited from the company."

Tiffany put her hand on her head. "Cliff, I agreed with your father last night because I wanted to keep him calm. The last thing we need right now is for him to go off the wall. Everyone in town knows what he is like when he is angry. Which he clearly is. I overheard him on the phone with a lawyer this morning. He is trying to contest his mother's will. He wants you out at *Knight*, and he wants us out of the house."

"Tiffany dear that is a non-issue at this point. If he contests my grandmother's will, then he has to contest my grandfather's will, as well as my great-grandfathers will. Not to mention my uncle will never allow him to take over the company again. I could honestly give a damn about the house."

"I just thought that since we raised our family there, you would care more about it." Tiffany started to cry.

"A home is nothing without the people inside it, and this family hasn't been a functioning unit in years. Hannah thinks we hate her. Hope thinks she gets whatever she wants based on her achievements when she has a terrible attitude. Harry was so afraid to tell us about his sexuality! Not to mention you have a terrible relationship with your sister..." Cliff just let it all out.

Tiffany looked at her husband in complete disbelief. "I have every reason to hate my sister."

If he stated the obvious, then it would be the end of their marriage. Cliff wasn't ready for that. "I'm going to be staying in the guest house for a while. Keep Rodrick out of my things. I'm going to go have breakfast. I have to go meet with a lawyer after this." With that, he walked into the kitchen where everyone was clearly pretending as if he hadn't just told off his wife. "Does anyone have anything to say?"

"Yeah, could you keep it down? I'm screaming at some twink website right now. It's hard to get my point across when you are screaming louder than Mrs. Templeton when she rents a man for the night..." Holly informed him.

Vivica took a sip of juice. "Is there anything you need me to do today?"

"No, I think I should have things under control. The lawyers think we should be able to take care of this rather quickly. If Harry was being blackmailed, then the kid who did this isn't going to stand a chance in court." Cliff explained.

"Good. Well, as you can see Holly has taken it upon herself to help out with the cease aspect of things. I could take Harry to the mall or something."

Lucy sighed. "I don't think that is the best idea Vivica. A large crowd is the last thing someone needs after a scandal like this." She looked at her phone. "I have to go. Austin wants to talk. I'll be back in an hour or so." She got up and left.

Cliff sat down. "I feel like an idiot."

"Why?" Vivica asked.

"I just do. I don't know how to explain it. I should have spoken up a long time ago about how my family has been going. We didn't see Hannah for months until she came back. Harry has so many insecurities. I love Hope, but she has her issues as well. I shouldn't be talking to you about this." Cliff might have been angry at Tiffany, but he knew the last thing he should be doing was talking about his marriage with Vivica. He wasn't trying to be heartless towards Tiffany. He didn't think he was at that point. He hoped he wasn't. Cliff walked into the living room. He heard footsteps behind him. He turned around to see Vivica. "Thank you for letting me stay here last night. I'll be in the guest house if you need to call a landline to reach me."

"Are you going to be alright?" Vivica asked.

Cliff shrugged. "If you are asking it if is the end of my marriage, well I don't know. I'm alright though."

The redhead rolled her eyes and walked closer to Cliff. "I could really care less about your marriage right now. I only care about you and the children. All of them."

"You really do..." Cliff could see if it now. The regrets started to pile in again. "Whatever happened to us, Weston?"

Vivica sat down on her couch. She didn't look at him. "We started to grow up."

"Yes, I'd like to file a complaint with hairless backdoor boys... I'll have you know that first off the boy in that video was hardly hairless, so that right there should be grounds for removing the video..." Holly screamed on the phone.

"You're ruining the moment Holly..." Vivica sighed.

VIVICA – 1986

She said nothing on their way to the construction site. She still was unsure why they were meeting her mother here instead of a hospital. Vivica looked out the window; there were fire trucks and police cars everywhere. The red-haired teenager wished she had more of a reaction, but she was still trying to find the proper response towards Rodrick. The man was always saying misogynistic things, and yet this really seemed to hit her in a way that everything else trumped in comparison.

The car stopped. The two looked at each other and then quickly looked away. "What on earth happened?" Vivica managed to say. Her step-father probably slipped on a rock and was making a big deal about it. That was typical of him. She stepped out of the car; she saw her mother from a short distance. She was holding on to Nadia Fitzpatrick. They were both crying hysterically. Vivica unsure of what was going on slowly walked over.

"Mother?" She said. She looked at her mother. She had never seen her act so hysterical. "What… What is going on?" All three of the local news stations were there. Vivica wasn't ready to admit to herself what was obviously in front of her. "Mother, where is DJ?" She looked at her mother who as just crying along with Nadia. "Mother?" Cliff walked over and grabbed her by the arm. She looked at him. "What is going on? Where is DJ? Did he get stuck in a hole or something? That sounds like something he would do…"

Cliff started to cry. "Vivica, I'm so sorry."

The redhead was confused. "Cliff, you never call me Vivica. Why all of a sudden are you calling me by my first name?" She looked around as more police showed up.

"DJ didn't make it." Cliff whispered.

Vivica looked at Cliff. She looked at the wreckage that was clearly in front of her. She looked at her mother and Nadia. "Cliff, that isn't funny. Why would you tell me that?" The curly haired boy tried to hug Vivica, but she wouldn't let him. "DJ isn't dead…" She screamed. It seemed that everyone was looking at her. She marched off.

This night was not going the way it was supposed to. She lost her virginity, and now everything was going to hell. Vivica believed in God, but this was ridicules. She has sex, and now she was an upscale whore, and her step-father was dead? The redhaired girl couldn't help but think about how mean she had been to DJ over the years. She did care about him. She knew that he loved her. She realized that DJ probably died thinking she hated him. She didn't though… "Why is this happening?" Vivica asked herself as she sank to the ground in the parking lot. Cliff ran over. She looked at him and whispered. "I can't do this…"

"What do you mean you can't do this?"

"I don't know. This all shouldn't be so hard." Vivica explained.

"Vivica I'm here for you." Cliff said. Tears are coming down his face.

She didn't want him here for her right now though. She tried to be strong enough to put herself together. "Cliff, I need to be alone right now." Vivica stood up and got herself together. "It's not that I don't appreciate you trying to help me. I do, it's just that right now is not the time."

"You can stop banging on the door... Oh, it's you?" Nial said as he personally answered the front door. He looked at Tiffany in confusion. "What exactly do you want?"

Tiffany marched in and slammed the door herself. "You need to take my sister back. I will do whatever just get her away from Cliff."

Nial looked at this woman he had called his pier for so many years. "While I'm trying, I don't think that it will work this time."

"You have married her three times. It's clearly meant to be. Otherwise you wouldn't keep coming back to her. You just need to stop cheating on her. It's that simple."

The blond doctor could tell that Tiffany was serious. He could also tell that she was desperate. "Tiffany has Cliff strayed from your marriage?"

She turned around. "I don't think so. I just am not willing to sit around and wait for him too. Why couldn't she have just stuck around Beverly Hills? She loves that damn city so much..." She started to stomp her feet repeatedly on the ground.

"Will you calm down? The floors are solid marble..." He grabbed her hand and guided her to sit down on the staircase. "Take a deep breath."

"I don't have time for that. Cliff is moving into the guest house. He slept at Vivica's house last night. He claims he slept on the couch, but I don't know." Her phone started to go off. She looked at it. "I'm needed in surgery... Damn it." She got up. She looked at Nial. "You need to think about this. Go back to your soulmate." She stormed off.

"Well, how intriguing..." Margot said as she walked down the stairs. "I adore the woman, but don't you dare go back to the whore from Beverly Hills. Three times was enough."

Nial sighed. "I can't help it, Margot. I love her." He turned around and looked at Margot on the staircase. "She is everything that I always wanted."

"So, were all my husbands. You don't see me going back to any of them." Margot said as she continued down the stairs. She quickly pivoted to look directly at her younger brother. "I want to make sure you heard me. Don't go back to her…"

"Oh, sister let me take care of things. I'm a big boy now…" He stood up and towered over her. "Vivica was not that bad. She was a saint in comparison to the other women." The smile he had on his face was slowly dropping.

Margot rolled her eyes. "Nial you have some real issues…"

He knew he did and they were only in small part because of Vivica. He knew he had been a bad husband. Nial sometimes regretted the things he did. "I'm not going to let that smug Knight get his way again." Nial said as he himself stormed out the front door.

"I hate Vivica Weston. Damn it!" Margot said as she stomped her foot.

"I can either get all the facts and have it made one hundred percent clear that Harry was the victim. Which he obviously is, or I can do a rush job and get the other kid sent away, but Harry isn't going to be walking out unscathed in this case." Lawson Stride, one of Cliff's lawyers told him. They were in Cliff's office. On his way up to his office, Cliff had to deal with many interesting facial expressions. Some wouldn't look at him. A few people who he knew would be on thin ice completely avoided him.

"I want this quick and I want Harry's reputation restored. He is a teenager, name a normal teenager who isn't somewhat sexually active? His sexuality should not play into this at all." Cliff pounded his fist on his desk.

Lawson typed something into his phone. "Well, here is the thing, if we can get Harry to be a new face of the LGBT community, then we might have something. LGBT issues are really in right now."

Cliff looked at Lawson straight in the eye. "My boy was taken advantage of and now is the only one suffering. We need to get this under wrap immediately. My Weston's maid is doing more damage control than you are right now." He then realized what he said. He hadn't called Vivica his Weston since they dated. Sure, she would always be his Weston, but she wasn't HIS Weston. This day was not improving. The door slammed open. Cliff turned to see who it was. "What do you want?"

"Ok, car boy you need to stay away from my girl." Nial threatened.

The automotive CEO walked over to the idiot doctor. "What on earth are you talking about? First off, she belongs to neither of us. She is a woman. Second of all, you left her in front of everyone in town… Do you just go back and forth between loving and hating her?"

"We both do. It's our thing." Nial stated.

"You have some serious issues, little boy." Cliff turned back to his lawyer.

Nial marched over to Cliff's view. "Don't ignore me. You have a wife. Stick with her. She is a good woman. That's what I hate about you. You are a giant hypocrite. Everyone around you is supposed to be perfect, but you are allowed to be flawed and accepted. That's bullshit, and you know it. That's why it didn't work out for you and Viv in the first place."

Cliff rolled his eyes. He leaned against his desk to show confidence. "You have no idea why it didn't work out for Weston and me in the first place. You never will because Vivica never shared anything about her life with you. She always has with me. I do love the ivory tower you have placed me in. That complete retcon to my life is laughable at best and insulting at worst." He walked over to the door. "I need you to leave. I'm trying to deal with my own family issues."

"What do you possibly need to deal with? Did one of the girls gamble away all her birthday money again? First world problems…"

"Little boy, the silver spoon that you were born with was shoved so far down your throat that you were choking on it. If only it had done the job… So, don't go around judging my family. You know exactly what I'm dealing with. Harry…"

The doctor looked at him with a blank expression. "The quiet boy? What on earth did he do?"

"Oh, don't act like you don't know." Cliff started walking back over to his desk. He wasn't going to talk with this idiot right now.

"I really don't know. I have a block on my phone keeping all news involving you and your family off it. It's not easy trust me…" Nial admitted.

Cliff could tell that he really was being serious right now. "Considering, that your son is helping Harry through this I will tell you. Then I need you to leave me be so I can deal with this… Harry was sexually taken advantage of and filmed during a sex act with another boy. The other boy published the video last night online and forced him out of the closet."

Nial gulped. "I should get to work. Tell me if you need anything. Anthony Costa owes me a few favors."

"I didn't hear that." Lawson said as he continued looking at his phone.

Nial walked out.

"There I something not right with that human being. I don't even think I can call him that." Cliff sighed.

Harry – 2018

He couldn't go online; he couldn't watch TV, he couldn't use his phone. He didn't even know where his phone was. Harry was so sick of all this. He wanted his life back. It was stolen from him in less than twelve hours ago. Really, it was stolen the moment he agreed to meet with that idiot Todd Roberts. He buried himself in one of Brad's pillows.

"You aren't going to sit in here sulking all day." Langley said as she walked in.

Harry turned and looked at the blonde girl. "What are you talking about?"

"We are going out. Brad is prepping downstairs."

"Langley, the last thing that I need is to go out and get recognized right now." He expressed.

Langley rolled her eyes. "Oh relax. No offense but we are in Michigan. No one is going to recognize you even if you are on the news. The only places you will get recognized are in this town and online. We are going to get out of the town for a few hours."

The curly haired teen sat up. "Where will we even go?"

"I know Grosse Pointe, Detroit, and St. Clair Shores. You and Brad can decide."

"What will we do?" Harry wondered.

The blonde teen shrugged. "I don't know. Shop? Eat? Rob a bank? Probably not that last one, my family doesn't need any more money-related scandals right now."

"I don't know... I mean..." Harry didn't know what to say. Langley sighed and yanked him at hand, dragging him out of the room.

***

220

Brad sat behind of the wheel of his car, Langley in the passenger's seat at Harry's request and himself in the back just sort of unsure of himself. They were on the freeway just sitting in silence. "Oh, this is ridicules… We can either talk out our feelings, or we can listen to one of my playlists. I like gangsta rap and heavy metal. So, talk it out?" Langley inquired. She looked at Brad who said nothing. Harry wasn't even looking at the two of them. "Ok, music it is then." She plugged her phone into the dock and turned the volume on full-blast. Very loud and very unpleasant music started to play. Langley was dancing to it, her hair all over the place and was singing along to it. Harry couldn't handle it anymore and ripped the phone out of the dock. "Please no more. What on earth even is that?"

"Some people just can't handle the classics…" Langley rolled her eyes. She crossed her arms. "So, let's talk about the kind of men we all like… I'm into broad-shouldered, puppy dog eyed, tall men, with a nice ass. Brad what about you?"

The blond boy looked at her. "Langley, I'm not into men…" He looked at Harry in the mirror. "Not that there is anything wrong with it."

"Ok, well that leaves Harry. Harry, what kind of men do you like?" She turned back in her seat to look at Harry who looked embarrassed.

"I don't really know…"

Langley sighed. "Well, we are going to have to work on that." She looked out the window. "Where on earth are, we?"

"I don't know just some city near Detroit…" Brad said.

"Oh, for crying out loud enough with the small talk. Harry, are you going to be alright?" Langley asked.

Harry had to think about it for a moment. He was out of the closet. It wasn't his choice to do so, and it would forever be remembered as being on his birthday. "No. No, I am not."

Brad pulled the car over. He turned back to Harry. "You have nothing to worry about."

"Brad, why did you stop the car? There is a man sitting at a bus stop, but I don't think he is waiting for a bus…" Langley screeched.

"I'm sure we will be fine Langley." Brad said. He turned back to Harry. "The worst of it is over. You don't have anything to worry about. Your family is still there for you."

He wasn't so sure about that after earlier when he heard his parents screaming from upstairs. "Yeah well, we don't really know that."

"Oh, good lord that girl has three different fast food takeout bags in her hand. I don't think she is sharing them with anyone." Langley said in horror as she stared out the window."

The two cousins looked at her. "Langley, I thought you lived in New York City?" Brad pointed out.

The blonde girl sighed. "New York City is a completely different battle-field than some random city in Michigan." She looked out the window. "Oh, yup the woman is eating French fries out of both bags. The man sitting at the bus stop just went for the third bag. Don't do it, buddy; she is not going to share. Uh-oh, that woman is beating him with her faux-designer purse. You show him, sister, just because you are wearing dollar store flip flops and probably have a hoagie in that purse of yours doesn't mean you can't be strong!"

"Well, we don't see that in Grosse Pointe." Harry chuckled.

"No, we just see women with sweaters tied around their necks and men wearing short pink dress shorts on one side of the street and a guy with a shopping cart on the other…" Brad stated out loud.

Langley sighed. "Well, there goes the hoagie all over the street… No sweetheart do not go after it. There are better things to do with your life… Well, so much for dignity." She turned to the two cousins. "Can we please get the hell out of here? I have mints in my purse, and I'm worried she will sniff them out and come for us."

Brad started the car back up. "Harry, look we will get things under control. My mom and Holly are working to get the press to lay off you. Your dad is your biggest supporter not in this car right now. Hannah is definitely on your side. Hope and your mom just need to get over the video. Things will be back to normal by the summer."

"If they aren't then you can always drop out of high school, move to California, become a social media influencer, and get a bunch of straight to streaming movie roles." Langley was checking her phone as she said this.

"That was oddly specific Langley." Harry pointed out.

"Men with large chests, toothpick legs, and scary faces are really big right now. Oh, and coming out as gay also really helps people online too. Especially, if you start making *documentary*-style videos and own the people, you hang around. Since you are actually a good person, I see a book deal almost immediately."

Brad looked at the girl. "What on earth are you talking about?"

Langley sighed. "We live in a fucked-up world boys…"

LUCY − 2018

"Why am I doing this?" She asked herself as she stood at Austin's front door. The door finally opened after a minute of waiting. She looked at her former fiancé. He was still the most beautiful human being that she had ever seen, but it didn't change what he had done to her.

Austin smiled. "You could have just walked in. You still live here Lucy. This is still your home."

Lucy reluctantly walked in. Austin closed the door gently behind them. It looked like Austin went off the handle a little. There were several empty beer bottles out and a broken vase. She looked at him again. So, beautiful but she couldn't let that fool her. "I don't live here anymore Austin. This is not my home anymore."

"You can't say that. You need to remember all the good times we had together. We spent years building a home. We were going to get married soon!" He pointed out.

The blonde woman needed to sit; she settled on the staircase. She put her hands on her head and sighed. "Austin, why did you cheat on me?"

The doctor gulped. "It was just sex. It meant nothing to me. She started it."

Her head was starting to hurt. She stood back up and crossed her arms. "So, what she forced herself on you?"

"Well, I mean not exactly…"

"Not exactly? She either forced herself on you, or she didn't. Though, the text messages and photos make me think otherwise of course. So, again did she force herself on you?" Lucy asked.

Austin sighed. "No. She didn't force herself on me, Lucy."

He was talking like a teenager being questioned by a parent on a bad choice. "Well, then I guess you don't have an excuse. You know I've been talking with Holly O'Dell about you…"

"Holly O'Dell? Oh, don't listen to anything she has to say. She had a crush on me in high school, and I didn't like her back. She claimed I was racist and tried to make the entire school hate me. It obviously didn't work."

Lucy rolled her eyes. "She didn't mention any crush but even if she did what does it matter? She is married with two children. Why would she still be jealous over a high school crush from over a decade ago?"

Austin stood in silence for a moment. "You know if you didn't spent so much time with Vivica and her family you wouldn't feel like this. I mean come on they aren't you."

"Do you mean rich? Austin, do you even know me? I might have ran out of my father's legacy, but I was raised in a similar way to all of those people. You are a doctor for heaven sake. Don't pretend it is because you actually care about people. You wanted money. Don't blame money and status on your cheating. Don't blame me either." Lucy screamed at him.

The doctor sat down on the couch searching for a beer bottle that wasn't empty. "You clearly aren't willing to move past this. Whatever, Lucy… I have to get to work in a little bit."

Lucy walked over to him. "I'd reconsider that if I were you. You are hung over and look terrible."

"I'll survive a shift. Thanks for thinking of me though…"

"I wasn't thinking of you. Just your innocent patients." Lucy started to walk towards the door. "I wish you well, but I'm not coming back here again."

Austin stood up. "I hate you…"

The blonde woman wanted to say something back, but she was holding back tears. She opened the door to find a man standing there. A man who happened to be Anthony Costa's, right-hand man. "I don't want to know…" She walked out and left them be.

Margot walked into her brother's office at GPGH. She found him sitting at his desk typing something up. "Well, deal is set in motion. I really wish you would have just ruined his life though. I was hoping to use that hit on someone else."

"For the last time Margot, you are not going to try killing Vivica… Again." Nial said as he sat up from his desk. "It was a worthy use of our understanding with the Costa family."

"You know how much I hate that family of scumbags Costa does know how to get the job done." Margot pointed out. "So, where do you go from here? A nice young blonde in Florida? Possibly, a visit to England with a brunet girl?"

Nial looked out his office window. "There is only one girl for me, and she is a redhead. You know that."

"I'm touched Nial, but I'm not into incest."

The blond doctor turned around. "Margot, just accept the fact that Vivica and I are meant to be together. We might stray from each other, but we deserve each other."

Margot rolled her eyes. "The only thing that bitch deserves is a slap in the face. Possibly, two. She is obsessed with the Knight family. Especially, Cliff. How can you be ok with that?"

"So, she can't get over a childhood crush. I never did either."

"I should point out that two weeks ago you were ready to marry that blonde bimbo with the fake tits." The older sibling pointed out.

Nial shrugged. "That was then this is now sister. I promise you that Vivica and I will be together again by the end of the year."

Margot groaned. "You really know how to make me proud don't you?"

VIVICA – 2018

"I'm going to check on Cliff at the office." The redhead told her maid.

"No, you aren't. You are going to sit right here and write a press release on your nephews' behalf. The last thing Harry needs is his parents breaking up right now because his aunt is a little too nostalgic." Holly informed her.

Vivica shot Holly a dirty look. "Oh, calm down. I just want to make sure that Cliff is alright. I have no interest in being the cause for that divorce. When it happens, it will be because my bitch of a sister cannot be a good mother."

Hannah walked in. "What about the bitch?"

"Hannah you really shouldn't call your mother a bitch. It's different when I do it." Vivica pointed out.

"Ok, what is my mother doing now?" Hannah scoffed.

"Oh, just being herself... We all heard her this morning. I don't understand how she can't support her child." Vivica lamented.

Holly sighed. "You know very well that isn't what she said this morning."

The redhead shot her friend a dirty look. "I'm just reading between the lines. I probably shouldn't talk like this in front of Hannah though." Vivica always tried very hard to keep her opinions of Tiffany from all the children. Even if everyone was well aware of what they were.

"I don't mind hearing. I'm not a child anymore. Not to mention everyone knows what you think of my mother." Hannah pointed out.

Holly gave Vivica another dirty look, but Vivica ignored her. "Well, I do love your mother deep down. It's just I don't understand how someone can do the things she did, and yet I'm the town whore..." She once again looked at Holly. "Not a word out of you right now." Vivica spat.

"Maybe I just remember her differently, but she never seemed like the same person after she came back from being kidnapped." Hannah pointed out.

"Oh, she is exactly the same person she was before the kidnapping only more self-righteous." Vivica had been arguing with her .

"I think the two of you need to remember that while I don't like Tiffany either, the last thing anyone needs right now is you Vivica going after their marriage." Holly repeated yet again.

Vivica rolled her eyes. "Holly I'm not going to go after their marriage. I gave up on going after their marriage long ago." She really had. There was no point in trying to break them up. Cliff made his choice twice, and he still wanted Tiffany. At least that is what he outwardly said. Vivica was definitely over courting Cliff, but she wasn't stupid. She knew deep down that while Cliff might love Tiffany, she wasn't his destiny. No, she wasn't because Vivica knew very well that it was herself that was meant for Cliff.

The things they had experienced together first. You just don't forget those things. The fact they stayed so connected after all these years helped show that. Tiffany screwed herself over by marrying him. It is probably what kept Vivica so close. Sure, there was a time when she outwardly fought to get Cliff back. Everyone from Margot to her mother tried to put a stop to it. Her entire second marriage to Nial was on the belief that she could be kept away. All the money in the world couldn't keep her away at some point.

Then Vivica finally had Cliff. She held herself off from going after him when they all thought that Tiffany had died. She volunteered to watch the children during the day. She hadn't been working often at that point. It was Cliff who went after her, and they finally were married, or so they thought. It was a wonderful few years together. They acted like an actual family. Then Tiffany came back… Vivica knew that legally she wasn't married. Cliff had the option to annul one marriage over the other though or even divorce Tiffany. He wouldn't erase what he had with Tiffany, and he obviously felt bad. Tiffany didn't feel bad for him though. She had always been jealous of her past with Cliff. Tiffany expected that things would go back to the way they were. The term you can never really go back home didn't apply for Tiffany. She demanded that things go right back to how they were when she left only several years later. Harry was a baby. He didn't even know her beforehand. Vivica suspected very much that Tiffany resented him for that. She wasn't even going to toss that theory out there though.

The redhead stood up. "I have to go see someone." She looked at Holly. "Don't worry… It isn't Cliff." She stormed out of the kitchen, into the living room, then foyer until she found herself marching herself across the street to North Pointe. Mrs. Templeton was screaming at her predominantly black staff about something as she did so. Like most of the town, she chose to ignore it. Instead, she started banging on the front door hoping that it wasn't Rodrick who would open. She had words to say to him, but they could wait for the time being. Finally, the door opened. "We need to talk." Vivica stated.

"What do you want little sister?" Tiffany asked.

Vivica walked in without being asked. "How can you abandon that little boy right now? He needs you."

Tiffany gave her a blank stare. "I have not abandoned anyone. I love my son. I just don't love his actions. If Brad did the same what would you do?"

"If Brad did the same, I'd be in complete and utter shock because he made me go to a purity ball with him once…" Vivica screamed hysterically.

"Vivica, I'm sorry, but you are not the one who has been receiving pity and bitchy messages all day from people. No that would be me." Tiffany spat back.

The younger sister wanted to punch her older sister. "Tiffany you will survive. You are a rich doctor. Your son while rich is a child still. He doesn't know any better. He has a million insecurities that we have been aware of since he was a little boy. Your reaction to this is not going to be good for him. He is going to go into a downward spiral." Vivica remembered the first time that Harry had a panic attack when he was only three years old. It came out of nowhere; he was supposed to go apple picking with a friend of his. He got panicky about being away from her for the day. She ended up having to cancel a photo shoot to go with him.

The older sister crossed her arms. "Vivica I know how to raise my own child. I don't need your advice."

"You don't know what any of your children need." Vivica started to walk away but then turned back. "Just so you know, when Cliff divorces you it won't be because of me. I'm going to leave him alone."

VIVICA – 1986

Vivica hated wearing black. It was inappropriate to wear anything else though. It had been nonstop arguing from everyone the past week as the adults around her argued the details of DJ's funeral. Her mother wanted a small memorial service with a luncheon held afterward in their backyard. Nadia wanted a large-scale event with the press involved. Brandon stood behind his wife obviously.

It never really hit Vivica until now, but DJ really held the family together. He was the only one who looked past the drama and looked for things at face value. He would have settled for something in the middle. She imagined that he would tell her mother that Nadia was making a big deal but then to keep peace allude to Nadia that Gale just didn't understand. DJ didn't grow up in a glamorous household. He grew up in a loving home at least that is what Vivica had been told to believe, and she had no reason not to believe it.

She had been looking at old photo albums. It wasn't by choice; Gale had asked her to put together a photo collage for the funeral. Vivica hadn't really wanted to, but she agreed to keep herself out of all the other nonsense. She was taking the week off of school. Gale had insisted, but Vivica would have regardless. Not because of DJ's passing but because she just couldn't handle being around other people at the moment. They kept wanting to give her their sympathy or pity. The issue was that as much as Vivica was sad that DJ was dead and she did indeed miss him, she knew looking back that she had been a terrible step-daughter.

The worst part of all was that DJ had never treated her with that label. She was his daughter as far as he had always been concerned. Vivica never really appreciated it until she looked at all the old photos. So, many pictures of DJ, Gale, and herself. She started to wonder where the heck her own father was during all of this. They saw each other once a year if that and it was never in Beverly Hills, which he knew very well she loved visiting. It was always for a few hours at a hotel or something. He wasn't a cold man, but he just didn't seem to be all that invested in her life. Yet, he would spend a majority of their time together talking about her older sister Tiffany.

Tiffany... She knew so little about the girl other than the fact that she supposedly was perfect. Vivica never understood why they were actually split up as children. She remembered them having a sisterly bond to some degree when they had been younger sort of. Yet, at the same time Tiffany never called, she never wrote, and she was basically a on existent person in her life. Her mother never seemed to talk with her either.

It almost seemed as though DJ's death was his last gift to her. It was a sick thing to think, but it had kept the subject her losing her virginity off her mind. The redhaired teen knew that she didn't regret losing her virginity going into things. Yet, now she did. She didn't know why though. Rodrick's words never meant anything to her in the past, and yet now they seemed to be stuck in her mind day and night when she wasn't thinking about DJ. Cliff had called, and she did take his calls. They would talk, but Cliff trying to be her knight in shining armor would try to keep the subject off of death and sex. Instead, they would talk about TV. Cliff actually had taken to recording *As the World Turns* and would give his opinions on the citizens of Oakdale. It was her favorite show; most people were still obsessed with *General Hospital,* but she could never get into it after Laura had left.

She sat down on her bed and cut out a picture of DJ and her fishing. She had no actual memory of this day. She rolled her eyes and laughed a little thinking about the idea of DJ trying to teach her to fish. That's when someone knocked on the door. It was Cliff. She turned to look at him. She tried smiling. "Hello." She said.

"How are you doing today Weston?" He asked as he sat down at her vanity. He put down a folder with her homework.

"I'll survive I suppose. Gale is still sobbing nonstop, and there is little I can do about it. Nadia comes over throughout the day, and they argue. Brandon then comes by with food. He keeps offering me a guest room if I need a place to escape to through all this. I keep turning him down. That brat of theirs Nial is back home for the funeral."

Cliff nodded to show he was listening. "Yeah, Brianna sends her love. She wants to visit tomorrow, but she is afraid you won't be up for it."

The redhead laughed. "If Brianna wants to visit that's fine. Just warn her that she will be walking into a disaster." Vivica looked at her boyfriends' eyes and noticed that something looked off. She got up and grabbed a tissue. "What is on your face Cliff?" He tried to stop her from touching his face. "Cliff stop moving." She finally got him to stand still and stopped wiped what looked to be makeup around his eye. "Cliff, did he hit you again?"

The young Knight didn't want to talk about it. "We should go over some of the homework. You don't want to get behind."

"Clifton Knight, we are not going to ignore this. Did that jackass hit you again?" Vivica demanded.

Cliff got up. "Look, I deserved it. Ok. I knew better than to argue with him but I did anyway. Shame on me." He crossed his arms.

"Why are you defending him? That man is not worth defending. After, all he has done to you."

"Vivica, I am not defending him. I was defending you ... Let's just leave it at that." Cliff said defensively.

She looked at him. "What are you defending me for? Is he still going on about us sleeping together? The man has slept with half the town ... If he is still that obsessed with me, he must be jealous. Congratulations Cliff you finally have something over your psycho father!" She rolled her eyes.

"Vivica how can you say something like that?" Cliff threw his arms in the air.

"Well, what do you want me to say? I still don't have an accurate perception on that night. I hate that your father ruined it, but I don't regret what we did." She didn't. At least she didn't think she did. Vivica honestly had no idea, but she wasn't going to let Cliff think otherwise.

CLIFF – 2018

It had been a long day. Each of his lawyers all helpful were also less than helpful. He was ready to fire each of them but stopped himself every time he got close. Cliff had been reluctant for the first time ever to look at the daily numbers. The Knight CEO had been expecting a phone call from his cousin Luke all day, but it hadn't come. He was grateful that Luke seemed to finally be mature enough not to call with threats or to taunt him with the fact that the company might be in trouble.

It wasn't in trouble though. It was 2018, who gave a damn if his son was gay? Half the country and definitely half the world... Still, his son was a teenager, and his sexuality had nothing to do with selling cars. On top of that Harry never once expressed any interest in being a part of the company. If he wanted to be part of it one day, Cliff would do his damn best to make sure that his child could be a part of the company though.

Cliff had many regrets in life. The number one being not as close to Harry as he possibly could. He never knew why. Hope had been easy to deal with growing up, and admittedly he saw himself the most in Hannah. It was Harry that was the odd one out for him. His son was quiet; his interests were staying in his room and going on walks by himself. He encouraged him in everything he could be it never seemed to be enough. It could have been for all he knew, but Cliff would never have known. Harry never opened up.

The Knight CEO walked into the guest house. It had been redone a few years ago. It was nice and more than enough room for the amount of time that Cliff expected to stay. He was hoping that he and Tiffany would be able to make up in a few days. Cliff just wasn't so sure that would happen though.

Fighting between him and Tiffany had become normal as time went on. When she came back from being kidnapped, she wasn't the same person. Cliff had felt guilty because of that. He knew it was in large part due to the fact that he had been living with Vivica under the impression they were legally married. While he did feel very guilty for that he had no idea that Tiffany had been alive. He witnessed the car explode; there were remains left that matched Tiffany's dental records… It wasn't as if he ran into Vivica's arms.

He sat down in the living room and sighed. That's when he heard a noise from the kitchen, and he turned around. "Well, I've been waiting for you to come home, all-day boy."

Cliff immediately jumped up. "Why are you here father?"

"I just wanted to let you know that I've spoken with members of the board. It will be announced next week that you will step down from Knight. I'll continue to allow you to live in the house of course. Now, don't worry I've arranged a nice severance pay." Rodrick explained to his son.

"If you think for a minute that I'm going to let you take the company back you are nuts. There is more to why you haven't been with the company in years than just me forcing you out, and you know it." Cliff yelled as he got up from the couch.

Rodrick stood at him face to face. "Boy you might be all grown up, but you are still a child. Don't take a tone with me."

Cliff rolled his eyes. "Old man, I'm not putting up with your bullshit. Terrorize the house staff for a few weeks, but don't think you are sticking around forever. If I find out you have been treating any member of my family and that includes Vivica badly, you will be out in a moment's notice."

"You still get hard for that little whore don't you. This town is full of red-heads with better upbringings than her. Move on boy! Tiffany might be her sister, but at least she has her head screwed on straight." Rodrick barked back.

"Vivica and my relationship or lack there of is none of your business." Cliff screamed as Tiffany walked in.

Rodrick saw this. "I'll leave you to alone." He walked out.

Tiffany walked over to Cliff and sat down on the couch. "I've had some time to think. I want you to move back in."

"Tiffany, I would love to, but if you don't agree with me, I don't see that happening."

"I know, but it is your house, and I think what would be best is that I move out." She shed a tear. "I've already made arrangements to stay at a hotel near the hospital."

Cliff sat down next to her and looked at her in the eyes. "Why would you move out? I said I would stay in the guest house. It's ridicules to leave."

"Do you love me, Cliff?" Tiffany asked.

"That is a stupid question. You know I love you." Cliff responded.

Tiffany shrugged. "I suppose it is. I guess the better question to ask would be if you are in love with me. Or if you ever have been."

He wanted to answer right away with yes, but he thought about it for a second. He never really thought about it. Yes, he did love her but was he in love with her? "I'm not sure. I think I do."

The doctor couldn't help but smile. "You know it is no secret I don't like my sister. My dislike boarders on hate but I do deep down love her to some extent. I know that for every terrible thing she has done to me, I've done something equally as bad. It all started when I came to town. She confronted me this afternoon…"

Cliff sighed "I'm sorry. I will make sure she tries to stay away."

"No, I don't want you too. I think we need time away from each other. You need to once and for all decide what you want. If it is Vivica then so be it. I won't say I'll be happy, but I'll understand. If it is me, then we will make an actual effort to fix our marriage."

"What if I want to fix now though?" Cliff immediately responded with.

Tiffany frowned. "Cliff, unfortunately, the only way I think the two of us can work is to get away from Vivica once and for all. I know that isn't possible for you though. So, I understand if you want just end things on a good note with me." She got up. She kissed him on the forehead. "Take a week or so to figure things out. I'll call you in a few days. I want you to know that I plan to make an actual effort on fixing things with Hannah and Harry as well."

"I love you." Cliff said crying.

"And I love you…" Tiffany walked out.

LUCY − 2018

Lucy had no idea why she was doing this, but she was. Vivica was with her because they had been having a working dinner making plans for the company's relaunch. She agreed to come with her to check on Austin. He had left her a text saying that there was an emergency at the house. She was reluctant, but it was eating at her throughout dinner. Lucy had obviously driven them both to dinner, so Vivica told her it was fine with her if she wanted to stop at the house to check on him. Lucy stopped the car.

"Why on earth did you stop here?" Vivica asked.

"This is Austin's house." Lucy said confused. "I just realized you never been here." Lucy said as she took her seatbelt off.

Vivica looked at the house with a blank expression. "I grew up in this house…" She finally blinked. "My step-father had grown up here as well. When my mother passed away, I sold it."

"I never realized that this was where you grew up. I just assumed…" She didn't know how to say that she assumed she grew up in a larger home.

"DJ refused to leave his childhood home. Between my mother's alimony payments, her job and his job they could have afforded somewhere nicer. Nadia constantly tried to get DJ to move somewhere nicer. She even offered to let us all move in with them on occasion. I always laugh at the fact that I ended up moving in by myself off and on for years." Vivica half smiled. She looked at Lucy. "Do you think that I could come in with you? I mean we are just going to tell him off anyway. I just want one last glimpse."

Lucy nodded. "Sure." They both got out of the car. They silently walked up the driveway to the front door. Lucy nocked, but it was half open already. The two women walked in. "Austin?" Lucy called.

"Well, it has changed a lot. I have to say modern furniture does make it at least a little nicer." Vivica admitted.

The blonde looked around. "Where the heck is, he? He said he was here." She walked into the kitchen as Vivica stayed in the living room. Lucy screamed. Vivica ran in. Lucy sank to her knees. Vivica saw the body and immediately got her phone out and called 911.

ONE MONTH LATER

Lucy hugged Austin's father as he got into the car to drive off. He had agreed to take his ashes with him. She walked over to Xander and Langley who were standing outside Austin's home. "Thanks, you guys for agreeing to help me pack up the rest of everything. His father took all he wanted."

"I want to make one thing clear. I didn't agree to any of this. I was told that I could either help out or have no phone for a month." Langley annoyed in tone said.

Xander gave Langley a dirty look. "We are happy to help. We know how hard it is for you even if things did end badly with Austin."

"I thought we would have been together forever." She admitted. She really did. Deep down she had been willing to forgive him. Lucy just needed the time. "I still can't believe he killed himself. He had so much life in him." Sure, he had turned out to be cheating on her but she still very much cared for him. The good times didn't just go away.

"So, what happens to the house?" Langley pondered.

"His father put it on the market. It probably will take a while to sell considering the death. However, it is a thought after area, so I don't expect it will be on the market for all that long." Lucy explained. "Why do you ask though?"

Langley shrugged. "I don't know... I'm just wondering... A girl can do that."

The male Kingsley rolled his eyes. "She is wondering because she doesn't want to leave Vivica's house." He crossed his arms.

The eldest Kingsley sighed. "Langley, we aren't going to live with Vivica forever. I want to be out by the end of the summer. I should have enough saved up by then."

"I wouldn't mind splitting with you, Lucy. I mean I've saved up a lot of money over the last few months. It would be cool to own some property."

"Well, we can definitely talk about it. I also have finally gotten around to talking with Vivica." She looked directly at Langley. "You are going to be going to Saint Agnes in the fall. So, long as you behave this summer. You have a few weeks left of school. I know you can get through this."

The youngest Kingsley smiled. "So, wait I'll get to go to school with Harry and Brad? And possibly people who don't think having a cabin up north means they have a second home?"

"What on earth do you think it means? You know what I don't care… Yes, it does mean that though." Lucy explained.

"No, for the thousandth time I wasn't forced into anything until after we had sex." Harry mumbled. He had been speaking with the lawyer that Cliff had hired all week long. It wasn't getting any easier. Saint Agnes had agreed to let him stay at the school and was allowing him to finish the semester at home. He only had a week or so left. If at all possible, he wasn't leaving his house Brad and Langley would come over daily though.

Things were not getting better. The curly haired teen had to shut down his social media accounts from constant bullying. His grandfather was apparently a very homophobic individual, and Hope had moved out along with Tiffany to the hotel. His mother had made an on-going effort to get to understand him though. Harry had to admit that he was grateful for that. That said he really didn't think that things were getting any better with her. It wasn't that Tiffany was homophobic. She wasn't. She just didn't seem to grasp who he was in general.

"I think that is enough for today." Cliff told the lawyer. "We should have enough for the trial this Friday. It should go rather smoothly." He stated.

"I hope it does…" Harry once again mumbled. He knew that it wouldn't change anything. He was going to be the gay Knight guy for the rest of his life. The one thing that Harry always wanted was taken from him. He never wanted his sexuality to define him. Yet, now it seemed that he had no choice but to flaunt it.

Cliff put his hand on Harry's shoulder. "Don't worry; things will get easier."

Harry groaned. These were the conversations he wanted to avoid. He never needed anyone in his life to know that he had ever had sex. It was the one benefit of being gay. Since getting pregnant was out of the picture, he could go through life with people thinking he was a virgin. Harry was more than ok with that assumption being made about him.

"So, what are your plans for the afternoon? Cliff asked his son.

"I'm probably just going to finish up my class work, and then Langley might come over." Harry said.

"Harry I just want you to remember you aren't in trouble. You are allowed to leave the house."

"So, if I were straight would I still not be grounded?" Harry was shocked he was able to ask that.

Cliff looked at him confused. "What do you mean?"

The teen sighed. "A video of me is doing stuff with someone else was released. If this had been a girl and myself would I still not be in trouble?"

"Well, I mean I guess the circumstances would be slightly different." Cliff admitted.

"Ok, so I am not punished because I'm a special snow flake now. Thank you for confirming that." Harry started to walk out.

Cliff walked over to him and stopped him. "Look, if you want to be punished you have to leave the house for three hours every day. You can't just go to your aunt's house either. You have to make a public appearance and take a photo of it, so I have proof. How is that for a punishment?"

The teenage boy shrugged. "I guess it is better than nothing…" Harry left.

He was trying his hardest to relate to Harry. Cliff didn't want to punish Harry because he had never in his life gotten into trouble. He felt bad telling his son that though. Tiffany even agreed with that. It didn't have anything to do if it was with a girl or not. He and Vivica got caught having sex in a broom closet once during their senior year of high school at school… He got a black eye from his father, but that was because he had to defend Vivica not because he was in trouble.

Cliff walked over to the desk in his home office and sat down.

"I don't need an appointment to see my brother-in-law!" Screamed Vivica as she made her way into the room. She slammed the door shut and looked at Cliff. She had a look of rage in her eyes. "Why are you avoiding me?"

"What are you talking about?" Cliff asked.

Vivica walked right up to him. "I have hardly said two words to you in a month. What the hell did I do to you? Holly told me I needed to keep my distance in light of all the things going on in your life. I agreed but only because Holly is the only one who knows how to work the laundry machine, and the coffee maker, and has the key to the liquor cabinet, and also drives me. Damn, I need to give Holly a raise…" She zoned out. "Anyway, why are you avoiding me? Is Tiffany making you keep your distance again?"

The curly haired CEO was shocked. "I thought you knew." He waited for Vivica to respond but she didn't. "Weston, Tiffany and I have separated. No one has told you about this?"

The redhead started to speak but kept stopping herself. She finally found the proper words… "I've been relaunching a business while helping my business partner get through the death of her fiancé. I'm so sorry that I'm not twenty-five anymore and climbing through your window at the first sign of trouble in your marriage."

Cliff remembered when she had done that. Tiffany had not been thrilled. "Well, I just assumed someone would have told you. Such as Tiffany."

"I blocked her phone number like two years ago. I try to avoid her at all costs. She blames me for things I have no control over such as the rain... You know, I'm not the one who stole her fiancé and yet that is the way people treat me." Vivica spat.

"Why are you acting so unhinged?" Cliff stupidly asked.

Vivica rolled her eyes. "Let's go over this one more time... I'm relaunching a business, and my business partner has been a chocolate mess. On top of that, the little blonde-haired girl that has been living with me is trying to get with my son."

"Langley?" Cliff asked.

"Yeah, sure let's go with that. I'm not particularly sure that I like her." Vivica's eyes widened. "Wait, a minute why are you and Tiffany separated?

"Things just haven't been working out as of late. I'm honestly shocked that you didn't know. I just assumed..." Cliff said.

Vivica looked at him. "Assumed what? That, I'd be running to you with an engagement ring?" She joked.

Cliff raised his elbows. "Well yes..."

Vivica gave him a dirty look. "Cliff once again, I'm not twenty-five years old anymore. If you notice over the past few years, I haven't been trying to get you back."

"I'm not saying you have. It's just in the past..." Cliff explained.

"Which is just that. The past." Vivica said confused at what he was trying to get at.

The CEO cleared his throat and got up from his chair. "I'm sorry. I just... I don't know what I assumed. You were just being so helpful with Harry and everything."

"Like I told Tiffany a few weeks back, I did help raise that boy when he was much younger. Even if I hadn't, he is still my nephew and your son. I'd move mountains to help someone I care about, and I've always cared about Harry, Hannah, and Hope." Vivica explained.

Cliff was unsure why Vivica was all of a sudden so upset. He honesty thought that she would have been excited at the prospect of him being separated from Tiffany. Then he realized the reason. He wanted Vivica back... Which meant... "I have to go see Tiffany." He grabbed his wallet and keys and headed for the door. He then turned back. "Can we have dinner tonight? Our place?"

Vivica looked at him with disgust. "I don't know... For all, I know you think I still watch reruns of *Bewitched* religiously every night."

"You have them all on DVD... I'll see you tonight." He left.

Vivica – 2018

"I'm not sure why you are so upset." Holly admitted.

Vivica sat down at the kitchen table with a cup of coffee. "I just am. I don't know... I guess at this point I just gave up on Cliff ever being single again."

"So, you aren't going to go after him?" Lucy asked.

"Well, I'm not saying no. It's just that this has been a year of change and while it hasn't been all positive in the execution, I've figured things out." The reality is she did want Cliff back. He was still the love of her life. He still gave her butterflies when she saw him. The issue was that when he mentioned he was single this afternoon, she wasn't jumping with joy. "I'm in my forties, and I think I've finally matured enough to not make rational choices."

Holly and Lucy looked at one another. "Vivica, you will never get to that point. It's not in your nature to do so." Holly explained.

"So, I'm not allowed to grow up? I have to be a caricature of a person my entire life?" Vivica couldn't believe what she was hearing.

Lucy put her hand on Vivica's wrist. "You are not the same person you were when you were sixteen. It's just well deep down you want Cliff. If he is indeed single are you going to attempt a relationship with him?"

She thought about it for a minute. "Well, of course I am. We belong together. I just don't want him or anyone else thinking that I've been waiting for him to be single."

"Haven't you though?" Holly asked.

"Not really. Well, ok yes." Vivica started to feel like an idiot. She had been waiting for him to be single. That said, she also knew that the chances of that happening before he was in his eighties was limited to none. It was one thing to flirt harmlessly. It was just harmless in her mind even if Vivica didn't think so. "It's a complicated situation."

Holly cleared her throat. "So, what will you do next?"

Harry – 2018

He had to give his father the benefit of the doubt. Cliff was trying, and he knew that he was. Harry knew though that his father could be a little too liberal at times, which was his own father's fault. Harry had seen very little of Rodrick Knight since he had moved in. Harry assumed that was due to Cliff being protective. That said, the house also was rather large, and it wasn't as if they ever ate meals together aside from his birthday.

The curly haired boy walked into the library at Saint Agnes. This was the only place he knew that he could go and not be bothered. He knew that Langley would criticize him for that, but he didn't necessarily have to tell her. Harry looked around and of course, saw next to no one. He didn't even see Sister Mary Newman at her desk, which he was somewhat relieved.

Harry went to his usual chair in the back corner and sat down. He grabbed a textbook and started to do his homework. Half-way through the chapter, he was completely hooked on his assignment when someone tapped him on the shoulder. Harry quickly turned, and it was the nun herself. "Sister Mary Newman? I didn't see you when I came in…"

"I haven't seen you in a few weeks. Where have you been?" She pondered.

"You didn't hear or well see?" Harry half mumbled.

Sister Mary Newman sat down on a stool. "Well, yes but I was surprised that you went into hiding. You have always seemed like such a strong young man."

Harry wasn't sure if she was just old and confused or what. "Um, that is like the complete opposite of my personality."

"Strange. It's just the boy that I've witnessed grow up over the years didn't seem like that at all." She shrugged.

The teen wasn't sure what to make of what she was saying. "I think you are confusing me with someone else."

"You are Harry Knight are you not?"

"Yeah, I'm Harry..." He confusingly admitted allowed.

"Straight A student, perfect attendance until now, you have two older twin sisters? One sort of a bitch the other kind of space?" Sister Mary Newman asked.

Now he was just completely unsure of what was going on. "Are nuns allowed to swear?"

Sister Mary Newman laughed. "You should have been around back when we were still encouraged to hit the children. I never did, but yes, we can swear... Though technically we shouldn't be in a Catholic school... The point I am trying to make Mister Knight now is that I'm disappointed in you."

Over the past month, he had received letters from distant relatives saying that he should be ashamed, his mother and sister had distanced themselves, and he had to delete his social media. Yet, an almost ancient nun being disappointed was what hit the hardest. "Well, I'm sorry you feel that way. I didn't mean to make the sex tape."

"Sex tape? Oh, who cares about the sex tape. Who doesn't have a sex tape nowadays? Well, I don't, but you know what I mean."

Harry was pretty sure that Langley had one or two that she was less than afraid of. "So, what are you disappointed about then?"

"I'm disappointed that you are not out there celebrating. You get to be yourself finally!" Sister Mary Newman declared.

"Wait, you mean you are upset that I'm not sashaying around town declaring my attraction to men?" Harry asked.

The nun nodded. "It's something to celebrate."

The boy put his hand on his forehead and rubbed it. "I'm sorry to disappoint you, but that is just not me."

Sister Mary Newman frowned. "Do, you know how many people I've known in this town over the years? I was friends with your great-grandmother. It was her, Susan Fitzpatrick, and me. We were the best of friends back in the 60's..."

"I never knew that. Who is Susan Fitzpatrick though?" Harry asked.

"One of the best people I ever knew. She was a lot like you. Quiet but intelligent. When you finally got her to open up, you could talk with her for hours about nothing. She was Brandon Fitzpatrick's older sister." Mary Newman explained.

Harry was shocked that he had never heard of this sister. Brad had never mentioned her, and he never saw any pictures of her anywhere in the Fitzpatrick mansion. "Whatever happened to her."

The nun frowned. "She, unfortunately, passed away very young. It was shortly after Brandon and Nadia's wedding. It was quite the event, and she was so happy she managed to live that long to see it. She had cancer." She looked at the teenage boy and could see he was calming down a little bit. "It was sort of a miracle that she managed to show up for the wedding. Susan had left town for some years before the wedding. Brandon was the one who wanted her at the wedding."

"What about her parents? Seamus and Ida? I think those were their names." Harry stated.

"Yes, Seamus and Ida. Two of the hardest working people I'd ever have the privilege of knowing. They had issues with Susan though. They loved her so dearly and, in the end, stood at her side. I was so happy that they were able to reconcile before she passed." The nun stood up from the stool and sat on the arm of Harry's chair. "Susan Fitzpatrick was a lesbian. The first gay person I had ever known."

Harry looked at the nun in complete shock. "I had no idea about her. If the family had made up then why are there no pictures?"

"Oh, like Margot is going to let that become public knowledge. The woman who slept with half the continent of Europe is embarrassed by a woman she maybe knew for about a month. There used to be pictures of her all over the house before Brandon and Nadia retired. You just are too young to remember probably."

"Well, I'm still not sure where you are going with this? Do I have cancer? Are you trying to tell me I have cancer?" Harry started freaking out.

Mary Newman put her hand on his shoulder. "Relax my child… No. You don't have cancer. I'm just trying to explain to you that you are living in a different era. You are allowed to embrace yourself in a way that Susan never was able to. I can only imagine what she would have been like had she not passed away."

The curly haired boy was now starting to realize where she was getting at with this. "I get it. I don't know if I want to be out and proud like some people. I want to live an average life."

"Well, who is to say you can't? You can embrace who you are without dying your hair shades or rainbows and demanding special treatment. I'm sure that there are things you always wanted to do when you were in the closet but never got too out of fear that it would label you as different." She pointed out.

She had a point. There were things he had always wanted to do. Things that he regretted he didn't do years earlier. "Thanks for the talk, Sister Mary Newman. I'd love to get to know more about Susan, and I'm sure Brad would as well."

"Oh, you are welcome my child. Nadia gave me her diaries quite some years ago. I've read over them a billion times over. I feel like she'd have liked someone like you to be able to read them. I can get them for you sometime."

VIVICA – 1986

The redhaired teen sat on the couch next to her mother. Gale had no moved from the couch in what seemed like a week aside from going to the bathroom. Vivica was worried about her but also had no idea what to do. The funeral had come and gone, and Vivica was unsure of how her mother would move on. "Do you want to go see a movie?" Vivica asked with frustration in her voice.

"Vivica, Erica, and Adam are yelling at each other right now. I'm trying to pay attention."

"You don't even like daytime TV." Vivica pointed out.

Gale looked at her daughter. "Well, maybe I just never gave it a chance. I tried watching that one you like. I couldn't get passed the upbeat theme music."

Vivica thought for a moment. "Mother I like *As the World Turns* not *Another World.*"

"Oh, who cares. They are all the same… Rachel, Erica, Tina… What the heck is the difference? I get why you like them though. It's watching other people suffer."

"I suppose that is why some people like them… Seriously, why don't we go to a movie or lunch?" Vivica once again tried suggesting.

Gale crossed her arms. "I don't have any desire to leave this house ever again."

"Well, then I guess I'm quitting school." Vivica stated.

The brunet mother looked at her daughter. "I never gave you permission to stay home all day."

Vivica laughed. "Who said I was staying home as well? If you don't leave the house, one of us has to work. Let's see what can a teenage girl without an

250

education do for a profession? Oh, I know prostitute. I'm sure Cliff will just love that."

"Stop being melodramatic… The money we get from your father along with DJ's life insurance will pay for us to live fine." Gale said annoyed.

Vivica got up. "Wonderful… You just sit on this couch and sulk mother. I'm going out." Vivica rolled her eyes. She headed towards the door and Cliff was standing on the other side ready to knock. "Let's go." She screamed at him and grabbed his wrist. Vivica slammed the door behind her, and they walked to the end of the driveway. "I want to be anywhere but here right now."

"So, you are talking to me again?" Cliff asked.

The teenage girl looked at him in anger. "What does that mean? Of course, I'm talking to you. You are my boyfriend after all…"

"Well, how would I know? I haven't spoken with you in three days. You avoided me completely at the funeral and ignored all my phone calls." Cliff barked back.

"I'm so sorry that I haven't been readily available to you while I dealt with my step-father's death. How selfish of me…"

Cliff realized how that sounded. "I'm sorry. I know you are dealing with a lot right now."

That was the understatement of the century. "I'm sorry too. Though I really shouldn't. You knew exactly what you were getting into when you agreed to be my boyfriend." Vivica laughed.

"I think it was more the other way around. You agreed to be my girlfriend." Cliff pointed out.

"So, seriously I want to be anywhere but here. I'd even take an afternoon watching Mrs. Templeton treat her staff like slaves." Vivica was still laughing.

The curly haired boy cringed. "Do you know how creepy that woman is? She literally lives down the street from me. I swear I once saw her baptizing squirrels in her backyard."

"This one Thanksgiving, she somehow ended up at the Fitzpatrick house for dinner. She spent half the meal discussing how much she hates the Irish and Spanish…"

"So, she was criticizing the entire room but your mother?" Cliff asked.

Vivica nodded. "Pretty much." The two smiled at each other. Maybe it was because Mrs. Templeton was batshit crazy and easy to make fun of. Vivica was just happy to be able to move forward with Cliff finally. She just hoped that her mother could find a comfortable life without DJ.

VIVICA – 2018

Vivica knocked on Brad's door, and he quickly opened. "We need to talk for a moment." She walked in without getting a response. She sat down on his bed. "So, I need advice, and I can't ask Holly or Lucy about it. Lucy is still dealing with Austin's death, and Holly is judgmental."

Brad sat down at his desk chair. "Ok, I'm listening…"

"Should I have another attempt at a relationship with Cliff?" Vivica asked.

The blond boy looked at her for a few minutes. "I think that is up to you." He finally responded with.

The redhaired mother crossed her arms. "Well, this would affect you just as much as it would be. I need your honest opinion."

"I've learned not to get my hopes up when it comes to you or dad's relationships. I think uncle Cliff is an awesome guy, but it is your choice if you want to get back together or not." Brad said.

"Well, you and Harry could be step-brother's again possibly." Vivica pointed out.

Brad shrugged. "I guess, but I already consider him my brother even without you being married to uncle Cliff anymore. I guess you finally heard about him and aunt Tiffany splitting up."

The mother looked at her son right in the eyes. "Even you knew before I did? Why didn't you say anything?"

The son looked at the mother. "Do I need to respond to that?"

She guessed he didn't. "I don't know what to do…"

"The only thing I want for you mom is for you to be happy. Uncle Cliff has always made you happy. Dad, not so much…"

He was right. "How did I raise such a smart son?" She asked aloud.

"So, do you know what you are going to do now?" Brad asked.

"Oh, not a clue," Vivica admitted. Someone knocked on the door. They walked in, and it was Langley. Vivica looked at the pretty young blonde girl. "Dear, what are you doing here?"

"Brad and I were going to go and visit Harry together." She said.

Brad got up from his chair. "Yeah, we will be back a little later."

She couldn't put her finger on it, but there was just something she didn't like about this Langley girl. Vivica wasn't going to get in the way of things for her and Brad though. "Well, have fun I guess…"

Vivica's phone rang. She looked at the contact. "Hello. Yes, I suppose we can meet. I will be there in a little bit."

***

The redhead might have been in charge of the hospital gala every year, but she was never very fond of Grosse Pointe General Hospital. It had such a cliché name and was no different than any other hospital in the area. She has given birth to both her children at the hospital and neither time went over well. She walked down a narrow hall until she found the office she was looking for. Vivica couldn't believe she was doing this. She didn't even bother to knock. "Hello, Tiffany."

"You can take a seat." The brunet doctor told her younger sister. "I think it is time we had a little talk about Cliff." Tiffany sat down herself.

"I suppose it is." Vivica couldn't stand the way Tiffany spoke in general. It was always as if she was better than everyone else.

The older sibling cleared her throat. "Cliff and I are separated. That doesn't mean we are divorced. So, go on your dates, kiss him, feel him up, do whatever… Just remember at the end of the day he will choose me over you."

That was something worth laughing about. "He picked you the first time because of a misunderstanding. He picked you the second time because Cliff wanted his children to be around their mother. Cliff has grown a lot in that time and is finally seeing things in reality and not just in the fictional world that you have created in your head."

Tiffany stood up and walked over to the window. She looked outside. "We aren't in college anymore fighting over a man. We are two grown women. I'm married, and you can't accept that."

"As I have already told everyone else, I'm not interested in fighting you or anyone else for that matter over a man. I don't mind being single at this point. Cliff will always be special to me, but if the time we spent together is all I will get from him then so be it." Vivica meant every word. She could go either way with Cliff. She loved the man but hated what he has become thanks to Tiffany's influence.

"Well, I hope you mean that." Tiffany responded with.

Vivica didn't respond. She just walked out of the office and slammed the door shut behind her. Her life was finally where she wanted it. The whore from Beverly Hills was finally her person. She took the title from Rodrick Knight with a sense of entitlement from him. Her phone started to ring, and Tiffany rushed out of her office. "Move. Rodrick is being moved to surgery." She spat at her as Vivica looked confused. The phone stopped ringing. It had been Cliff. Hannah then left her a text message asking if she needed a ride to the hospital. Rodrick had a heart attack.

CLIFF – 2018

The emergency room was the worst part of the hospital. He had personally paid once for it to be remodeled, but it still had a bad attachment to it. A nurse had assured him everything would be fine. Cliff had so many things going through his head. The man and him had never gotten along. Rodrick was his father because he had gotten his mother pregnant and that was about it. He wanted a son for superficial reasons. They never played catch together, he never helped him with his homework, and he never gave him any solid advice. Yet, he was worried about him at this moment. The CEO sat down on a chair because he started to feel dizzy. He closed his eyes for one second and then he felt a hand. He turned to look. "Weston?"

"So, remember that time Brianna made us watch that Molly Ringwald movie like five times in a weekend? That girl just has an unhealthy obsession with read heads." Vivica went on.

"Well, who could blame her? She had a pretty good taste." Cliff smiled.

Vivica shrugged. "It's a good thing she grew up in a town filled with redheads. There must be something in the water. Then again, I'm from Beverly Hills."

They were talking as if they were in high school again. This was the distraction that he needed right now. "Thank you."

"Oh, Cliff. You have always been my Knight in shining armor. It's time the queen of Grosse Pointe pays you back."

"Weston, you have so many times over." Cliff started to randomly think about all the thing that Vivica had done over the years. Even within the last few weeks. Vivica had taken so much charge in helping Harry through everything. She was the confidant that Hannah needed as well. He realized that the best thing for him to do was just to shut up and wait.

Hours passed. Hannah and Xander showed up. Hope came back and forth between breaks and downtime at the hospital. Harry even showed his face along with Langley and Brad until the other two had to get ready for school in the morning. They all had finals but insisted on sticking around. Cliff could tell that Vivica was uncomfortable with how close Langley was getting with Brad. He had to admit it fascinated him; he was reminded of them at their age. He could also tell that his two daughters were about to disagree on yet another subject. This one being who got possession of the Kingsley boy. Cliff had been told that Tiffany was overseeing everything, which did help him a little bit.

Suddenly he woke up after what seemed like days. It was just the middle of the night though. Tiffany walked over. "Good. You are awake." She looked at Vivica who was passed out next to him. "He is awake and is ready to see you." Tiffany explained. She put out her hand, and he grabbed it.

"Is he able to talk and move alright?" Cliff asked.

"I wouldn't recommend he get up from his bed, but his speech does seem to be alright. It was touch and go for a while. Personally, I don't think he needs any visitors but he said that if you were around that he needed to speak with you right away." She led him right to the door of Rodrick's private hospital room. "I'll leave you both alone." She walked away.

The current Knight CEO opened the door and took a deep breath. Rodrick was lying on his back. He looked vulnerable. Cliff had never seen his father look so vulnerable. "Hello, father."

Rodrick raised the bed so he could be sitting up. It was slow, but it managed to find its way up. He looked at his son. "I suppose you thought I was going to die?"

"I wasn't sure what to think. I didn't know you were having heart problems." Cliff admitted. He had spoken with Rodrick's primary doctor only a few hours earlier for the first time. The man acted as if this was all important information that any child of an aging parent should have. Cliff didn't disagree, but Rodrick was far from his parent. "You are supposedly alright now."

"Well, I'm not going anywhere anytime soon. As soon as I get out of this room, the first thing I am doing is getting you removed from Knight." The old man stated.

This was just never-ending. His father would never be voted in as CEO again. His management of the company was terrible. Rodrick was in big part of the downfall of the 2008 crash, and he hadn't even been forced out two years before that. "If you say so." Cliff said monotone. He wasn't going to argue with a man in bad health even if he was Rodrick Knight. The man who never treated him right. "Phillis called. She sends her love."

"That disappointment of a daughter said no such thing. Did my brother call? Your namesake? Let me guess he didn't have anything to say?" Rodrick pondered.

Cliff rolled his eyes. His sister Phillis did send her love… Reluctantly but none the less. "I was able to get in contact with Uncle Clifton. He said he hoped you felt better." That part was the lie. His uncle was beyond estranged from the family. He had tried to reunite with the family back in the nineties, but it didn't work out. "Luke wishes you well as well." This was true. Vivica had texted him, and he sent him a text after the fact. Cliff hated the fact that Vivica still talked with Luke on occasion.

"Oh, good lord… I don't know what to believe. I'll figure it out when I get out of here and am back in my office." Rodrick stated proudly.

"Do you honestly think it is the right time to get back to work? Take my job. I don't care, but in all honesty, do you think you are ready?" Cliff asked.

The old man grimaced. "*Knight* is my birthright. My grandfather always said so. It was wasted on my father in the same way it has been wasted on you."

As much as he hated to admit it, Cliff often thought the same thing. The company was never his dream; he got stuck with it because Tiffany was insistent upon it. "Why do you even want the company back?"

"Well, for starters I want to make sure that your fagot never is employed even as a janitor in the company. Don't think I won't use my connections to get him blacklisted everywhere else as well. The little fruit's life is over as he knows it. At least he knows how to turn tricks for the camera."

"So, do you old man …" Cliff spat out.

Rodrick looked at his child. "What did you say?"

"My son liking boys is not important to who he is as a person. Until he has slept with every man in town like you did every woman you have no room to judge." Cliff crossed his arms. He wasn't going to allow his father to bad mouth or belittle his child.

"You are weak. You always have been. Cliff, you are a Knight. Knight's take charge, we protect ourselves though. Just like I did back when I found out my father had another child." Rodrick rambled.

Cliff looked at him. "What do you mean your father had another child? Aside from you and Uncle Clifton?"

He laughed. "Oh yes, my father was a sleaze bag just like myself as you would put it. He fucked the maid on the side. Only to get back at grandfather though. Grandfather sure did love our maid. I'm the only one who ever knew. I was fourteen at the time."

The son thought about this for a minute. The entire town knew the story of Brandon and Nadia. Brandon was a rag to riches story. Nadia was his childhood sweetheart. Her mother had been the Knight family's maid… "DJ Brash was my uncle?"

"Ugh, who calls a grown man DJ? Yes, David Brash, the second was your uncle. You and Nial Fitzpatrick have even more in common than you thought. You both like near incest experiences. Personally, even I'm not that disgusting."

Cliff started to feel dizzy. The man who he spent most of his childhood making small talk with was a blood relative. "How are you certain all this happened?"

"Benton was ambitious. He went after what grandfather wanted and practically had. One day I got off early at school and walked in on Benton and the maid. Whatever the hell her name was. It was far from traumatizing, but grandfather heard me and walked in beside me. I didn't tell mother because I didn't quite care for her in the first place. I never really did. Benton had other affairs, but this one was just sex for him. I think it was a one and done deal. I will give props when deserved though. That maid hated him beforehand."

Something that Rodrick had said earlier hit Cliff. "How did you take care of DJ?"

"Oh that… Well, do you remember when you were so against me firing the *Fitzpatrick Group* as the contractors for that dealership? Well, I simply wanted to get DJ blacklisted back then. You wouldn't leave things be. I had no choice; I couldn't risk anyone finding out about DJ. I paid off a few of his co-workers and made sure he was crushed to death." Rodrick had a giant smile on his face.

His father was a monster. Cliff knew this though. He had always known this. The son just never realized how horrible he could be until now. He looked at his father who was now laughing. There were so many things he wanted to say. Cliff couldn't say them though. Instead, he ran for the door and kept on running. He accidentally bumped into Vivica about halfway from Rodrick's room. "I'm sorry."

"Are you alright? Tiffany refused to tell me if he was going to make it." Vivica looked at her former lover and could tell something was wrong. "What's going on?" She asked confused and scared.

"We... We will talk later." He walked quickly out of her sight. He couldn't face her right now.

VIVICA – 2018

The redhead had known Cliff for so long. She knew that as brave and noble as he was there was one person who could always rip him to shreds. Not anymore. Vivica marched herself towards Rodrick's room. She walked in and slammed the door shut. The old man turned and looked at her. "What did you do to Cliff?"

"I think the real question is what didn't you do to Cliff? How is my little whore doing? Oh, wait how rude of me. How is my big whore doing?" Rodrick laughed.

Vivica walked right up to his bed and looked him straight in the eyes. "I'm not a sixteen-year-old anymore. Neither is your son. I won't let you talk to him that way anymore. Do you understand me?" Vivica demanded.

Rodrick looked at her for a second in a serious stature. Then he started laughing. "I don't listen to whores. If you want money, by all means, go for my wallet. All you have to do is what your nephew did to that boy."

"You bastard!" Vivica slapped him across the face. "Let me make one thing clear. You can call me a whore all you want. You can rip me to shreds. You will not ever again utter a word about Harry or Cliff ever again. For that matter, you won't utter a word about Hope or Hannah either. If you do, I will personally end your life. Do you understand?"

"You don't have it in you… I will say what I want about my family. If it weren't for me none of them would be here right now." Rodrick crossed his arms. "The little fag will soon be removed from just like I am his father."

Vivica looked around the room. She noticed his IV. She yanked it from his arm. "What did I tell you?"

"What the hell is wrong with you?" Rodrick screamed. He went for his alert button, but Vivica grabbed it before he could press it. "I need that put back in me." The redhead said nothing. She just stared at him. "If you don't think I won't sue you I will."

"I hope you can find a very good lawyer in hell because that is where you are going. Actually, you might be in luck down there…" Vivica made a joke. She always made jokes when she was nervous. Could she go through with this? The man was horrible, but she couldn't take someone's life. The redhead dropped the pager. "You aren't worth prison…"

Rodrick laughed. "Awe the little whore is giving up halfway. Just like all your marriages." Vivica slapped him clear across the face. "That hardly hurt."

This man had long been a burden on society. The year he was exiled was one of the best of her life. "You know what. I truly do hope you burn in hell one day. I'm going to go and find your son who with any luck will bury you in a cardboard box." Vivica screamed as she stormed out of the room. As she walked, doctors started to run towards the room. Tiffany was one of them. Vivica could hear a noise in the distant. She peaked back in the room. "Oh, thank God…"

HARRY – 2018

After giving it much thought, he knew that Sister Mary Newman was right. The curly haired boy looked at himself in the mirror of his bedroom. He was wearing a white tuxedo. The funeral of his grandfather was in a few hours. Cliff had informed him that the family was making a statement by wearing white to the funeral. The guests in attendance were not going to be made aware. Harry thought it was petty, but at the same time, it wasn't as if his grandfather had ever been very good to him.

"Is it alright if I come in?" Hannah asked without even knocking. "Good. I need to talk with you about the Kingsley family."

Harry turned around. "Why?"

"Do you think that I have a chance with Xander?" Hannah blurted out.

The brother looked at his sister in confusion. "Well, I mean if you want then I guess you could go for it. I thought that Hope liked him though."

Hannah sunk her face in one of his pillows. "She does... Or well she likes him because I like him."

"I'm not really sure what you want me to tell you. I mean... I love you?" Harry said.

The older sibling laughed. "I love you too. I hope that you do know that."

He sighed. "You and everyone around me doesn't have to remind me of that every five minutes." His mother had been sending him text messages non-stop lately. He was sick of people reminding him. "Do you know how you can show me you love me? Just let me be me."

"Alright. If you want to be a moody and anxious teenager go for it." Hannah explained.

"That's all I ever wanted." Harry put on a small smile.

"That may be the most I have ever seen you smile." Hannah joked.

"What are you two going on about? We are going to our grandfather's funeral." Hope said as she walked in the door.

Harry honestly couldn't tell if she was serious at first, but she was. This man had tormented their father and aunt for years. Hope was acting like they had reason to mourn his loss. "Why would you be sad about grandpa dying?"

Hope's eyes widened. "Just because he was less than a good person doesn't mean he wasn't our grandfather. Honestly, Harry the things you say and do lately…"

The other twin decided it was her turn to speak. "Hope dear, it's time to get the stick out of your ass already. Harry has done nothing wrong."

"Well, sure you wouldn't think so my dear sister." Hope smiled and walked out. "We are leaving as a family in five minutes." Hope screamed from outside the room.

The curly haired boy looked at himself in the mirror one last time. He smiled. "This might sound morbid, but I honestly do look at today as a new beginning."

"That's a good way to think about it. If only I wasn't into Xander…"

VIVICA – 2018

"Well, how do I look?" She asked as she walked down the living room staircase of her house. Lucy was on her computer and Holly was pretending to dust in a dress.

Lucy looked up. "Oh, you look nice. You always look nice though. Vivica we might have a bit of an issue."

Vivica walked over to Lucy and sat down next to her. "What could possibly be the issue?"

"Mrs. Templeton… She has written bad reviews on every platform about us. I think she might even have sock puppet accounts." Lucy explained as she scrolled through a webpage. "Such as this one… *The worst party I ever have been too. I asked for a French salon style party. I got a five-dollar pizza and a clown. I think the owner of the businesses maid might be a hooker on the side.*"

"That closet case wishes…" Holly said as she dusted the air.

The redhead shrugged. "Well, then we will get out of the party planning business. There are so many other things we can get involved in. I did cosmetics for a while." She thought about it for a moment. "Actually, we can't go back to that. Margot owns the rights to all my cosmetics."

The blonde rubbed her forehead. "We can't just randomly change businesses mid into a relaunch."

"Sure, we can Lucy. I randomly change my mind constantly, and it always works out for me." Vivica explained.

"It's true. Just ask Cliff, Nial, and Luke…" Holly said under her breath.

Vivica turned around. "We aren't talking about my love life. Let's put a pin in this for the moment. I need to talk to you both about something serious."

"What could be more important than our business?" Lucy asked.

Holly sat down on one of the armchairs. "Cliff Knight."

"Exactly!" Vivica admitted. "I've decided that I am going to flirt with the idea of going back to Cliff."

"So, then you are going to get back together with him?" Holly asked.

"No. I am going to consider it though. I need more time to think about things. I do think that things could work in our favor though." Vivica was still on the fence. She wanted to be with Cliff more than anything in the world. She just needed more time to decide properly. "This is a big decision for me. I'm no longer twenty. If I decide to get married again, then I plan to do it with the assumption that it will be the last time."

The maid did a facepalm. "You shouldn't be going into marriage at any age thinking that it won't last."

Vivica shrugged. "My second marriage to Nial was based around money. I initially married Luke as a way to piss off Cliff. Cliff is the only one that really has ever mattered."

"So, you didn't love dad?" Brad asked as he walked down the stairs wearing a white suit.

The mother stood at the question asked by her son. She looked at her maid and business partner. "I need a moment alone with my son." The two understood and walked in the kitchen. "Holly turn the music on. You aren't listening in!"

"I know your actual birth year woman!" The maid screamed back.

"Just pretend you didn't hear anything for once..." She crossed her arms and walked over to the staircase. "Your father and I have always had an interesting relationship."

Brad looked at his mother. "You asked me if I was alright with you marrying uncle Cliff. I want you to be happy, but mom he has never been able to commit to you."

Vivica looked at her son. "Well, neither has your father." She remembered Nial hitting on her maid-of-honor at their first, second, and third weddings. "One day when you are older you will understand what it is like to want something so badly that you are willing to wait."

"A person who married your sister over you was worth it? He was given a second chance to make things right. This town loves to talk. We all know he had his choice and he still picked aunt Tiffany." Brad reminded her.

All these things were true. She had thought about them over and over again. Day after day for a year. Her son had a point though. There was a knock at the door before she could try responding. "That must be the car. We will be going with Cliff and the children. Lucy and Holly are being driven straight behind us with Xander and the girl."

"Langley?" Brad stated.

For the second time in a short period, Vivica facepalmed herself. "Don't remind me of the girl again. I swear she better be wearing an appropriately fitted skirt." This little girl was making her sound like her mother. It pissed her off. "Remind me to call your grandmother later. I owe her an apology." After all these years Vivica finally realized how Nadia felt when Nial and her announced their engagement.

CLIFF – 2018

It was forecasted to rain that day, but it didn't. It was bright and sunny and near-perfect weather. The public funeral had been the day before. People of all walks of life showed up. Factory workers who had been around when Rodrick was a child. Cliff was honestly shocked. His father was far from a good man, and it was public knowledge. If he had to guess half these people only showed up to make sure he was finally dead.

Cliff had been in contact with his lawyers as well as Rodrick's. It was clear that there were more surprises in store for him after the funeral, but he didn't care. He looked around the cemetery as a group of high up executives sat around. It didn't seem like anyone was crying or sad. Hope had a few tears, but Hannah and Harry were rolling their eyes on both sides of her. Tiffany was sitting next to him and Vivica on the other. It was odd, but Tiffany didn't seem to mind it at all. They had spoken the night before and agreed they would go public with their divorce at the end of the month. It was the most civil conversation the two had, had in months.

They had a prenup already, so there wasn't anything to discuss. Harry would split his time between them. Tiffany didn't want his life to be interrupted. He didn't either. She even offered to give him her wedding ring back, but Cliff told her to keep it and give it to one of the girls one day. Something had changed in Tiffany, and he was grateful for it. He would have stayed married to her. They both knew that wasn't for the best though.

His sister Phyllis, uncle Clifton and aunt Dallas were not in attendance. He received calls from each of them explaining why it wouldn't be appropriate for them to be there. He understood. If it hadn't been a PR nightmare, Cliff himself wouldn't have shown up. His cousin Luke, however, was in attendance.

Rodrick had always treated Luke well, but only because he knew it pissed him off. Rodrick had always been public about this.

Now that he knew that his father was responsible for DJ's death, it really made everything that much easier for him. Cliff wasn't going to miss him. He never was in the first place though. He knew that he would have to tell Vivica soon about this, but as much as he didn't care if his father's funeral was ruined, he didn't want Vivica to embarrass herself.

The priest had stopped speaking, and now everyone was looking at Cliff. He stood up and walked towards the coffin that held Rodrick's body. The CEO cleared his throat. "My father lived his life the way he wanted. He didn't care what anyone thought about him, and if he ever did, he made sure that he won in the end. I think the turnout today is a great indication on his legacy. A legacy that will never be forgotten. We learn from our parents and hope to do better than them. Rodrick wouldn't agree with that. I thank you all for coming today. We will be meeting at the banquet hall in an hour." It was short, to the point, and the press knew better to report anything but the words he said.

He told his family to go on without him. Tiffany took the children. His dear friend Brianna Belle had flown in for the occasion. She was now sitting where Tiffany had been, and Vivica remained on his right side. It truly felt like the good old days for a moment. "He would have hated all of this."

"He really would have." Brianna said with a smile on her face.

"The bastard can rot in hell." Vivica half whispered.

They had waited until the body was buried. Cliff stood up and reached for Vivica's hand. "This is long overdue."

"What do you mean?" Vivica asked confused.

Brianna laughed. "Oh my gosh! I almost forgot about this. Let me find a good song for you."

VIVICA – 1986

"We are getting you out of that house Cliff!" Vivica screamed as they waited in the ER at GPGH. Rodrick had just punched his son in the face after an argument again. "My mother is completely off her rocker right now. You can stay in the guest room. When he comes to collect you, we will take him to court."

Cliff sighed. "I'll be ok Vivica."

The redhaired teen took out her makeup mirror. "Can you see how bad it is this time? Look with your left eye because your right eye might never open again..."

"I can't just leave. He will never allow it." Cliff explained. "One day after high school and college we will move far away together."

"He will never rest. Rodrick will make you miserable as long as he lives." Vivica crossed her arms. Brianna ran over.

"My parents gave me the message that you and Cliff were going to the hospital. I'm so sorry." She looked at Vivica to indicate that she could see that this was not good.

Cliff rubbed his forehead. "As I was telling Vivica, one day we will move far away from Grosse Pointe and never see or hear from my father again. We will only return when we hear a word that the old man has healed over."

"Why would you want to return for his funeral? He doesn't deserve your mourning." Vivica pouted.

"Who said we would mourn? No, we will return to dance on his grave..."

VIVICA– 2018

"So, can I have this dance, Weston?" Cliff smiled.

It all came back to Vivica. She looked at the freshly filled grave. "You know when I originally pictured this I thought there would be grass. I also thought that we would not be wearing white." She took his hand. "I'll just throw the dress out if it gets dirty…" She stood up. Brianna pressed play on her phone. Cliff put his hands on her waist, and she rested her face on his shoulder. "You know in a way; this is exactly what Rodrick always wanted."

"How is that?" Cliff asked.

"He would have liked having a whore dance for him on his grave."

Cliff looked at her. "I see no whore. Just a queen."

She hated when people called her the queen. Except right now… They danced for what seemed like an eternity…

HANNAH – 2018

Since they slept together, Hannah and Xander had grown closer. Yet, they were somehow even farther apart. Hope was like a wolf in that way. Hannah doubted her twin knew of the one-night stand, but she smelt blood none the less. Xander had asked Hannah over for lunch today though. She sat on Vivica's patio as she waited for him to appear. It didn't take long. He walked out with a tray of food in his own hands. Something she had never seen a man or anyone who wasn't a servant do in her life. "Hi." Hannah said.

Xander smiled and sat down. "So, I have some news."

"Oh really? What kind of news?"

"Well, I didn't want to say anything until anything was confirmed. It is now though. I've put my two weeks in at the dealership. My credentials are finally available. I will be training with the Grosse Pointe Police department. I realize it isn't as big a deal as say the NYPD, but it is a great start really." Xander explained.

Hannah's heart sunk a little. She wouldn't be working with Xander. "Oh, well I'm going to miss you."

The blond boy grinned. "Well, we will still see each other a lot. I'm still living across from you for right now. Lucy and I have been looking for a new place to rent though."

Hannah nodded. She was happy for him. She just didn't know where they stood. Then she walked out… "Did you tell my sister the good news?" Hope asked as she came out carrying a cake. "I'm so proud of you." She kissed him on the forehead. Xander kissed her back.

"Well, this is all great. I will leave you two to celebrate then." Hannah got up.

Xander stood up as well. "I thought we were going to all have lunch together?"

Hannah was never made aware that Hope would even be here. This was not what she agreed to. "I have to go into work." She lied. She walked back into the house and made her way into the living room.

"You know just so we are clear. I did win." Hope said from behind her.

Hannah turned around. "Sure, you did…" Hannah would have moved on if it weren't for that. This was war as far as she was concerned, and Hannah was due to win.

LUCY – 2018

Lucy told Langley she would be picking her up on her last day of school. Langley had wanted to wait for Harry and Brad to pick her up, but with all the death and everything lately, she realized that it was time she made an effort to get to know her sister more. They sat in traffic.

"I don't know why you went this way. We could have been home by now." Langley said with her arms crossed.

"Well, maybe this is a good time to talk. What exactly are your plans for the summer?" Lucy asked.

Langley looked at her. "How the heck would I know? I'm obviously not going to South Hampton like normal. Do we even own that property anymore?"

The older sister had no clue and didn't honestly care. "Well, at least next school year you will be back in a private school."

"With Harry and Brad!" Langley said. She emphasized Brad's name.

Lucy groaned. "Please, don't do anything stupid with Brad. The last thing we need is Vivica and Nial going after you or the two of us."

"Oh relax. Brad is not some fragile child. Besides, nothing is official between us yet." Langley looked at her sister and smiled. "We need to find you a man too."

"I think I need to take a break from having a romantic life for a while." Lucy almost choked on nothing. She meant it though. There was no reason for her to get back into the dating scene so soon after a breakup and the death of that same man. The police were still investigating the suicide.

They finally parked the car at Vivica's. Langley quickly got out of the car as soon as she saw Harry.

HARRY – 2018

Harry waved to Langley as he sat on his aunt's front porch along with his cousin Brad. "So, I have good news." He explained

"You met someone?" Langley guessed.

"Who on earth would I have met? No… Anyway, so my lawyer told me that the judge had made his verdict. I'm off the hook for everything. Todd is going to trial, and I will more than likely be called in to testify, but I think I will be able to handle it."

Brad put his hand on Harry's shoulder. "When that day comes, I'll be there."

"I will too. I can be all *Legally Blonde* and what have you." Langley added in excitement.

"I also have joined a gay/ straight alliance group in town. I don't know if I will be a regular member, but it will be interesting just to be able to talk with other people my age who also happen to identify as not straight." Harry explained. Sister Mary Newman had given him the pamphlet along with Susan's diaries. He had gotten through the first fifty pages of one of them, and Susan's thoughts were compelling.

Langley got out her phone. "Do they have a website? I'll sign up to. We can go together!"

A few months back Harry was sitting alone in his room reading by himself. He would talk with people at school but never see them outside of campus. Things had changed for him. He had his cousin back. He also had a best friend. Sure, she was completely over the top and possibly a little bit crazy, but she meant well, and it was clear that she genuinely thought of him as a friend. His father was making an effort to speak with and get to know him. His mother was trying her hardest to repair their relationship. Hannah demanded to spend time with him at least once or twice a week. Hope was still distant, but she was distant before he came out. They always loved each other in their own way.

It was a beautiful day. The first day of summer, he passed all his exams like he knew he would and he honestly was excited for once to be off school for three months. It meant he would get to spend time with his friends. The future was bright.

TIFFANY – 2018

The last few months had been hell for her. She lost her husband, her son went wild, and her one daughter returned to taunt the other as far as she was concerned. The only thing that seemed to help her as of late was therapy. Tiffany had been seeking the help of a resident therapist at GPGH. Doctor Nora Logan, she had been a friend of Tiffany's for years and was helping her recover from everything that had been transpiring. "I listened to your advice, and I'm just not sure that it is helping." Tiffany said distraught.

"Well, we have to fix some of the messes that the people who are supposed to be there to help you destroyed. Cliff has never been good for you. I encourage this separation and divorce. It should have happened years ago." Nora told her.

"I guess you are right." Tiffany responded.

"I'm always right." Nora said.

The door opened and in walked Margot. "Are you ready for lunch Tiffany?" She looked around the room. "I swore I heard a second voice."

The doctor looked at Margot confused for a moment. "Oh, I was just getting off a phone call with a friend of mine." Tiffany stood up. "Yes, I'm ready. Let's go somewhere nice. Anywhere but that diner that Cliff and Vivica love so much."

"We will go to the yacht club. Like, I would go to a diner. Lunch is on me."

Tiffany grabbed her purse and looked back at Nora who was still in the room. She gave her a gesture to be quiet while she left. "I love the yacht club."

"Who doesn't?" Margot asked in response.

VIVICA – 1986

The redhaired teen walked into her home only to be shocked. Her mother was not on the couch. "I'm home…" She called out in confusion. It was the last day of school. She had not yet looked at her final grades and honestly just didn't care at this point. It had been less than an idea year in her opinion. She didn't know anyone who would disagree with her. "Mom?"

"I'm in the kitchen!" Gale called out in a chipper voice. Vivica didn't know what she was going to be walking into, but she did anyway. There sat Gale with Nadia. They both were dressed properly and were smiling. "Finally, you are home! We have been waiting for you all day."

"I've been at school." Vivica reminded her mother.

Gale laughed. "Well, I suppose that must have slipped my mind. So, I think I owe you a bit of an apology."

Vivica had just dealt with several weeks of her mother being miserable and now all of a sudden, she was happy. Not only was she happy but she was with Nadia Fitzpatrick of all people. "Well thank you." She wasn't going to bother asking why she was saying sorry. "Cliff is going to be over in a little bit. I'm going to go and get changed out of this hideous uniform."

"Oh, Vivica I actually need you to babysit Nial tomorrow night." Gale explained.

'Why?" She asked confused.

Nadia put her hand on Gale's. "We are going wine tasting together. Brandon will be at the office late, and I don't trust Margot. It will only be for an hour or so. Don't worry; we will pay you for it. If Nial does anything wrong just tell us and we will punish him."

"Nadia, we are not accepting your money. We are family always and for-ever. Vivica will be happy to watch her cousin."

Vivica hardly considered Nial family. Her mother was in a good mood though, so she was willing to play along with whatever charade they were up to though. "I'll be in my room for a little bit…" She walked out of the kitchen and headed upstairs. Vivica honestly had no clue what had transpired in that kitchen today, but she was glad to see her mother not depressed. She had no clue what the future held, but she was happy that she seemed ready to return to the real world.

She walked into her bedroom, and the phone started to ring. Vivica quickly answered it. "Hello!" Vivica said.

"*Weston, it's me.*" Cliff said.

"How is my shining Knight? Ready to celebrate the end of this horrid year?" Vivica asked. This would be their first summer together as a couple.

"*I actually can't go out tonight.*"

"Why not?" Vivica asked.

"*Rodrick has booked me a ticket to Amsterdam. He wants me to spend the summer with my aunt and uncle.*" There was a sound of reluctance in his voice. "*The plane boards in a few hours. I had no clue about this until like five minutes ago. He already packed my bags.*"

Vivica sat down at her vanity. This couldn't be happening. This was supposed to be their first summer together as a couple. They were supposed to stay up all night together, go to Canada, and travel to New York, possibly Beverly Hills. "How long will you be gone?"

"*Honestly, I have no idea. I promise I will call you every day.*"

"Call me the minute you land. I love you, Cliff."

"*I love you, Weston. More than anything in the world.*" Cliff sounded as if he was fighting back the tears.

The redhead hung up the phone. She knew that he wasn't doing this on purpose. This was Rodrick's doing. The bastard just couldn't let either of them be happy. Vivica would spend three months hanging out with Brianna and her other friends. Plus, she had a bad feeling that her mother and quasi-aunt would be forcing her to watch Nial a lot more. She could learn to handle Nial. It's not like she had to love him to tolerate him. Cliff would hopefully be back before the beginning of the school year.

CLIFF – 2018

The CEO walked down the staircase of North Pointe and took a look at the family portrait of his great-grandfather, grandparents, uncle, and father. His father was the only one smiling in the painting. It was disturbing. With Rodrick finally gone, it seemed appropriate to finally put that horrid portrait in storage or something. He would handle it later.

Cliff walked into the kitchen where he found Hannah looking at something online. He happened to notice it was a job application. "Don't tell me you are planning on moving out?" He asked.

Hannah looked up. "I'll be honest, with mom gone I might be able to handle living here. Hope might push me though. I'm just thinking of using my business degree a little more. Car sales are far from the career I was looking for." Hannah admitted.

"Well, I had a talk with your manager the other day. You realize that you and your friend Xander are both tied at top place in sales?"

"Xander is actually leaving. Regardless though, top sales or not if I have to sell one more car to Mrs. Templeton, I'm going to rip all my hair out." Hannah explained.

Cliff sat down. "Hannah, I know you want to make your way in the world but would you consider coming on in a more business-oriented position at Knight?" He asked his daughter.

Hannah sat in shock for a moment. "I'm honestly going to have to think about it dad. I just need to try a little harder to make it on my own. It isn't about spiting you though. I hope you know that."

"No, I understand. It's just that well with Hope going to med-school and the fact that Harry doesn't seem interested in cars at all, you would make the most sense as my prodigy. You don't have to take the position though. Don't take that as me guilting you or anything. Rodrick forced my hand in it and made me work for the company after college. I don't want you or your brother to feel the same obligation ever. Think about it this way though; you would be the first female CEO. Rodrick would have hated that." Cliff joked.

"I will think about it. I promise." She closed her laptop. "So, how are things going with you and aunt Vivica?" Hannah asked.

Cliff turned a little red. "I have no idea what you are talking about."

The daughter looked at her father. "The entire town is talking at this point. Mrs. Templeton told Jackie Costa who told Margot who told Holly that you are an item again. None of who are happy about this."

"Why doesn't this town just stay out of my love life?" He sighed.

"It'd be too easy… So, are you dating aunt Vivica?"

Cliff had no answer. "Would you be ok with your aunt and I being in a relationship again?"

"Dad look I realize that Hope needed you to be with mom back when she came back from being kidnapped. She is grown though, and this is between us, but Harry was telling me the other night that he didn't even realize that Vivica wasn't his mother until mom came back. Ask the entire town; your names are written in the stars to be together. I want you to be happy." Hannah admitted.

"Hannah, I realize that you have issues with your mother, but she does mean well." Cliff sighed. He was already ready to make things official with Vivica. He went into his pocket and took out a ring box. He opened it. "Do you think she will like it?" He asked.

"I don't know. Why don't you go and ask her right now?"

Cliff laughed. "Well, I was going to take her to dinner later in the week."

Hannah stood up. "You two have been waiting since you were twelve for this. Can you honestly wait another minute?"

The curly haired man stood up himself. "I love you. I hope you know that." He kissed her on the forehead and walked out of the room.

VIVICA – 2018

Vivica walked down her living room staircase and smiled. Brad was sitting in the living room with Harry and Langley. They were all just laughing and having fun. Langley had her hand on Brad's lap which concerned her, but she would deal with that later. Lucy was on the phone in the library making strides towards whatever the heck their next career was going to be. She didn't care, Vivica would be successful regardless. She refused to plan otherwise.

The redhead walked into her foyer. She was planning to go to lunch with Holly that afternoon. She invited Lucy but Lucy was I work mode, and it was pointless trying to break her out of it. Holly walked down the front staircase. "I didn't see you upstairs. What were you doing?"

"It's a big house Vivica. I'm the head maid." Holly reminded her.

"You are the worst maid ever. You do know, that right?" Vivica asked.

Holly shrugged. "I might be the worst maid ever, but I'm the best friend you have ever had."

Vivica hugged her friend. "Don't you forget that. I wouldn't have been able to get through everything the past few months without you." The doorbell rang. Brad and Harry ran in with Langley following them.

"We ordered a pizza." Brad explained. He opened the door only there wasn't a pizza delivery guy. Instead, the CEO of *Knight Motor Company*. "Oh, hey Uncle Cliff."

Cliff walked into the foyer. "Hi." He looked around the room. "Um, could I maybe talk with Vivica alone for a minute outside?"

"Why can't we just talk right here?" Vivica asked.

Holly looked up from a text message from Hannah. "Vivica I think you might want to go outside."

Vivica took a deep breath and walked outside with Cliff. They closed the door. "Holly, you better not be listening!" They both said in unison.

"Don't tell me what to do!" The maid screamed back.

"So, what did you want to talk about?" Vivica asked.

"We've known each other for a while, right?" Cliff wondered.

The redhead laughed. "You could say that." She admitted.

Cliff sat down on the porch and Vivica followed. "So, then you would say that in that time I've maybe made one or two mistakes?"

"You could say that as well."

"I don't regret marrying your sister all those years ago. It was a happy mistake. That said, Tiffany was never the love of my life. I'm looking at the love of my life." He got down on one knee. Cliff took out the ring. "Weston, will you marry me?"

After all these years. After months of everyone assuming this would happen. After three marriages to a toxic man. Vivica gave the only answer that she could. "Cliff, I love you more than anything in this world. You are my shining knight and always will be. I've spent a lot of time lately thinking about what my answer to this question would be. So, my answer is not yet…"

Will Vivica say yes eventually? What about Langley and Brad? Will they get together? Has Hannah given up on Xander or will she continue to court the Kingsley boy? Where will Lucy move? What about Mrs. Templeton? Will she succeed in bringing slavery back to America? Then there is Tiffany and her mysterious therapist. What is Margot's role in all of this? Will we ever learn why Tiffany was kidnapped? Will Nial be caught in the murder of Austin Martin? All these questions and more will be answered in the continuing saga of Between Heaven and Hell!

ACKNOWLEDGMENTS

I have wanted to be a storyteller since I was three years old. A lot of career aspirations have come and gone but the idea that I would one day publish a book always stuck around. Whether I'd be writing a short story in third grade or playing with terribly self-drawn paper dolls to act out the stories of characters I would one day write about. There are so many people I feel deserve to be recognized in helping me get my dream to fruition.

First and foremost, while I already dedicated the book to you, I want to once again thank my late mother, Lisa Marie. She played a special part in the inspiration for this book, and I cannot thank her enough. I had let her read the very first story bible back in 2010. So, I am glad that she at least was able read that. If it weren't for her though, I'd never have discovered the hidden treasure that are daytime dramas and this book would never have existed.

My amazing cover and promotional artist luviiilove. Follow them on their Deviant Art account right now! It was so important to me that my characters be envisioned a certain way and you went above and beyond to make every detail beyond perfect. The fact that the Knight, Fitzpatrick, and Kingsley families each look like they are related is just one of the small details taken by this phenomenal artist.

Nikki Baker, I've known you since 2010 when we bonded over a mutual love of theatre and acting. It's perfect that we both transitioned from the two mediums practically at the same time. We have been everything from business partners to critics of each other's works. Thank you so much for the advice and help you have given me in this book. If it were not for you, Vivica would be wearing (tasteful) lingerie on the cover of this novel.

Thomas Fitzgerald, you are so special and important to me in general. You are the only person I have let read a lot of my drafts and stories, and your opinion means so much to me. I let you read the terrible first draft of this book many years ago. If it weren't for you, the character of Harry would never have been able to exist as he does today.

Josh Patterson and Mercy Rogers, if it were not for the two of you in general over the past year, I'd probably be sitting in a mental institution. The support, curiosity, and excitement you have both shared for this book has meant so much to me in ways no one will ever realize. I cannot thank you both enough for the support and friendship.

I'd also like to give a shout out to Vicki H (yup you are in the book), Sue Ann F, my forever baby brother Manny, my other brother Alexander, and my father, Ralph.

About The Author

L A Michaels is a Michigan native having also lived in Wichita, Kansas and Rock Hill, South Carolina over a two-year period. L A is passionate about reading, writing, theatre, the art of drag, world history, and art. An avid soap opera viewer L A Michaels has worked with online publications over the past decade with web content.

You can follow L A Michaels on the following platforms:

Twitter: @lamichaels1995

Instagram: @lamichaelsauthor

Facebook: L A Michaels

lamichaelsauthor.com

Please also check out the artist for *Between Heaven and Hell*, luviiilove on their Deviant Art page.

deviantart.com/luviiilove